VICIOUS GRACE

'Kim,' I said, pushing the power out into my voice. 'Wake up.'

I didn't take my eyes off the red-haired man, but in my peripheral vision, I saw her fall out of the pattern. She put a hand to her head and looked around. The red-haired man was trembling now, shaking with barely restrained violence. Two of the nurses behind the station put down long gray folders and stepped out into the hallway behind him. A blond woman in a business suit came out of one of the patient care rooms, her hands at her sides like claws. King Mob, closing ranks. Their synchronized breath filled the space: a single, huge, animal sound.

'Jayné?' Kim said.

'Just stay cool, and when I tell you to run, run,' I said. And then, 'Okay. *Run!*'

By M. L. N. Hanover

VICIOUS GRACE

the black sun's daughter

3

M.L.N.HANOVER

www.orbitbooks.net

ORBIT

First published in Great Britain in 2012 by Orbit
First published in the United States in 2010 by Pocket Books
a division of Simon & Schuster, Inc.

Copyright © 2010 by M. L. N. Hanover

The moral right of the author has been asserted.

Excerpt from *Killing Rites* by M. L. N. Hanover
Copyright © 2011 by M. L. N. Hanover

*All characters and events in this publication, other than
those clearly in the public domain, are fictitious
and any resemblance to real persons,
living or dead, is purely coincidental.*

A CIP catalogue record for this book is available from the British Library.

ISBN 978-0-356-50124-6

Typeset in Garamond 3 by Hewer Text UK Ltd, Edinburgh
Printed and bound by CPI Group (UK) Ltd, Croydon, CR0 4YY

Papers used by Orbit are from well-managed forests
and other responsible sources.

 MIX
Paper from
responsible sources
FSC
www.fsc.org FSC® C104740

Orbit
An imprint of
Little, Brown Book Group
100 Victoria Embankment
London EC4Y 0DY

An Hachette UK Company
www.hachette.co.uk

www.orbitbooks.net

To Sigrid Drusse

Prologue

Kim arrived at the fMRI suite twenty minutes later than she'd intended. It was in a wing of the hospital she rarely passed through, and late at night, there were few people to ask for directions. As she swiped her card through the pass-key protection, she had a sense of being tardy for class. The doors opened silently onto a long, empty corridor. Only one in three lights glowed, giving the space a sense of twilight and darkness. The smell of antiseptic and electricity seemed to cover something deep and earthy. The closed doors of the individual rooms couldn't quite shut out the clanks and thumps of the machines. A man in a white coat much like her own leaned out of a door halfway down the hall, his eyebrows raised and his mouth set in a scowl.

'I'm here for Dr. Oonishi,' she said, and his scowl shifted into something odd—relief, perhaps? Anticipation?

'You must be Kim,' the man said, waving her forward. 'I'm Mohammed. He's in his office. He said to send you back as soon as you came.'

Kim forced a tight smile and nodded curtly. She knew her reputation in the hospital and at the university, and she more than half expected this all to be a prank. It wouldn't be the first time someone had seen fit to make fun of the kook, and Kichirou Oonishi had a reputation of his own. Media appearances, popular books, combative letters in the journals, appearances before Congress. Large grants for flashy, headline-grabbing research. He had a lot of pull in the academic hierarchy, and his sense of humor wasn't to be trusted.

But even if she was walking into her own private *Punk'd* moment, she would see the research in progress. That was worth something. And she trusted that she could maintain her dignity. God knew she had enough practice at that.

Oonishi's office could have belonged to an accountant. Desk, filing cabinet, worn carpet with old stains, the smell of stale coffee. Only the sixty-inch touch-screen monitor on the wall hinted at the grant money behind the project. Oonishi leaned on the desk, his gaze flickering over the computer screen. Six individual panes were open on it, each showing confused jumbles of grainy black-and-white images. A seventh pane spooled green characters on a black background too quickly for her to process. The wallpaper image behind it all was Oonishi shaking hands with a former president.

He glanced up at her and then back to the screen. His face wasn't rugged so much as cragged, and the white at his temples made Kim feel younger than she was. Or at least less qualified.

'So,' Oonishi said, without preamble, 'you understand how all this works?'

Kim crossed her arms.

'It isn't in my area of expertise, but I imagine that I

understand the theory. At least as well as you understand parasites,' she said.

He blinked at her. The light from the monitor blued his skin and deadened his eyes.

'I don't know shit about parasites,' he said. The matter-of-fact tone might have meant anything: that her work was beneath him, that she wasn't expected to understand his experiments, or that even a mind as broad and deep as his own had its limits. Kim took a deep breath. If it was all a joke, the best thing she could do was be gracious. Kill him with kindness and let him look like the asshole.

'Fair enough,' she said. 'I know a little about what you're doing here. I read your article about the Miywaki study. Computational neuroimaging. Using blood flow to specific parts of the early visual cortex to reconstruct observed images.'

'Yeah,' Oonishi said, his gaze shifting back to the flickering screens. 'The bitch of it is the neocortex isn't all one-way streets, you know? There's more neurons feeding up to it from the deeper parts of the brain than there are coming in from the eyes. We don't have a baseline for that feedback, so that's what I'm looking at. What visual activity you get when there's no conscious direction or sensory input.'

'Watching people's dreams,' Kim said.

Oonishi shifted his shoulders, an impatient expression ghosting across his face. It wasn't, apparently, a description he liked. Never mind that it was accurate.

'It's not as hard as it sounds. We spent a few months with the subjects doing standardizing studies. Seeing which regions fired when the subjects saw particular lines in particular parts of their visual fields. Building up functional maps. Then when they're asleep, we see what's firing, and use the maps to put the puzzle back together. Simple. Worst part was finding people who can sleep in an fMRI machine. Bastards are loud. And the subjects can't move. But . . .'

He pointed to the screen. The gray, grainy images on the monitor flickered and danced. For a moment, a face appeared in one, openmouthed and distinctly feminine despite image resolution so blocky as to approach the abstract. Another showed something that might have been a house with a wide staircase rising up to the door. The image flickered, replaced by something that was clearly a moving object, but too blurred for Kim to make out.

A little thrill passed through her at peeking into another person's private world. The theory was interesting enough, but the experience had a dose of voyeurism more powerful than she'd expected. And more than that, the sense of witnessing something . . . not miraculous. *Better* than miraculous. Something unexpected and reproducible. Standing witness as the limits of human knowledge changed. If it had been in her own field, she might have fought with a little professional jealousy. As it was, she started running down how Oonishi's machines could be adapted for measuring parasitic behavioral modifications. She'd almost forgotten the man was in the room with her when he spoke again.

'You're looking at five years of my life. I've got twenty

graduate students who have put their hearts and souls into this research. They're betting their careers on this.'

'It's good work,' Kim said. 'Very impressive.'

Oonishi shook his head. He pressed his lips so tight, they all but vanished. The silence in the room was fragile. Kim felt a little clench in her belly. If this was a joke, the setup would begin here. She had to stay on her guard. Oonishi tapped on the huge screen, closing the dusty windows into the sleepers' minds.

'Look at this,' he said, tapping an icon and resizing the resulting window with a sweep of his fingers. Again, six windows flickered. The time stamp in the corner said September 4. A little more than a week earlier. A bare breast appeared in one of the screens, almost startling in its detail.

'Subject three,' Oonishi said, smiling at her reaction. 'We can always tell when he's been watching porn.'

'Tell me that isn't why you asked me here.'

'It's not,' Oonishi said. 'Here. Now. Watch.'

The six screens shifted. A cooling fan within the computer kicked on, as much hiss as hum. Kim's neck began to ache, just at the base of her skull. All six images shuddered at once, and then synchronized. Not perfectly, but almost so, like six cameras trained on the same object. In the blocky gray scale, it could have been anything roughly rectilinear—a box, a machine, a coffin—set into a lighter gray. Black, with strong lines. In each screen, the thing cracked, arcs of whiteness pouring out. The lighter gray around the opening lid shifted like soil. Dark earth. Kim's breath was suddenly ragged, her heartbeat faster than it should have been.

The box burst open, light pouring out of it. What color was it, she wondered. Had they dreamed this as the clarifying yellow-blue of dawn? The red and gold of sunset? There was something inside the light. She had the impression of a forest of glasslike teeth, an eye, a hand with fingers splayed and proportions out of true. The screens fluttered, shifted, and fell out of sync. A moment later, they were all different again, each mind on its own, individual journey. Oonishi stopped the playback.

It was a trick. She couldn't let herself fall for it.

'Interesting,' Kim said. 'Data corruption?'

'I've been through the data streams. They're all fine.'

'Well, it's clearly *some* kind of equipment failure,' Kim said. 'Unless you mean to suggest that all your subjects magically started sharing the same dream.'

She let it hang in the air between them. Even if all of his research assistants were secretly recording the exchange, an upload link to YouTube standing by, Kim was not going to come off looking like the idiot. Let him come to her.

'You have,' Oonishi began, 'something of a reputation for—'

'I got drunk at a Christmas party four years ago,' Kim said. 'I said some things that have been wildly misinterpreted.'

'Do you believe in spirits?'

'I am a research scientist. Maybe not in a field with as much respect and clout as yours, but I'm not some kind of crystal-humping, incense-burning new age fake. No matter what you may have heard.' Her face felt hot, her throat thick with an anger she hadn't expected. She swallowed, cursing herself for rising to the bait, even that much.

'Then you don't believe,' Oonishi said.

Kim gave herself a moment before she spoke. She had to keep better control.

'I believe there are many, many things we haven't figured out yet,' she said, pushing back a stray lock of hair. 'If no one ever came across evidence that didn't fit theory, I wouldn't have a job.'

The concession softened Oonishi's expression. He sat on his desk, leaning over his own knees. His feet didn't reach the floor, and his heels tapped against the side of the desk. Kim had a brief, powerful image of what the man would have looked like as a young boy sitting in a chair too big for him. When he spoke, his voice was low, almost a whisper.

'If I have . . . artifacts like that when I publish, the *best* thing that will happen is Boaris and Estrahaus at Stanford will accuse me of faking the data. My career will be destroyed. And not just mine. Every coresearcher on the project will be guilty by association. Their careers will be over before they've begun,' he said. And then, slowly, as if each word cost him, 'I'm in trouble here.'

Cold and dread filled Kim's belly. He looked lost. He looked empty.

It wasn't a prank.

'Show me again,' she said.

Oonishi rose, tabbed back the playback, and they

watched again. The dark box, more than half buried. The uncovering. The flashing, pouring light. Teeth. That misshapen hand. Kim found she'd pressed her fingers to her mouth without realizing she'd done so. Oonishi stopped the flow of images.

'I know you've caught some hell for talking about this kind of thing,' he said, his voice very careful, preemptively apologetic. 'But can you help me?'

'I can't,' Kim said. And a moment later, 'But I know someone.'

1

I lay as flat as I could on the carpet of old pine needles, my rifle hugged close against my cheek. The world smelled of soil and gun oil and sweat. I kept my breath soft, my hands steady. In the crosshairs, Chogyi Jake crouched beside a huge pine tree, one hand on the rough bark to steady himself. He had a rifle of his own, held low against one hip. The sun was setting behind me. If he looked in my direction, the light would dazzle him. From my perspective, it was like God was shining a spotlight on him. The targeting sight magnified his familiar face. To someone who didn't know him, who hadn't spent over a year day-in, day-out in his company, he might have looked fine. To me, he radiated the same physical exhaustion I felt. I let the crosshairs drift down to his body. Shoot for the center of mass, I told myself. Go for the biggest target.

Gently, I put my finger on the trigger. I breathed out as I squeezed. My rifle coughed, and a wide swath of bark two feet above Chogyi Jake's head bloomed neon green. He looked up at it, and then out toward me with an expression that said *Really? That was your best shot?* just as three sharp impacts drilled into my side. Baby blue splotches marked my autumn-leaves camouflage fatigues. Aubrey's color. I rolled onto my back and said something crude.

'Okay, Miss Heller,' Trevor said in my earpiece. He always called me Miss Heller instead of Jayné. I had the impression that even after he'd heard it pronounced correctly—zha-*nay*—he was afraid he'd refer to me as Jane or Janie. 'I think we're calling it a day.'

I fumbled with the mic. Somewhere in the exercise, I'd pushed it down around my collarbone.

'Got it,' I said. 'I'll see you back at the cabin.'

I lay there for a moment, the wide Montana sky looking down at me through the trees. The setting sun turned a few stray wisps of cloud rose and gold. The ground under me felt soft, and the sting of the paintballs faded. A breeze set the pines rippling with a sound like something immense talking very gently. I thought that if I closed my eyes, I could fall asleep right there and dream until the bears woke up next spring. My muscles felt like putty.

I felt wonderful.

I'd gotten Trevor Donnagan's name from a cop friend of mine in Boulder. He'd said that Trevor was hands-down the best place to go if you absolutely, positively had to train yourself into a killing machine in the minimum possible time. A former Green Beret and five or six different kinds of black belt, Trevor had spent the better part of his life meditating on how to dislocate joints, shatter bones, and immobilize bad guys without having the same happen to him. His cabin sat on eight square miles of fenced-off woodland, and he was charging me enough for a month of private, intensive training to pay for eight more. Considering the shape my life had taken in the last year, it was cheap.

I'd been coming up on my twenty-third birthday when my uncle Eric died. I went to Denver knowing that I'd been named his executor. I didn't know that I was also his sole heir, or that he had more money than some small countries. Or that he'd made his fortune as a kind of spiritual fixer, dealing with any number of parasitic things from just outside reality that could take over people's minds and bodies and do magic a thousand times more powerful than a normal person could manage. Vampires, werewolves, shape-shifting demons. The generic term was rider.

Now I was almost a month into twenty-four, and several times in the past year, my learning curve had approached vertical.

Aubrey walked up from my left. I knew from the sound of his footsteps that he was at least as tired as I was. I turned my head. His camouflage was smeared with Day-Glo yellow over his right shoulder and left hip, meaning that Ex had gotten the drop on him at least once during the day. His sandy hair stood at ten different angles, and a smear of mud darkened one cheek. I raised my left hand. He took it and hauled me up to my feet. I followed through, collapsing against him a little, my forehead resting in the comfortable curve where his shoulder met his neck. I felt his chuckle as much as heard it.

'I have never been this tired in my life,' he said, threading his arm around me. 'I'm getting too old for this.'

'Poor ancient man,' I said. 'Can't keep up with his bouncing baby girlfriend.'

'My poor childlike sweetie looks like she could use some rest too.'

'I'm fine,' I said, leaning against him a little more. 'Just lulling you into a sense of safety.'

'Besides, I'm not that old.'

'Men's physical peak is, like, twenty-five,' I said. 'You're ten years past that. Your teeth should start falling out any minute now.'

'You keep me young,' he said with a mock sourness, and spun me back toward the east and our walk to Trevor's cabin. The sun blazed on the horizon, glowing like a fire among the trees. The shadows of the low, rolling hills splashed against the landscape, and the green and yellow of the cottonwood trees nearest the cabin standing out against the evergreen pine. It was at least a half-mile walk, down a long, gentle slope to the path that curled around to the north. We walked together, our rifles slung over our shoulders, our paint-stained uniforms glowing in the twilight like we were veterans of the battle of Playskool Ridge. The wind cooled. The sky faded from blue to gray, darkness creeping up the eastern sky. Missoula was an hour-and-a-half drive away, and not even a smudge of backsplash on the nighttime clouds.

The cabin itself was two stories of stained wood and black iron with a wide, flat expanse on one end like a military parade ground and a barn in the back that was really a gym and dojo unlike anything I'd ever seen before. Our rented minivan squatted beside a dusty three-quarter-ton pickup truck. His bumper stickers suggested Trevor was unlikely to vote for a Democrat. Inside, warm, thick air carried the scents of curry and fry bread. A sudden near-raging hunger hollowed my stomach. Trevor stood in the doorway to the kitchen, nearly blocking out the light behind him. The man was built like a refrigerator.

'Soup's on in twenty, Miss Heller,' he said. 'Should give all of you a shot at the showers.'

'Thank you,' I said.

'You can leave your weapons in the case there. I'll get them stripped and cleaned.'

I knew I should have objected, should have insisted on doing it all myself, if only to prove that I wasn't just some poor little rich girl hauling her male friends on some kind of weird Outward Bound retreat. I let the fatigue win.

'Is Ex already here?' I asked instead.

'Upstairs,' Trevor said. 'Jake's there too.'

Aubrey tilted his head like he'd heard something strange.

'Is something wrong?' he said.

Trevor crossed his massive arms and looked uncomfortable.

'Nothing we can't talk about after dinner,' he said. 'Twenty minutes.'

On the way up the stairs, Aubrey exchanged a silent look with me. It hadn't been so long since I'd been in a more traditional learning environment, and even though I knew I was the one paying Trevor, part of me got nervous at the thought that teacher was pissed off about something. At the head of the stair, we split, Aubrey heading down the left-hand hallway while I went to the right. Alone in my little monastic cell of a room, I stripped off my fatigues and sweat-soaked T-shirt. As the only woman, I got the cell with the private bathroom; an undersized toilet crowded against a tiny sink, with a shower the size of a postage stamp. The closest I had to an amenity was a soft towel and a full-length mirror. After I'd washed the bits of pine needle and dirt out of my hair, I paused and took stock of my new bruises. There was a nasty one, blue-black on my left hip where I'd landed wrong when Trevor threw me. Four light ones across my back, legacies of paintball failures. Or five, if I counted the one hidden by the half-finished tattoo at the small of my back. A raw, red patch on my shin from slipping during a fast scramble up a stony ravine. And with the scars I had on my side where a possessed man had shoved knifelike fingers into my ribs last August, and the long, white-pink mark where a voodoo god had split my arm open in the spring, I looked pretty beat-up. Well seasoned, Trevor called it.

As soon as I was dressed again—blue jeans, Pink Martini T-shirt under a wool cardigan, white sneakers—I headed downstairs. Aubrey wasn't at the dinner table yet, but Ex and Chogyi Jake were. Ex was in his usual priestly black even though he'd dropped the whole Jesuit gig long before I'd ever met him. His white-blond hair was tied back in its severe ponytail. Chogyi Jake had skipped his usual sand-colored linen shirt for the kind of white sleeveless T-shirt my big brother used to call a wifebeater when our parents weren't around. His scalp was freshly shaved and shining, his smile as genuine and enigmatic as ever. I pulled out a chair and sat down. Our rifles were, I noticed, already disassembled, cleaned, reassembled, and put away with nothing more left behind than a slight hint of gun oil under the curry.

'Holding together?' I said.

'We're fine,' Ex said.

'It's a more vigorous lifestyle than I'm used to,' Chogyi Jake said, 'but I have high hopes that the training effect will kick in.'

Aubrey clomped down the stairs nineteen minutes after we'd gone up, and Trevor emerged from the kitchen with the food a minute after that. Pineapple chicken curry with saffron rice. Fresh nan bread. Sag aloo. Trevor grinned as we all made appreciative noises. If he'd brought out cheap, greasy drive-through burgers, I probably would have thought it was the best-looking meal ever. This was like something out of a very good dream. Trevor sat at the head of the table and bent his head to say grace. Ex and Chogyi Jake did likewise, Ex with his eyes squeezed hard and Chogyi Jake with the polite air of following someone else's form. I didn't bow my head, and because I didn't, Aubrey didn't either. When Trevor opened his eyes, we ate for half an hour straight without pausing to talk.

Afterward, we students cleared the dishes, Ex brewed a pot of Café Du Monde French roast and chicory, and with our coffee cups in hand, we walked down the cold, dark path to the barn. Stars filled the sky like flakes in a snowstorm.

Trevor waited for us by the practice mats. He wasn't in

his gi, for which I was secretly thankful. I had hired him to kick our collective ass into shape, but having at least part of a night off sounded very, very appealing. He had an old monitor hooked up to a cheap DVD player sitting on a folding table at the edge of the mat.

'All right,' Trevor said, crossing his arms. 'What did you see out there today?'

We were all silent for a moment. Chogyi Jake spoke first.

'I think we focus too much on Jayné.'

'*You* do,' Trevor agreed. 'The morning session, you practically ignored Aubrey. There were three times you could have taken him out, and instead you focused fire on her. And you'—he pointed at Aubrey—'put yourself in harm's way each time in order to protect her.'

'I . . .' Aubrey said, then sighed. 'I didn't mean to.'

'Ex, on the other hand, was just the other way around,' Trevor said. 'Focused too much on taking Aubrey out of the picture. You people have to play the whole board. And we can work on that. What else?'

I raised my hand.

'I can't hit the broad side of a barn,' I said. It was the truth. I'd never been good with firearms, and I didn't seem to be getting much better. The only time in my life I'd even gotten close to hitting my intended target, it had been point-blank range with a 30–06, and the wizard I'd been shooting at caught the bullet anyway.

'No,' Trevor said. 'You really can't.'

I was a little embarrassed that he'd agreed so quickly. There's something awkward about being self-deprecating when everyone around you thinks you're stating the obvious. I looked down at my hands, but Trevor had already turned to his DVD player.

'And the shooting is only part of the problem,' he said. 'This is the training session from yesterday.'

Ex and Aubrey both glanced over at me, nervous on my behalf.

'I am sorry about that,' I said.

'Don't be,' Trevor said. 'Just watch.'

I popped into life on the screen. The camera had been set up at the corner of the practice mat we were all sitting on now, high on a tripod so that, through its glass eye, I looked even smaller than I actually was. The audio feed scratched and echoed. We weren't going to watch the whole session, then. Just the bad part. On the screen, Trevor stepped toward me.

Even with the camera angle, he looked big. We circled each other, Trevor lunging in one direction, me scrabbling to get away from him. Now that I was watching from outside, I could see what he meant about my needing to keep one leg strong, even when I was moving fast. He shifted, and the Jayné on the screen side-stepped toward the wall. I squinted and held my breath.

Trevor paused the frame.

'Look here,' he said, pointing at my legs on the screen. 'See how her hips are behind her? And her elbows are in at her sides. She's like this.'

He took an awkward stance that I thought exaggerated my position, but the others nodded.

'Defensive,' he said. 'She's trying to engage the fight, but she's also trying to back away from it. Women do that all the time. Hardest thing to teach a woman is to stop being nice in a fight. So all this? It's normal. Now—'

He took off the pause. On the screen, Trevor rushed me. I danced back a step, my arms pulling into my body, and then he was around behind me, one thick arm around my neck, the other digging into my spine while he bent me back.

'I'm pushing her here,' he said. 'Making her uncom-fortable.'

In the moment, it had felt a lot more like he'd been trying to kill me. The on-screen me flapped her arm, trying to tap out, give up, say uncle. I could see the fear in my expression. And then I dropped, curling to the side. On-screen Trevor grunted, the arm that had been around my neck suddenly at a strange angle. I hammered an open palm into his side twice, making him yelp on the second strike. And then he was airborne, crashing into the barn wall hard enough to make the camera shake. It was over in less than a second. I felt chagrined, watching myself hurt him. And maybe a little pleased. Trevor paused again, backing up frame by frame until he was once again chok-ing me as I bent backward.

'There,' he said, then shifted to the next frame forward. I didn't see any difference, except that maybe in the second frame I looked a little more angry than scared. 'Right there. That's where she changed. See how her knees bend? She gets her center back. Her feet dig into the mat. Right there,

18

she goes from a white belt fresh off the street to someone who can kick *my* ass. And that, ladies and gents, is not normal.'

'What do you make of it?' Chogyi Jake asked, leaning forward.

'That she's a typical girl white belt until she feels directly threatened, and then turns into someone else?' Trevor said, shaking his head. He let the action play out, watching himself go flying like it was a puzzle he wanted to solve.

'Adrenaline rush,' I said. 'That's not weird, right?'

'That's not adrenaline,' Trevor said. 'That's technique. And I can't train it.'

We all knew—meaning the four of us who weren't Trevor—that Uncle Eric had left me with more than just money. He'd put some kind of magical protection on me that meant I was better in a fight than I had any right to be. I was also harder than your average bear to track down using magical means. Sort of an instant ninja package. Chogyi Jake had been disquieted that we never found references in any of Eric's places to what exactly he'd done or how exactly it worked, but this was the first time I had a hint that its mere existence might be a problem.

'Can't you train the white-belt me?' I said. 'The early one?'

He turned off the monitor. The image died, leaving all of us reflected in the dark glass.

'Miss Heller, I don't mean any disrespect, but I don't train with people I can't trust, even if that just means trusting them to be inexperienced. I've been at this for more years than you've been breathing air, and nothing I've seen matches what I saw there. I can train these guys, no trouble. I can help you with strength training. Flexibility. But I'm not getting in the ring with you again. I'd be stupid if I did.'

Trevor went on for half an hour, going over the recordings of Aubrey, Ex, and Chogyi Jake taking their turns. It turned out Chogyi Jake had had some previous training. Ex and Aubrey were just about the same as I had been in the first part of the recording. I drank my coffee and felt like a balloon with half the air sucked out. I understood exactly what Trevor was saying, why he was saying it, and I still felt rejected. It might have been dumb of me, but that didn't keep it from being true.

When they were done, we walked back to the cabin, rinsed out our coffee mugs, and Trevor headed up for bed. I sat at the dinner table, looking out at the night. The clock on the wall was manufactured to look old; fake black cracks ran down the white face. It was only a quarter to eleven. It felt way past midnight. I heard Ex walking down the stairs, heard him hesitate when he saw me alone, and then come the rest of the way into the room. I knew he had a little crush on me, and I hadn't found a better strategy than to ignore it with the same ferocity that he did.

'Hard night,' he said. He'd let his hair down, a soft, near-white flow draping to his shoulders. It softened his face.

'Disappointing, at least,' I said.

'Are we going to stay?' he asked.

'It depends,' I said. 'I don't think it's a bad idea for you guys to get some training. It's not like hanging out with me doesn't put you in danger sometimes. But part of why I wanted to do this was—'

'Hey,' my dead uncle said from the front room. 'You've got a call.'

I headed for the door. The leather backpack I used instead of a purse hung on a wrought iron coatrack. The side pocket was glowing.

'You really need to—' Ex began.

'To change that ringtone,' I finished. 'I know. I know.'

I didn't recognize the number. The area code was 312, not that it meant anything to me other than it was probably somewhere in the continental United States. Very few people called this number, and even fewer expected to find me on the other end of it. I'd changed the voice-mail message to an explanation that Eric had passed on, and that I was his niece, so that I wouldn't have to go through it all in person again. For a moment, I thought about letting this call drop. But then curiosity won, and I thumbed it on.

'Hello,' I said.

'Jayné? Is that you?' It was a woman's voice, tight and controlled and serious. She'd pronounced my name correctly. It took me less than a breath to place it, and then my heart ramped up. Aubrey's ex-wife. The one who'd still *been* his wife the first time I slept with him. The one who'd confessed to me that she still loved him. The one who, in spite of everything, I kind of liked.

'Kim,' I said. 'Hey. What's up?'

2

When, fifteen minutes later, I dropped the call, Ex had gone upstairs to his room. I sat for a while with my phone in my hand. The windows looked out over the moonlit night, trees and scrub in monochrome and about a thousand times more stars than I was used to. I could call her back. I could say that something had come up. Hell, I could even tell her that I just wasn't comfortable. What was she going to say? That I had to get comfortable? I had the choice, so I had the power.

Aubrey's room was even smaller than mine, his bed little more than a cot. I always thought of sleep as making people look younger, but it only changed the shape of his face a little. Softened his eyes and let his lips relax. His breath was deep and regular. I sat next to him, willing my gaze alone to wake him. After about a minute, I put my hand on his shoulder. He took one breath that was almost a sigh and opened his eyes. A few months sleeping together and he didn't even startle when I touched him.

'Hey,' I said.

'Hey. Rough night?'

'Sort of. Kim called.'

He frowned. Even in the faint moonlight, I knew that the softness had left his eyes.

'What's the deal?' he asked. Which, oddly, was better than either *Is she okay?* or *What did she want?* though I couldn't quite have said why.

'High weirdness in Chicago. Something about a sleep study with funky results. A lot about blood flow and visual cortex layers. Upshot is she wants to call in the troops, see if we can make sense of it.'

Aubrey sat up and I slid in next to him. With a bed that small, it felt like we were sitting on a bench together.

'Do you want to?'

'I don't know,' I said. 'I mean, yes. Of course. It's Kim. She came through for me when I called her for help. We should absolutely return the favor.'

'But,' he said. He didn't have to say the rest. But he was her ex-husband. But the divorce hadn't been finalized until about six months ago. And add to that the things I knew that Aubrey didn't. That she'd been having an affair with Uncle Eric when she'd still been with Aubrey. That the reason she'd left Colorado was to get away from both of them. That she'd still had feelings for him as recently as last year. I scooped his hand up in my own. He had a scar on his thumb, right below the nail bed. I'd noticed it before, but I'd never asked where it came from. I bet Kim knew.

'I think the Miss Manners center of my brain is having a little seizure over it,' I said.

'Would it help if I reminded you that she and I have been separated for almost four years, and that she was seeing other men a long time before you and I fell into bed together?'

'It couldn't hurt.'

'We've been separated for almost four—'

I nudged against him, feigning annoyance. Then I smiled.

'Look,' he said. 'If it's too awkward, we don't have to go.'

'Of course we have to go,' I said.

'Whatever you pick, I'll back your play,' he said.

I leaned into him with a sigh. He smelled of soap and clean hair and the small, elusive scent that was just him.

'You break the news to the troops?' I asked.

'Now or in the morning?'

'It'll wait,' I said.

'All right, then.'

One of the nice things about dating men who are past their twenties: snuggling for the sake of snuggling becomes an option. Even on a cot.

In the morning, I told Trevor we were going to cut things short and popped up my travel-site bookmarks. The way I saw it, we had three options: a direct flight in coach that lasted around five hours, a first-class flight that went seven hours with a twenty-minute layover in Denver, or wait until next week. My own mental calculus said that this week was better than next, and big seats at the front of the plane beat tiny little seats in the back.

The big drawback was my irrational unease about Denver itself. I hadn't been back, even just to pass through the airport, since Uncle Eric had been murdered by a rider cult called the Invisible College. And while we had finished Eric's work—killing the cult leader, breaking his magical influence, and scattering the Invisible College to the winds—it had nearly killed me at least twice. Aubrey had had to use the Oath of the Abyss, a magic so raw and destructive it had taken a year off his life, just to get me through my first brush with a rider. Ex and Kim had barely managed to keep an evil wizard from pitching me off a skyscraper. Just breathing Colorado air seemed risky. They say that lightning never strikes the same place twice, but I had the feeling that was because no place survives being struck. Leaning against lightning rods seemed dangerous, even if the sky looked blue.

But living in a world of possessing spirits, magic, wizards and werewolves, and vampires didn't make me a superstitious nut. I booked the flight to Chicago through Denver, leaving Missoula just after noon, and put it on my nifty American Express black card just as Aubrey and Chogyi Jake came down the stairs, packed bags in hand. We loaded into the rented minivan, said our last good-byes to Trevor, and started back to civilization.

I rode shotgun, Chogyi Jake and Ex in the backseat, Aubrey driving. The same configuration as always. Behind us, Trevor's private boot camp turned into just another swath of trees preparing themselves for an autumn that wasn't quite here yet. The winding gravel road that led out to state highway 83 shuddered under our wheels and left a low cloud of white dust behind us.

'Well,' Chogyi Jake said, not looking up from his laptop and our still-in-progress wiki. 'According to the lawyer's documents, you have a condominium in Chicago.'

'You're sounding tentative,' I said.

'It has two of Eric's annotations.'

'What kind?' Ex asked.

'It was listed in the Lisbon papers with YNTH and DC1,' Chogyi Jake said.

'And do we know what he meant by those?' Aubrey asked.

'No, we don't. Except that the only other DC1 entry was the place in Los Angeles.'

I groaned. The Los Angeles property with the DC1 annotation had been a royal pain. A converted warehouse in a bad section of the city, it had undocumented locks on every gate, extra dead bolts on the steel doors, and a system of wards and countermeasures that would have made the place impossible to get into at all if they'd been at full strength. But since Eric's death, no one had been around to do the upkeep, and so working together, Chogyi Jake, Ex, and Aubrey had been able to untangle that knot in six twelve-hour days. And I'd spent a small fortune on locksmiths.

'There are four other YNTH entries,' Chogyi Jake said, 'but we haven't been to any of them yet.'

Since I'd put the three guys on my payroll a year ago, most of our time had gone into trying to make sense of Eric's world. The list of properties he owned—that I owned—was pages long even if you single-spaced it. After we'd left Denver, we'd gone to Santa Fe; New Haven; New York; London; Athens (the one in Greece, not the one in Georgia); New Orleans; Savannah (but only briefly);

Eugene, Oregon; Los Angeles; Barstow, California; Tulsa; Lisbon, Portugal; Gdansk, Poland (for a day and a half); Shiprock, New Mexico; and Bangor, Maine. We'd also taken a two-week vacation in Portland, Oregon, specifically because my uncle hadn't had anything there that we needed to explore, catalog, or decipher. All in all, it made for seventeen locations in thirteen months, with the contents of each place cataloged—books, objects, the contents of storage facilities, the names of people we found who had known or worked with him. We'd made a good dent, I thought, but even once we got the whole list of things, there would be years of work after that making sense of it all.

Half the time it felt like a permanent occult Christmas with new surprises every day. The other half, I was just overwhelmed.

'I'll call my lawyer as soon as we get to Missoula,' I said. 'She'll probably have keys and information.'

'Not that they helped in Los Angeles,' Ex said.

'If it's another high-security site, that'll be a good thing, right?' Aubrey said. 'I mean, then we'll know what DC1 means.'

'By small steps, we achieve wisdom,' Ex said in a voice that made me think he was quoting someone. Probably ironically.

As if the universe knew that Denver made me uncomfortable, the layover took two hours longer than it was supposed to, the second leg of the flight delayed by bad weather in Missouri. The four of us ate a long lunch of pizza and salads at the Wolfgang Puck Express, then scattered to kill time in the shops. Retail therapy—usually one of my first resorts—wasn't working; I felt like a cat that smelled pit bull. After fifteen minutes, I gave up, headed back to our gate, and fidgeted there instead. I tried meditating, focusing the vital energy called qi in my belly and slowly pulling it up my body. But as I did, my mind kept wandering back to the reasons Chogyi Jake and Ex had taught me this kind of little magic. Like being hunted by cults of evil wizards who could disguise themselves with cantrips or fighting spiritual parasites hidden inside apparently normal people. My focus was for crap.

I tried crowd watching. And then giving my attention to the constant babble of news on the televisions in the concourse. And then going to the bathroom and washing my hands and face. When I got back out, Chogyi Jake was sitting in the plastic chair with one of those Mylar bags of Cracker Jacks. I plopped down at his side, and he tipped the bag toward me. I took a handful. The popcorn's okay, but I've always been a sucker for the caramel peanuts. Something about the salty and the sweet together. The white noise of voices and rattling roll-away suitcases and incomprehensible, garbled PA announcements gave us a kind of privacy.

'All well?' I said.

'Well enough,' Chogyi Jake said. 'You?'

'Got a little too much extraneous stuff on my plate,' I said. 'But I'll pull it together. I'm fine.'

The slightest of all possible frowns touched his brow as

he popped another cluster of popcorn and sugar into his mouth.

'I'm sorry that the training didn't go better,' he said.

'Yeah, well. It was worth a shot,' I said. 'We can go back later, maybe. For you guys, at least.'

'I'm not particularly concerned with us,' he said.

'You're worried about me? I'm the one who flipped Trevor the Ninja King into his own wall. I appear to be fine.'

'That's what concerns me,' he said. 'After all we've done, there's still nothing that tells us what protections Eric placed on you. What the parameters were.'

'How to change the oil. When to rotate the tires,' I said.

This was a conversation we'd had before. Magic fades. If we didn't figure out what exactly Uncle Eric had done, sooner or later it would go away. Probably when it was under stress. Like in the middle of a fight when something was trying to kill me.

'I don't know what else to do,' I said. 'We're looking, right? We've found a lot of stuff. We'll find more. Maybe we'll get the part that tells us what's the right kind of juju. Maybe we won't. But—'

'But you took us to Trevor so that you could build defenses of your own,' Chogyi Jake said. 'Something you understood and controlled. Only the attempt failed.'

From anyone else, it would have stung. If Chogyi Jake had a superpower, it was that he could say things that should have hurt and make them seem like they were just more information. He would have made someone an excellent mother.

'It did,' I said. 'I don't know that it was a bad idea, though.'

'It wasn't. It seems absolutely the right impulse.'

'And yet,' I said, rooting through his bag for another peanut, 'here I am going into fieldwork without actually following through on it.'

'Yes.'

'I don't think I have an option,' I said. 'Even if it wasn't Kim, I don't see how I can wait until I'm ready for everything before I try doing anything.'

'I understand that.'

'Then what are you telling me?'

'Be aware of what you are. Of what your limitations are. Respect them.'

'You know, that's *really* vague.'

Chogyi Jake took a deep breath, letting it out slowly through his teeth. He let his head fall back until he was staring at the ceiling. Behind us, an older woman was scolding a little boy in a loud, grating voice. A pack of five Japanese kids in matching black outfits hurried past, staring at the gate numbers. I took another handful of popcorn and sugar, and I waited.

'I do know,' he said.

'I can try not to count on things I don't understand, but it isn't like I've been swaggering around looking for trouble. I don't think of myself as the badass warrior princess whatever.'

He nodded, but I could tell he didn't quite mean it.

'When I was eighteen,' he said, 'I was living in a

two-bedroom apartment in South Carolina with five other people. We were taking a lot of drugs, so we were very hesitant to call the landlord if something was wrong. For instance, there was a raised patio outside with a split in the railing. We all knew about it. We respected it. But we were junkies. It wasn't something we cared about. And it was solid enough. Strong enough. Reliable enough. I knew it was untrustworthy, but every time I leaned against it, it supported me. Every time I put something heavy on the rail—just for a moment, of course, because I knew it was broken—it held.'

'Until it didn't, right?'

'But by then, I trusted it. Yes, I knew better, but all my experience had trained me to believe otherwise. It was classical conditioning,' he said. 'You have won every fight you've been in. Even when it ended with you in the hospital, you've won. Those successes have an effect. They teach you that you can succeed, and that Eric's protections are reliable. And you'll be right. Until you aren't.'

A man got on the speakers, announcing with mushy consonants that our flight would be boarding in half an hour and thanking us for our patience. Chogyi Jake ate the last of his snack, crumpled the bag, and tossed it neatly into a garbage can four seats down.

'What happened?' I asked.

He shook his head, asking a question with the gesture.

'When the rail broke,' I said. 'What happened?'

'I fell over. The patio was only raised by a few inches, and we had a lawn. I didn't get hurt.'

I laughed. I didn't know why I'd expected something dark and tragic, but I had. Chogyi Jake's constant smile took on a rueful cast. Far down the concourse, I caught sight of Ex and Aubrey walking together. Ex was moving his hands in short, sharp gestures while he spoke. Aubrey's head was canted toward him, listening intently. Despite the fact that Aubrey was my acknowledged lover and Ex his unacknowledged rival, the two of them got along well. Or maybe not despite. Maybe it was because we all recognized the tension but didn't talk about it that they both made the extra effort. Whatever it was, it worked.

'Look,' I said, 'I can try to be careful. Not push my limits. But since I don't know exactly where my limits *are*, the only way I can find out for sure is to go too far.'

'That's what Eric did,' Chogyi Jake said. 'He went to the limit of his ability, and past it, and the Invisible College killed him.'

My stomach went a little tighter.

'Yeah, okay,' I said. 'So I shouldn't do that.'

'Not if you can help it.'

The flight into O'Hare was ugly. The storm front that had delayed our flight in the first place left enough turbulence behind it to shake the airplane like a terrier. The sun set behind us, and the clouds far below glittered and flashed with lightning. Even in the first-class cabin, people were feeling testy and miserable, myself included. Aubrey, beside me, seemed to be asleep, but there was a green cast to his skin and his hands were balled into fists. My own stomach was unsteady, and I turned away the meal the flight attendants offered.

I knew I had a style. A set of habits that I fell into, time after time. I rushed in where angels feared to tread as a matter of course. I'd done it when I'd burned my bridges at home and gone to a secular university. I'd done it when I'd gotten involved with my first real lover and his friends, and again when I left for Denver after that all fell apart. I hadn't known what I was doing when I went against the Invisible College. When we'd gotten into the mess that had been New Orleans, it had been me in the lead, charging ahead without knowing what I was charging into.

But this was different. It was Kim, who knew a lot about riders and possession to begin with. Ex and Aubrey and Chogyi Jake were all with me. And if I didn't have a set plan, it was only because the idea was to go there first, and then see what the situation was. This time, it was different.

The captain's voice blatted through the airplane. The flight attendants scurried.

We began our descent.

3

There had been a time not that long ago when MapQuest printouts had been part of my routine. The GPS was better. Rain was still coming down hard, and traffic on the highway was thicker and faster than I liked. The cheerful little map glowed in the dashboard, encouraging us on, making the city around us seem like a known quantity. The skyscrapers of Chicago glittered and glowed through the storm, towers of gold and darkness. We got off at Division Street, heading east. The low brick buildings seemed to crowd the street, leaning in toward us, and gray-white rain flowed angrily in the gutters. We followed the GPS directions, and the buildings we passed grew taller, the bars more like places college kids went when they wanted to be edgy. Then banks and restaurants. A Starbucks. My head had been filled with the stories I knew about Chicago—Al Capone and Millennium Field, Buddy Guy and deep-dish pizza. I'd never been here before, and looking out at the same corporate coffee joint I'd been to in every city I'd seen, I felt like I'd driven through someplace—some real, genuine Chicago—and wound up at a convention center. I half wanted to turn back.

And then, the city ended. Between rain, darkness, and

the four intervening lanes of I-41, I couldn't see Lake Michigan itself, but the darkness was sudden and extreme. Aubrey turned us north at the GPS's gentle, vaguely British suggestion, and the world on our right was towering electric light, glass, and concrete and on our left, blackness. I'd never lived on the water, and the contrast made me jumpy. Or maybe I was already jumpy, and it was just something to latch onto.

The building we wanted looked like a hotel. Pale stone rose over twenty stories above us, lights glowing in over half the windows. Black-barked trees rose up the sides, their canopy covering the street and making the bulk of the building behind them seem even larger. The GPS announced that we had arrived. From the backseat, Ex whistled low.

'We're sure this is the right place?' I asked.

'I think so,' Aubrey said, squinting past a parked FedEx truck as he drove. 'Anyone see an address?'

'This thing's half the block,' Ex said. 'Let's park and find a security guard to ask.'

'Right,' Aubrey said. 'Anyone see where we park?'

We circled the block twice, pulling in at a locked loading dock and then back out again before a figure darted out from the sidewalk. A brown-haired man in a suit and tie waved tentatively, and Aubrey paused, rolling down the window. The blast of air smelled of rain and cold.

'Jayné Heller?' the man asked, pronouncing it Jane.

I raised my hand.

'I'm Harlan. Harlan Jeffers. I work for the building

management,' he said with a smile, as the rain dripped down his cheek. 'Your lawyer wanted me to meet you. Sorry if I'm late.'

'Where do we park?' Aubrey asked. Harlan pointed him to a bush-camouflaged ramp and handed us a radio passkey before stepping back and promising to meet us inside. We turned the car down the ramp and around a sharp corner. A wide steel gate slid open before us, and we went in.

The lobby of the building belonged in an architectural magazine. Gentle archways of butter-colored marble rose and fell all along a wide central court, and a fountain of black basalt in the center had water sheeting down the stone as if spouting up in the air would be too nouveau riche. Classical music played through hidden speakers like Muzak's grown-up, sophisticated sister. The smell of rain wasn't completely gone, but it was lessened. I more than half expected the security guard to stop us and ask for our papers. My traveling T-shirt and jeans seemed about as appropriate as an evening gown in a mosh pit. But Harlan appeared again, his hair slicked by the rain and his smile almost painfully eager to please. I wondered how much he knew about us, or if my lawyer had just put the fear of God into him by implication. She had that knack.

'I'm really sorry I left you hanging,' Harlan said, holding out a manila envelope. I accepted it with a smile.

'No trouble,' I said. 'We weren't out there long.'

The envelope held a ring with two keys, a magnetic key card, a sheet of paper with what looked like a four-digit

PIN, and a restaurant guide. I pulled out the restaurant guide.

'That's mine,' Harlan said. 'I mean, it's from me. I knew you were new to the Windy City, and I thought it might help. While you got your bearings.'

'Do they *really* call it the Windy City, or is that just for tourists?' Ex asked, and Harlan's smile got a little more nervous.

'One thing,' I said, breaking in before the guy could dig himself in any deeper. 'I know we've got it listed in the database, but could you just remind me what floor and room we're heading to?'

'Nineteenth floor,' Harlan said. 'You've got 1904. Just turn right when you get out of the elevators and it'll be halfway down on the right. Beautiful view of the lake.'

'Have you been in it?' Chogyi Jake asked. 'Not the lake, I mean. The apartment?'

Harlan looked nonplussed.

'We have very strict instructions about 1904,' Harlan said. 'We don't go in or out unless the owner or the owner's listed agent is present. That's a very solid rule.'

'So you've never been in,' I said.

'No, miss,' he said. 'Never.'

I looked at Aubrey, who raised his eyebrow a millimeter. For someone accustomed to dealing with the rich and powerful, Harlan was a rotten liar. The man seemed to sense that he was on thin ice. When he spoke again, his voice was louder and more cheerful.

'My card's in there too. It has the office number and my

private line. If there's anything I can help with, just let me know. Any time.'

He beat a hasty retreat, and the four of us hauled our suitcases across the wide lobby to the bank of wood-paneled elevators. It took me a minute to figure out that the car wouldn't move until I waved the magnetic key card over a flat black sensor panel, but then we rose up smoothly, almost silently.

'Well,' Ex said. 'That was interesting. I guess getting into the place isn't *too* hard.'

Compared to the Los Angeles property, 1904 was simple. Two locks, corresponding to the two keys. A simple magical warning system and a network of aversion wards that made the place feel unwelcoming and dangerous until Chogyi Jake placated them with a handful of salt and a drop of my blood. And the place itself . . .

Imagine a good, solid cottage on the cliffs above a cold sea. Three bedrooms, a living space, a kitchen. Wooden floors, white walls, thick wool rugs of gray and fading red. Rough-hewn wood furniture filled five rooms, and old woodblock prints in cheap frames were the only art. The dining room table was big enough for eight, but with only three chairs. The kitchen had wide, pale linoleum counters and a freestanding gas stove in green-and-cream enamel that looked like it belonged in the 1930s. When I pulled back the thick cotton curtains, the rainstorm, silent behind the triple-paned glass, and the overwhelming view of the black lake framed by skyscrapers to the south was like something out of a Magritte painting. Too implausible to be real. We all walked through the place for a few minutes, just to get our bearings. Everything was covered with dust. Eric clearly hadn't popped for a cleaning service.

Aubrey was the first one to put his finger on what was so dislocating.

'There's nothing *here*,' he said.

Every one of Uncle Eric's properties had shown the effects of his occult life. Strange books and unsettling objects were arranged in boxes, crates, and shelves all around the world. This place was so simple, so clean, so *empty* that it felt wrong. I saw it in their faces that it set us all on edge.

'Do you think . . .' Ex began. 'Did Harlan *rob* the place?'

'We wouldn't know if something was missing,' Chogyi Jake said. 'There's no inventory to compare it with. And it does seem . . . spare, doesn't it? I thought it would be bigger too. Did anyone else expect it to be bigger?'

We stood silently, each of us looking at the others.

'Okay,' I said at last. 'Is there anything we can do about that?'

After about a heartbeat, all three of them shook their heads and made negative grunts.

'Then let's table it and move on. How about we see if there's any food here, then unpack and clean up a little, and I'll call Kim.'

An hour later, Kim was sitting on the cow-skin couch. She had a new haircut that softened her features and left her looking a little less like Nicole Kidman. Still, the last year hadn't been kind to her. She'd put on five or ten pounds, and they didn't actually suit her. Her skin was paler than I remembered, and her eyes had a sunken look. Her expression was the same, and I had to remind myself that her closed, brittle manner had put me off the first time I'd met her too.

Ex had moved one of the kitchen chairs into the living space, Aubrey sat in a chair that matched the couch, Chogyi Jake sat on the floor with a cup of green tea in his hands, and I stood in the door frame to the dining room as if I wasn't sure I was supposed to be there.

I hated it that my gut went tight, seeing her with Aubrey. It had been easier that first time in Denver. Aubrey had been in a coma, for one thing. By the time he'd come back, she'd left. From the way they talked now, you wouldn't know it was the first time they'd seen each other in years.

'But what's this Oonishi guy trying to prove?' Aubrey said. 'I mean, does he *have* a hypothesis?'

'It's an exploratory protocol,' Kim said. 'The idea is to provide a baseline for further work. And yes, it's hey-look-at-me science and exactly the sort of study that pisses you off. But what can I tell you? He gets grants.'

Aubrey shook his head, but his expression was easy. Yes, he thought the sleep guy was doing lousy science. Yes, it pissed him off. But the fact that Kim knew all that even before she started talking pulled the sting. All this was part of a conversation they'd had countless times before I knew either one of them, complete with the private shorthand that comes from knowing someone well for a long time.

They didn't mean to exclude me. It just worked out that way.

'So the weird dreams,' I said. 'Are they the only thing we're seeing? Or is there something else we can go on, maybe get a toehold on the problem?'

Kim turned to me.

'It's the only hard data,' she said. 'But I've been asking around a little bit since I called you, and . . . well, there are stories. Anecdotal evidence.'

'What kind?' Ex asked.

Kim settled back into the couch, her brow breaking into half a dozen tiny lines. She waved vaguely with one hand, holding her fingers as if she had a cigarette between them. I wondered if she'd ever been a smoker.

'Little things,' she said. 'One of the recovery room techs was talking about people coming out of anesthetic saying words and phrases in languages they don't speak. And apparently there's been a huge upswing in walk-aways in the last year.'

'Walk-aways?' Chogyi Jake said.

'Patients on the care floors go missing,' Kim said. 'Walk out on their own, AMA.'

'Against medical advice,' Aubrey said, anticipating my next question.

'Any signs of riders?' Ex asked.

Kim's sigh was sharp.

'*I* can't find anything,' she said carefully. 'I used some of the things Eric taught me. The Mark of Kadashman-Enlil and de Lancre's candle meditation.'

'De Lancre?' Chogyi Jake said, a little taken aback.

'What's de Lancre?' I asked.

'Seventeenth-century demonologist,' Ex said. 'Witch-finder. Burned a lot of women and Jews. He's not generally very well regarded.'

'Be that as it may,' Kim said, 'I can't find anyone who seems like a good suspect. I won't say there aren't any riders in the hospital, but if there are I haven't found them. And I can't explain what I *have* seen.'

'Meaning Oonishi's data,' Aubrey said.

'Yes,' said Chogyi Jake. 'Could we actually see that recording?'

While Kim fished around in her purse, I went back to my bedroom to get my laptop. I had the master suite with my own bathroom and a king-size bed and a window that would probably look better in the morning. Aubrey's bags were in there too, open and empty. I stopped for a few seconds to open the dresser and see his socks there beside my own. The little bits of cloth tangled together calmed me, and I went back into the living room feeling a little more grounded. Kim handed me a thumb drive, and I popped it in one of the laptop's USB ports. It took a minute to get the right application up, but then a huge window opened. We all crowded close to watch. The resolution sucked, but if I squinted, it was like seeing some old silent horror film. Count Orlok rising from his grave. The dream images went white, then flickered with strange things. An eye. A mouth. An oddly shaped hand. I felt a deep stillness in me, like they were things I recognized except for the bit where I didn't know what they were.

'Well,' Aubrey said from just behind me, 'the box looks like maybe an interment binding?'

'Symbolic burial,' Chogyi Jake said with what sounded like agreement. 'But if it's leaking like this, not a totally successful one. It could also be some kind of historical echo.'

'What about that hand?' Ex said. 'Did that seem familiar to anyone?'

'Couldn't tell much about it,' Aubrey said. 'It was pretty blurred.'

'Could it have been a Masonic reference?' Kim asked.

'Maybe Daughters of the Nile,' Ex said, but his voice carried a weight of skepticism.

The conversation dove into references and occult theory deeper than my personal bookshelf went. I detached myself from the group and headed for the kitchen. When they'd hashed it out, I'd get the FAQ version. That was how it usually went, and the scheme worked for me well.

There wasn't much. Eric hadn't stocked the place with anything that wouldn't last more or less indefinitely. Some canned beans. A few boxes of antiquated tea. The only thing in the cupboard was a box of Twinkies. None of it looked appealing. My cell phone said it was already after midnight. I'd woken up in Montana, and now, looking out over Lake Michigan as lightning arced over the water, I let myself feel a little tired. A hard gust of wind bowed the dark glass of the window, and in its dim reflection, the door opened behind me. Kim stepped in.

'Hey,' I said, turning to her.

'Is there any tea water left?' she asked.

'Can be,' I said, scooping the kettle off the stovetop. As I filled it, the tame water from the tap like a parody of the falling rain outside, Kim stood behind me, her arms crossed.

'How have you been?' she asked.

'Busy as hell. You?'

Kim pushed a lock of hair back from her eyes and I lit the fire under the teakettle.

'The same,' she said. 'Half the time I'm writing grants. I got on a good study with some guys I know over at UIC's public health department tracking *Toxoplasma gondii* strains. The data's not all in, but I think we're going to have some pretty good papers coming out of it. I'm linking the extent of behavior modification in the host with the virulence of the strain. The correlations are pretty nice.'

'Sounds good,' I said.

'It's kicking my ass,' Kim said. 'And the politics get old fast. Everyone's jockeying for money and attention. And there's a more or less constant war between patient care and research at the hospital. I get tired.'

'Yeah,' I said.

'And . . . and it's good to see you again. All of you,' she said. 'There's really no one in Chicago I can talk to. I slipped a few times when I first came here. Said things about riders. I'm still paying for it. Getting to let my guard down is . . . it's nice.'

It struck me harder than I'd expected. Standing there,

her arms across her chest, her lips just slightly pinched, her shoulders tight and unmoving—this was Kim at rest. Unguarded. Relaxed. I wanted to ask if she was seeing anyone, but that was answer enough. I wondered how I would have met someone new, knowing all that I'd learned about the secrets of the world. Would I have brought them into the fight too or kept it secret or given up the attempt and accepted my own isolation? I could see it going any of those ways.

'How about you?' she asked. 'What have you been doing?'

I ran down the past few months. Kim listened. The flow of words relaxed me, slowly. By the time I caught up to the present, I felt almost like we were just two old friends, catching up. And maybe gossiping a little.

'Does Ex have a little thing for you?' Kim asked.

'Um,' I said, glancing at the door. Then, quietly, 'A little one. I think it's little anyway. We don't make a big issue out of it. Is it obvious?'

'A little,' Kim said. 'Aubrey looks really good, though. It's nice to see him happy.'

It was the olive branch I'd been unconsciously asking for. My chest felt warm and softer, and laughter I didn't expect bubbled up out of me.

'Christ, I'm glad you think so,' I said. 'I can never *tell* with him. It's like if I was driving him crazy, I think he'd act just the same. How would I know, you know?'

Her smile was pure sympathy, and she reached out to press her fingertips briefly against my arm.

'Makes you crazy, doesn't it?' she said. 'About two years ago, I made the mistake of sleeping with a psychiatrist a few times. Whenever we had a disagreement, he'd start his active listening routine. Half the time I didn't know whether we were fighting.'

The kettle made a soft plopping noise and steam began to wisp up from the spout. I turned off the fire.

'It's good seeing you too,' I said.

'Good,' she said, and grinned. When she did that, the extra weight looked a lot better on her.

We went back into the living room together. Ex, Chogyi Jake, and Aubrey were all busily talking over one another, each of them apparently keeping track of what the others had said and responding even as new points were being made. Their excitement spilled over into me as I sat down.

'Hey. Hey!' I shouted. Anything more gentle would have been whispering in a windstorm. 'Have we figured anything out yet?'

The three men looked at one another.

'There's not enough here. We need more information,' Ex said, as if he was delivering a challenge. 'I'd like to examine the site.'

Maybe my relief at having a little ice-breaking moment with Kim blinded me. Maybe I was tired and careless. Or maybe I was too comfortable being who I had always been, rushing in again where angels feared. I didn't think. Didn't ask or even consider what the risks might be. I didn't feel a moment of apprehension or fear.

'Okay,' I said. 'Let's go.'

4

Two hours with a strong cup of morning coffee, Google, and Wikipedia yielded this:

When it was built in 1921, Grace Memorial was the second largest hospital in a city that was thick with them. Cook County Hospital was only a mile away, and Grace's redbrick towers and colonnaded walks, cathedral-style entrance, and massive network of wards and offices were a response to the older hospital's preeminence. But the original buildings changed fast; almost as soon as Grace opened for business, the construction crews came in.

In 1929, the Bureau of Prohibition raided the hospital, recovering enough gin, rum, and beer to feed Chicago's speakeasies for a week. The men responsible for building the network of smuggler's tunnels and secret warehouses fled or were arrested, and the hospital itself almost didn't survive the scandal. All through the 1930s, Grace Memorial had a reputation as Chicago's hospital of last resort. A prostitution ring ran out of it from 1936 to 1939. One whole wing was demolished as structurally unsound.

The Manhattan Project came to its rescue in 1942. While Fermi conducted the first controlled nuclear reaction at the University of Chicago, the Army Corps of Engineers quietly took control of Grace Memorial, retooling it for research on the effects of radiation. When, in 1946, that project ended, a new group stepped up with the stated intention of making Grace Memorial a functioning hospital again. President Truman himself signed the documents that transferred control of the buildings away from the army. Over the next half-decade, Grace Memorial became a cause célèbre among the highest ranks of Chicagoan society. Mies van der Rohe and Declan Souder—the two great lights of Chicago architecture—competed for the chance to redesign it, with van der Rohe dropping out at the last minute to go work on the Farnsworth House.

In the 1970s, it entered into partnership with the University of Illinois at Chicago—one of the largest medical schools in the nation—and became a teaching and research hospital with the joint missions of serving the poor and supporting cutting-edge medical research. If that particular pairing sounded a little ominous to me, no one else seemed to blink. The worst scandal it had been involved with since then was a 1998 report about failures to conform to the Americans with Disabilities Act.

Nothing online mentioned ominous dreams or boxes in dark earth. None of the graphics were of weirdly staring eyes or improbably jointed hands. I hadn't really expected the Internet to deliver all the answers, but there was nothing there to give me traction. My little spate of research did give me enough background to understand what I was looking at when, after a half-hour drive through the rain-scrubbed streets, we got there.

'Wow,' I said. 'Ugly.'

Ex craned his neck as Aubrey drove us all past.

'It looks like ten other buildings that got in a car wreck,' he said.

'It's worse inside,' Kim said. 'When I was interviewing for the job here, they asked how well I read maps. I thought it was a joke.'

She was understating the case. After we stuck Kim's permit to the window and found a space in faculty parking, she led us to her office. The public areas of the hospital were pleasant enough—well lit, with living plants and relatively humane paint jobs—but as soon as Kim used her key card to get us past the wide metal Authorized Personnel Only doors, things got weird. We passed through two long, looping hallways to an elevator that said we were on the second floor even though we were still at street level. Then up three levels to floor 5-East (as opposed to 5-West, which was actually the floor below). Kim led us through two more sets of locked doors with bright orange biohazard markers on them, and we stepped into a cramped area wider than a hallway but too narrow to be a room where three desks huddled together. A black man with thinning white hair nodded to us as we passed.

'This has got to be a joke,' I said as Kim unlocked the final door. 'Who designed this place, and where'd they put my cheese?'

'All hospitals are like this to some degree,' Aubrey said. 'My postgrad research was a collaboration with some MDs at the University of New Mexico. I always had to meet people at the front of the place and guide them in.'

'I remember that,' Kim said. 'Grace is worse.'

The office was too small for all of us to fit comfortably. There wasn't even space to put down the backpack I used as a purse. A thin window had wedged itself in one corner, daylight spilling across one wall. Kim's computer hummed and whirred, a screen saver cycling through images that I assumed fit in with her work: X-rays of skulls, bright pink-and-white pictures of what might have been flesh, drawings of complex microorganisms with joke labels on them like 'extra cheese' and 'On the Internet, no one knows you're infectious.' The air smelled of oil and old carpet.

'We do our actual lab workups down in Pathology or over on the UIC campus,' Kim said as she dug through a small metal filing cabinet, 'but the paperwork's all here.'

'Who are you working with?' Aubrey asked.

'Alepski and Namkung,' she said.

Aubrey crossed his arms and leaned against one wall.

'Didn't expect to hear *those* names again,' he said.

'Namkung's the official lead, but she came here because Alepski and I were willing to sign on if the study was based out of Grace. They ask about you sometimes.'

'And what do you tell them?' he said with a laugh in his voice.

'That you're traveling the world,' Kim said. 'They're comfortable with that. It's a good team. One of the nice things about working with them is that sometimes the residents will actually consult with me.'

'Why wouldn't they?' Ex asked.

'I've got a PhD. Alepski and Namkung both went on to get MDs, and so I'm respectable by association,' Kim said, as if that explained everything. When she stood up, she had a card in her hand. I caught a glimpse of an old picture of Aubrey on it and a silver magnetic strip. 'I got guest researcher access for Aubrey on the strength of the papers we did together. It won't get you on the medical wards, but if you need to get in there, you can use it to sweet-talk the nursing staff.'

'And the rest of us?' Chogyi Jake asked.

'Are limited to public areas or else going chaperoned,' Kim said. 'Or you can get a white coat, carry a clipboard, and scowl a lot. That's usually enough to keep anyone from bothering you.'

'Security *would* be difficult with this many people,' Chogyi Jake said.

'More than people, it's the different systems,' Kim said. 'On any given ward, you've got the nurses and technicians who work there, and the doctors who come in and out. And then the therapists. And the social work staff. And security and the physical plant guys. Janitorial. Kitchen staff. Compliance inspectors from the state and the fed. And the researchers like me. And the patients. And the families. And everyone answers to a different set of management, if they answer to anyone at all. Everyone has different methods for interacting with everyone else. It's a complex tissue. By and large, if you aren't keeping someone from doing their job, they don't much care whether you're there or not.'

'So don't piss off the security guys,' Aubrey said as he clipped his new ID card to his belt. It was just a little square of plastic, but it made him look like he belonged there. It was such a small thing to be a disguise.

'That should be all right,' I said. 'We're just getting the lay of the land, right? Basic recon.'

'Fair enough,' Kim said. 'Where did you want to start?'

'I assume there's a chaplain,' Ex said. 'Resident priest might have more of an idea of the spiritual state of play than the other staff.'

'And is there a mental health service?' Chogyi Jake asked with his customary smile. 'Possession can be mistaken for mental illness.'

'There are three, actually,' Kim said. 'Adult, pediatric, and geriatric, but the psych wards are high privacy. They're strict about keeping patient information away from anyone but physicians and family. If we get someone specifically that we want to look at, I can try to talk to the attending. But even then it'll be tough.'

'Maybe just the commissary, then,' Chogyi Jake said. 'Where the nurses and technicians would be likely to eat.'

'Is there something you're looking for?' I asked.

He spread his hands in a gesture I took to mean *anything interesting*.

'I'd like to see Oonishi's lab,' I said. 'Dreamland. If that's where this thing is showing up, that seems like a good place to start.'

'I'm fine with any of it,' Aubrey said. 'How do you want to do this? All stick together, or split up the party?'

The last questions were directed at me. All gazes shifted. While it was true that I was responsible for signing all the checks, I still hadn't quite gotten my head around being the boss. Moments like this one left me squirming inside, but I put my brave face on.

'Let's split up,' I said. 'Cover some ground. I figure the chaplain is going to be someone you can get to without going through restricted-access areas. The staff commissary, maybe not. So how about Ex tackles the priest, Aubrey and Chogyi Jake can go schmooze with the locals, and Kim can introduce me to Oonishi. It's eight thirty now, so find out what you can, and we'll plan to meet up for lunch and compare notes.'

'I think we have a plan,' Aubrey said.

'We should set a solid meeting place and time,' Kim said. 'Cell phones are kind of tricky in the buildings.'

We settled on half past twelve in the main lobby. Kim wrote detailed maps to get Ex, Chogyi Jake, and Aubrey where they were going, and then we headed off. It didn't take long before we were in the public parts of the hospital again. We passed a waiting room where an oversized television was blasting *SpongeBob SquarePants* to a shell-shocked, unsmiling family. In the hallway, a guy who was just about my age hunched over his cell phone, saying something about lab results and trying not to cry. The air smelled like cleaning solution. Outside the windows, blue sky and fluffy white clouds hung high above the buildings, pretending there had never been a storm. The Sears Tower—now officially the Willis Tower—peeked out from behind smaller, closer structures, and I tried to pay more attention to it than to the thousand small human dramas we were walking past. It seemed polite.

'What a difference a year makes,' Kim said. Her voice sounded tight. Clipped.

'You think?' It hung halfway between question and agreement, and it got a hint of a smile. She didn't elaborate, and I didn't press.

Thinking about it as Kim led me confidently down the corridors and wards, I realized there was something to what she said. It wasn't that the others wouldn't have listened to me before—well, except Ex, and that was more about his own weird paternalistic streak. But when Kim had first met me, I'd been younger. And it was more than just the months and weeks. It was the mileage.

Being Eric—taking over the work he'd left behind—had put me in harm's way more than once, but it had also given me chances to figure out who I was. To try being the sort of person I wanted to become. I was more confident than I'd been the first time she met me, more in control of myself and the people around me. I wondered if my parents would have recognized me as the same girl who'd hurried through the kitchen on her way to school and church, or if I'd become someone so alien to my own past that I'd be a stranger to them. I wasn't sure if the idea left me sad or proud.

I was still lost in thought when it happened.

We passed through a set of automated swinging doors, a blue-and-white sign above them announcing the rooms

within as the Cardiac Care Unit. The hallway marched out
before us, the glass walls of patients' rooms arrayed around
a wide, high nurses' station, the same panopticon architecture as a prison. Half a dozen men and women in hospital
uniform and almost that many in civilian clothes stood
behind the desk or before it, engaged in at least three
separate conversations. I didn't see the man until I bumped
into him. It was like stumbling against a wall.

'Sorry,' I said.

'*You*,' he said, and then, 'What the hell is your
problem?'

He was red-haired and freckled, his jaw wide and starting to sag a little at the jowls. He stood a head and a half
taller than me, which put him on the large side, even for a
guy. His scrubs were powder blue, and an ID tag much like
Kim's hung from his neck. The rage in his eyes unsettled
me.

'I'm sorry,' I said. 'I was thinking about some—'

He moved in front of me, blocking my way with an out-
thrust chest. A red flush was climbing up his neck.

'You were thinking?' he said. 'You've got to be shitting
me. That's you *thinking*?'

I looked at Kim looking back at me. I had hoped—expected,
even—outrage and maybe an echo of my own sudden fear.
Instead, she was considering me like I was an interesting bug.
Everyone at the nurses' station had turned toward us. All the
conversations had stopped. A nervous glance over my shoulder, and I saw the patients in the fishbowl rooms staring at me
too. I lifted my hands and took a step back.

'Look, I said I was sorry. I just bumped—'

'You piece of shit.'

His voice was low and shaking with rage. I felt the cold electricity of adrenaline hitting my bloodstream. Kim didn't say anything.

'You piece of *shit*,' he said again.

The fear didn't leave me—nothing simple as that—but an answering rage started to bubble up alongside it.

'Hey!' I said. 'I don't know what your problem is, but I've had about as much—'

The red-haired man drew in a long, rough breath.

And so did everyone else.

Each nurse at the station. Patients watching us through the open doorways of their rooms. Breath is a small thing, a subtle thing, until it's coordinated, and then it's devastating. A moment ago, I'd been having a surreal encounter with the poster boy for steroid rage. Now, that soft, vast sound made me something very small in the middle of an unexpected battleground. I felt myself go suddenly, dangerously calm. It wasn't quite the I'm-not-driving experience of being in a fight, but I could feel myself leaning in toward that. The man's breath quickened, and the other people matched it. I took a step back. His hands were balled into huge fists.

'Kim?' I said, but her breath was keeping time with the sharp panting that rose up all around me. Whatever this was, it had taken her too. I licked my lips and pulled my qi—the vital energy that fuels magic and life—up from my belly and into my throat.

'Kim,' I said, pushing the power out into my voice. 'Wake up.'

I didn't take my eyes off the red-haired man, but in my peripheral vision, I saw her fall out of the pattern. She put a hand to her head and looked around. The red-haired man was trembling now, shaking with barely restrained violence. Two of the nurses behind the station put down long gray folders and stepped out into the hallway behind him. A blond woman in a business suit came out of one of the patient care rooms, her hands at her sides like claws. King Mob, closing ranks. Their synchronized breath filled the space: a single, huge, animal sound.

'Jayné?' Kim said.

'Just stay cool, and when I tell you to run, run,' I said. And then, 'Okay. *Run!*'

5

We bolted.

Behind us, the mob roared with a single voice. Kim and I burst through the doors at the ward's entrance hard enough that my arm stung. Kim took a sharp left, and, only skidding a little on the traffic-polished linoleum floor, I followed her. She ran like a sprinter, her body straight and aligned, her arms pumping along with her stride, her hands flat. She'd kicked off her shoes.

Just as we reached the wide, triangular space before a bank of brushed steel elevators, the red-haired man caught up. He surged up behind me, swung a wide arm, and pushed Kim's racing body into the wall. The impact sounded like a slap, and she fought to keep her balance before she fell. Between one heartbeat and the next, I found myself quietly behind my eyes while my body took over. I ran toward the elevators, the red-haired man hard behind me. Like something out of a Hong Kong action flick, I ran up the closed metal door, pushed off, and flew for a second, backward and down. I landed on both feet and one hand, our opponent's broad back in front of me. He tried to turn, but I jumped forward, driving the heel of my palm right about where his left kidney was.

He grunted once and went down like a sack of flour.

Kim was still getting to her feet. I tried to call out to her, to ask if she was all right, but my throat didn't respond; the wards and protections were driving, and my body was not yet my own. It took half a second to understand why. The red-haired man had been the fastest, but the others were coming. The low rumble of their feet was like a small earthquake. From the opposite direction, an older man in a white lab coat walked toward the elevators, saw me, saw Kim and the groaning man on the floor. His eyes widened, and he backpedaled fast. Smart cookie. The mob rounded the corner.

Seven of them ran toward me, mouths in square gapes of rage. When they saw me, they started screaming together, one voice from all their throats. The blond woman who'd come out of the patient's room leaped for Kim. I shifted forward to protect her, but the others were on me. I kicked hard into someone's knee, feeling it give way. An elbow got me in the ribs, but not hard enough to break them. A man in a nurse's uniform lifted me by my shirt and the waist of my jeans like he was going to throw me. I brought my knee up into his jaw and my palm down on the bridge of his nose. His blood spattered my belly, and he dropped me.

I caught a glimpse of Kim wrestled to her knees by the blond woman. A dark-skinned man with a salt-and-pepper beard drove his shoulder into my gut, pushing me back by main force. I dropped my elbow into his neck, and three new attackers rounded the corner. Watching from the still space behind my eyes, I was afraid for Kim, I was afraid for the men and women boiling out of the cardiac ward with murder in mind, but from the moment the red-haired man fell, I wasn't worried about myself. I'd fought riders before, and they didn't go down this easy.

A man threw a clipboard at my face, and I knocked it away as I dodged one of the new women's kicks. I sank my foot into the softness of a fat man's belly, his breath gusting out as he collapsed. Someone grabbed me from the back. When I dropped, turning into them, and brought my foot down on their instep hard enough to crunch, the grip at my neck went slack.

They were fighting, but they were fighting like people: fragile, untrained, inflamed with anger, but not technique or supernatural power. I put my faith in Eric's protections, and my body danced around the blows as I worked my way toward Kim. More of the mob's reinforcements came, but each group that arrived seemed weaker and slower than the last. The people who couldn't run as well catching up. I started to wonder if the cardiac patients would show up too, throwing IV stands and catheter bags at me.

I got to Kim's side as the elevator behind us chimed, a red down-pointing arrow glowing. My fist sank deep into the blond woman's throat, and I lifted Kim up. Her hair was tangled, and a trickle of blood marked her hairline.

'I'm okay,' Kim said. The elevator doors slid open. An elderly woman in a wheelchair and a girl who must have been her granddaughter started to come out, then hesitated. There were a dozen bodies on the floor, either unconscious or incapacitated and groaning. I pushed Kim into the elevator car past the wheelchair and turned back. Five of the mob were struggling to their feet, chests rising and falling together, and none of them coming close enough to make a real attack.

As the doors closed, they screamed. Frustration, anger, despair. The sound of a predator whose prey has just made it down the rabbit hole. I sagged against the wall, my body my own again. I felt bruised and spent and jittery. Kim was on her feet, wiping at the trail of blood on her face, her efforts smearing the mess more than cleaning it. The elderly woman and the girl stared at us nervously.

'Insurance problem,' I said, my voice whiskey-rough. 'No big deal.'

The old woman nodded and smiled like I'd made any sense at all. My knuckles ached where I'd skinned them on something. On someone. When Kim spoke, she sounded as calm and businesslike as ever.

'We need to get to the others,' she said. I nodded. If we were in danger, they were too. We had to get them out. I willed the car to go down faster. The numbers kept moving at the same, deliberate speed.

'I take it this hasn't happened before,' I said.

She didn't dignify me with an answer.

It took us ten minutes to find someplace in the hospital with cell reception, but we got through to Aubrey and Ex on our first calls, and after that, it was like a fire drill. No running. No questions. We all walked quickly and deliberately out of the buildings, to the street, and away. In the full light of the sun, I felt the first tremors of my coming

61

adrenaline crash. Mentally, I felt fine. Emotionally, I had no problems. It was just that my hands were shaking and I was a little nauseated. It would get worse before it got better, and I'd do my level best to ignore it then too.

As we walked, I brought the others up to speed. What had happened, how we'd dealt with it. We'd covered three long city blocks before I could bring myself to stop at a sidewalk café and sit for a while. It was Greek food, and the blue-and-white sign promised real Greek coffee. We took a wide, steel-mesh table set back in a patio of cracking cement that might have been a basketball court, once upon a time. The fading blue umbrella stood in the center of it like the mast of a sailboat, but it was thin enough that we could all still see one another. When Kim sat and started rubbing her feet, I remembered that she'd ditched her shoes. Three city blocks was a long way for bare feet on concrete. If she'd said something, I would have stopped sooner.

'It wasn't possession,' Ex said after a thin, olive-skinned boy who looked about thirteen took our orders. 'If they'd had riders, Jayné wouldn't have been able to snap Kim out of it with an improvised cantrip.'

'So magic, then,' I said. 'Someone with a rider who could throw some kind of mass mind-control mojo? And who knew we were there?'

They were all silent for a moment.

'There's some holes in that,' Aubrey said.

'Like?' I asked. It came across sharper than I'd meant it to, but he didn't take offense.

'Well, for instance, how did he know you were there? Eric's wards are supposed to keep you from being found, right?'

'What if he wasn't using magic to find me?' I said. 'It's not like you can't take a picture of me. Or see me if you look across the room. The villagers didn't pull out their pitchforks and come after you guys. Kim's been there for years without anything taking a swing at her. I have to think he was after me specifically.'

Kim shook her head.

'That doesn't scan either,' she said. 'If someone's using mundane strategies to find you, why use some kind of proxy magic to attack you? Why not just shoot you? And for that matter, why shoot *you* in the first place? Unless that was supposed to be some kind of warning.'

'Maybe it was reacting to Eric's wards and protections,' Aubrey said. 'You know. Watching for someone with the most armor and figuring they're the one that poses the biggest threat?'

'Or an autoimmune response,' Kim said. 'Magic that saw other magic as not-self?'

'There's a comforting thought,' I said.

Chogyi Jake leaned forward in his chair. His fingers laced his knee, and when he spoke, his voice was thoughtful.

'We're missing something. What did it feel like?' he asked. I was on the edge of telling him it felt like being the soccer ball at the World Cup when I realized he wasn't talking to me. Kim brushed back her hair with one hand.

'Like dreaming,' she said. 'I didn't have the sense of

63

being ridden or out of control. But my logic and reality sort of fell out from under me. Jayné was Jayné, but she was also . . . an outsider? Foreign? Something like that.'

'A threat,' Chogyi Jake said.

'Yes, definitely. And one that I recognized,' she said, then frowned and looked down.

'What is it?' Aubrey asked. Kim looked up at him. I couldn't read her expression.

'I can remember it from other perspectives,' she said. 'The shift nurse at the station? If I think about it, I know what we looked like through her eyes, Jayné and I both. The big guy who started the trouble? I remember Jayné bumping into me as if I had been him. I can remember it from any perspective until she woke me up.'

'Even Jayné's?' Aubrey asked.

'No. Not hers.'

'Okay,' I said. 'So what does that mean?'

'It means we don't know what we're dealing with,' Ex said.

The big debate after lunch was how—and whether—to go back for the car. On the one hand, we didn't know what was going on at the hospital or how far out the danger extended. On the other, it was a rental and it had Kim's parking permit and some of Ex's stuff in it. There was the option of hiring a tow truck, but sending a civilian to spring a trap meant for us had some ethical problems.

Once we agreed to go back, there was the question of whether I should go on the return trip because Eric's wards and protections would help fight off any assaults or stay behind out of fear that they might be drawing some kind of spiritual attention. In the end, Aubrey and I went for the car, the others staying at the café drinking the muddy coffee and eating baklava. The walk back was shorter than I'd expected. Escaping from Grace into the still-unknown streets of Chicago had given every block an exaggerated distance. I was surprised by how quickly the hospital's awkward, looming bulk came into view. I kept scanning the other people on the sidewalks, waiting for them to start moving together or breathing in sync.

A taxi driver to our right leaned hard on his horn, shouting obscenities at the truck that had cut him off. The air smelled of exhaust. Grace Memorial loomed across the street, hundreds of windows catching the light like an insect's compound eye as we walked briskly past it toward the parking structure. A little shiver crawled up my spine, and I walked faster.

Aubrey walked with his hands in his pockets and his brow in furrows. I'd seen him like this before—worried, but trying not to talk about it for fear of worrying me. It was a deeply ineffective strategy.

'Spit it out,' I said. We were stopped at a traffic light, waiting for the signal to cross.

'It's nothing. I just wish I'd known Eric better,' he said. 'I worked with him on and off for years, and I always . . . I don't know. Respected his boundaries? Gave him his space? I never pushed to find out things he didn't want to tell me about. He would have known what this was. Just from what we've got now, he'd have known. And I don't.'

'Neither does anyone else.'

'Yeah,' Aubrey said with a rueful smile. 'But I'm not responsible for them.'

'It'll be fine. We'll be careful,' I said. And then, 'How are you doing with seeing Kim again?'

'Fine. She's . . . just the same.'

'No return of old feelings? Regret about signing the divorce papers?'

Aubrey's eyebrows rose, and a small, amused smile tweaked the corners of his mouth.

'How are *you* doing seeing Kim again?' he said.

'Standard insecurity,' I said.

'You could stop that.'

'Nope. Don't think I can. I'm aiming for having a good sense of humor about it.'

He leaned in, his fingers twining around mine.

'Jayné,' he said. 'You're great. And I love you. And if you and I weren't together, I still wouldn't be with Kim. I think she's a good person. I enjoy her company, and I admire her intelligence. We have a lot of history, but we broke up for a reason. I'm pretty sure she was seeing someone else, even before she left Denver.'

A totally different kind of fear bloomed in my chest. It was stupid. Kim's affair with Eric wasn't even my secret, except that I knew about it. And still, at that moment I wished I'd spilled her beans a year ago.

'How do you know?'

'I don't,' he said. 'Not really. It was just the feeling I got. Some unexpected long nights. Some inexplicable crying jags. I knew she was unhappy, and when she decided to leave, I told her it was the right decision.'

I stopped in the concrete archway. Rows of tightly packed cars stood in the shadows. Aubrey paused, looking back at me.

'Would you want to know now?' I asked, trying to make it sound hypothetical. 'I mean if you could know now what was really going on with her back then, would you want to?'

'What would the point be? We did what we did,' he said. 'And I think we've got enough to worry about without hauling all that back from the dead.'

In the parking garage proper, we had a moment's panic that the minivan was gone, but as soon as we figured out we were on the wrong level, everything went smoothly. We were back on the streets in a few minutes, and if Aubrey chose a longer, looping route back to the café rather than drive past Grace, I didn't object.

I leaned against the door, watching out the window as we drove. Men and women stood or walked along the gray, urban streetscape. It wasn't as gray and overwhelming as Manhattan had been, but had almost more of a sense of being a living, human city. A black man in a neatly pressed suit drove a sports car alongside us, his eyes on the street ahead even as he talked with a lighter-colored child in the car seat behind him. A painfully thin Asian woman sat at a bus stop, her arms crossed, her mouth set in a scowl. A pack of teenagers in matching black-and-orange uniforms that said Leo Catholic High School held up traffic by running through the crosswalk as the lights changed, bubbling with laughter and shrieking with delight at their danger.

The city was alive. Almost three million people with lives as complex and intersecting as my own, navigating the daily pulse of rush hour on the 90, the 94, the 290. Riding the elevated trains. Every day, they were eating their dinners and talking with their friends and cheating on their lovers. And in the middle of all this normal, rich, oddly beautiful human life, *something* was happening. Something at Grace Memorial. And the more I let my mind wander, the more a growing knot in my belly told me it was something very, very bad.

6

Looking back at my childhood, I couldn't say my father had done me many favors. The lessons he'd tried to instill in me—things like 'never wear a skirt that goes above the ankle' and 'Jesus died because kids sneak into movie theaters'—never really took. But that's not the same as saying I never learned anything from him. Throughout the weird, judgmental, just-barely-repressed Christian rage-fest that was my childhood home, I'd picked up quite a bit about how the world works. Not all of it had immediately applied, but some bits still came in handy.

For instance, when I was ten years old, the doctors found a suspicious lump on my big brother Jay's spinal column. My mother called from the doctor's office in hysterics, saying that no one was telling her anything, and they were running tests she didn't understand. I could hear every word she said, even though my father had the telephone handset to his ear. He sat at the kitchen table, scowling and fighting to interrupt my mother's litany of fear and confusion. He was in a white T-shirt and the battered canvas work pants he always wore on his days off. In the end, he told my mother to sit down, be quiet, and wait. Then he told me to find my little brother, Curtis, and get him in the car. That I was too young to stay by myself, and he didn't have time to find someone to watch us. His tone of voice left no room for disagreement.

By the time I'd done what he said, little Curt squirming in his car seat and demanding cartoons, my father had transformed himself. His hair was combed back. He had a good gray suit on with a deep red tie. He smelled of cologne, and he looked like a movie star or a president. I'd never seen him this way, even for church.

When we got to the doctor's office, he dropped Curtis and me in the waiting room with my mother, and went back to speak to the doctors and nurses. Five minutes later, he came out with answers to every question Mom had asked him. My mother drank all the information in—yes, Jay was going to be admitted overnight; yes, cancer was a possibility, but it wasn't the best suspect; no, there wasn't cause for immediate alarm. I watched relief pour over her like cool water on a burn. But I didn't miss my father's little smile or my mother's near-subliminal frown. The gray-suited man had been given a level of courtesy and respect that a woman couldn't get.

Lesson learned.

Truth was, Chogyi Jake looked amazing in the right outfit. Brown linen so light it was almost blond, a black linen vest of matching cut, pin-striped shirt and tie that coordinated like a symphony perfectly in tune. He'd let the stubble of hair grow out just enough for the scattering of gray at the temples to show. When he chose not to smile, he could look seriously dangerous. By comparison, Aubrey, even in his best suit, never quite gave off the air of command, and Ex's long hair wasn't quite overcome by his quasiclerical black and humorless attitude. And me? Yes, I was the money behind everything. Yes, I was the one Kim called. Yes, I was Eric's heir and successor with the weird supernatural powers and protections. I was also twenty-four and a woman, and even in my best clothes and most understated makeup, I looked more like Jennifer Connelly than an international demon hunter and occult expert. So by common agreement, Chogyi Jake took point.

'Thank you for joining us, Dr. Oonishi. I'm sorry we couldn't come to your office.'

'Thank you,' the man said. 'It's probably good if we don't meet at Grace.'

'There are reputations to protect,' Kim said, only a little bitterness in her voice. Her dress was sherbet green and didn't suit her. She wore it like a smock.

The restaurant sat on the river, broad windows looking out over water glowing gold with sunset. A yacht had tied up while we were being seated, and now a young man had climbed up one of the deck ladders and was paying for his to-go order. The skyscrapers of downtown rose up around us like trees above rabbits, and the cool evening breeze mixed the smells of water and freshly grilled steak. Oonishi sat forward with his elbows on the table. His gaze shifted between us, restless and uneasy.

'I take it,' he said to Chogyi Jake, 'you understand why I need help with this problem?'

'Of course,' Chogyi Jake said. 'And I understand why

discretion is important. We have experience with this kind of issue. You don't have anything to worry about.'

He delivered the lines with a conviction that almost had me forgetting that we'd had a small riot on the Cardiac Care Unit earlier in the day. Oonishi either hadn't heard about it or hadn't put it together with our arrival, because he looked reassured.

'What can you tell us about the problem?' Ex asked.

'You've seen the data sets?' Oonishi asked, turning his head almost imperceptibly toward Kim. When Chogyi Jake nodded, he continued, 'We've been running the tertiary tests for almost three months now. Three nights a week, the subjects come to the lab. There are anomalies as early as the second session.'

'Can you give me the date on that?' I asked. It was a safe question. The kind of thing that even a jumped-up secretary might ask.

'I've brought a copy of the study logs,' he said. 'Everything's there. Dates, names, times.'

'Great,' I said, keeping the annoyance out of my voice. I'd asked him for a piece of information, not where I could go to look it up. But I let it slide.

'At first, it wasn't simultaneous. It was only a common set of images. I thought it was day residue.'

'I don't follow,' Ex said.

Watching Oonishi shift from embarrassed client to popular scientist was like watching the playback of myself in Trevor's dojo. He didn't exactly move, his expression didn't quite change, but he was suddenly more grounded than he'd been before. His nervous half smile vanished.

'What we're learning about perception,' he said, 'is that it's very dependent on priming. The actual experience of vision, of seeing, is associated with activity in the V1 and V2 layers of your visual cortex. What the neuroanatomists have found is more neurons enter V1 and V2 from the deeper parts of the brain than from the optic nerve.'

'Implying what?' Ex asked.

'That your conceptual and emotional knowledge affects not just your interpretation of what you see, but what you actually see,' Oonishi said. 'Five years ago, a man in Madison, Wisconsin, had a heart attack. Fell over in the street. An off-duty paramedic happened to be there. He started administering CPR.'

'They shot him,' Aubrey said. 'I heard about that.'

'Yes,' Oonishi said. 'The paramedic was black. One of the passersby saw a young black man straddling an older white man and shot him. When the police arrested the shooter, she swore the paramedic had been stabbing the man. She'd seen the blood. She'd seen the knife. There had been no blood. No knife. But she was adamant she'd seen it.'

'And you say she did?' Aubrey asked.

'I say she did. Not because it was there, but because she expected it to be. There are any number of simple experiments that prove your knowledge and emotion affect your actual perception. If you look at a sign just at the edge of your visual range, you can experience the letters becoming sharper when someone tells you what they are. This isn't even controversial.'

'Okay, but back to the data,' I said. 'The thing in the dreams. Day residue?'

Oonishi glanced his annoyance at me. I wasn't doing a great job of letting Chogyi take point, but the further we veered from the issue at hand, the more impatient I got. I saw Kim nodding as if in agreement. Someone at the table behind us laughed at something, a high, masculine sound.

'If there was something,' Oonishi said, 'that all the subjects had seen—a movie or a popular commercial—I would have had an explanation of the image's recurrence. They would all have seen it recently, and so when they lost the input from their optic nerves, they would be primed to impose that image on the visual cortex from below, as it were.'

'Didn't work out,' Chogyi Jake said.

'No. It didn't. I talked to the subjects after that session. None of them identified the images. They didn't even remember having dreamed them. And then, when the images started coming at the same time . . .'

'So it began two months ago,' Ex said.

'This did,' Oonishi said. 'My study did. But I wasn't looking before then. It might be something that's been happening for years. Decades.'

Kim didn't bring up the anecdotal evidence she'd heard—the walk-aways or the people coming up from anesthetic saying foreign phrases. She was paging through

Oonishi's study logs. Her mouth pressed thin, and her eyebrows drew in toward each other.

'Do your subjects have any recollection of the dreams now?' Chogyi Jake asked.

'I haven't asked,' Oonishi said, and then, pronouncing each word very carefully, 'I have been afraid to.'

'We may need to explore it,' Chogyi Jake said.

In the uncomfortable silence, our waiter appeared with our meals. I'd gotten the fourteen-dollar BLT. I took a bite as the waiter passed the other plates around and asked if he could get any of us anything. My tomatoes tasted a little like cardboard, but the bacon was good. Oonishi was quiet until the waiter had gone, and even then spoke in a low voice.

'I would rather that we kept this among ourselves,' he said. 'I haven't even spoken to the other researchers.'

'They must know something's up,' Kim said. 'Unless you invite parasitologists to your lab at midnight on a regular basis, they'll wonder why I was there.'

'They think I'm trying to bang you,' Oonishi said. Kim's eyes went a degree wider, and I felt some of her shock. My cough meant I was offended on her behalf, but Oonishi only gave a surprisingly boyish smile and shrugged. I found myself liking him less.

'We can be discreet,' Aubrey said coolly, 'but we can't work without evidence. Would you prefer that we address the subject outside your study, or would you like to present it as part of the research?'

Oonishi looked to Chogyi Jake in appeal, but he only

got an enigmatic smile in return. After a long moment's silence, he gave in.

'I can interview them about the dreams,' Oonishi said. 'You'll need to tell me what to ask.'

'One of us should be there,' I said, and Ex scowled at me. Having one of us present at the interviews would probably mean going back into Grace.

'We'll discuss that,' Chogyi Jake said. 'But we should also address the price.'

'Price?' Oonishi said.

Chogyi Jake spread his hands toward the plates before us.

'We have to eat somehow, Doctor,' he said.

Over the next fifteen minutes, Chogyi Jake and Oonishi haggled quietly while the rest of us ate. I didn't care what the answer was. My attention was on the others. Kim chewed slowly, her face a blank, but her eyes kept moving to Oonishi. I couldn't tell what she was thinking. Aubrey was watching her too, and the anger on his face was like the perception experiments Oonishi had told us about. Even though it was subtle, I could see it clearly because I was prepared to see it. What I couldn't say was what it meant.

They settled on three hundred dollars a day with a one-month cap, payable when the inconvenient data stopped appearing in his study. Any longer than a month, and he wouldn't have time to get enough fresh data, and he'd have to push back publication of his reports. We'd build a list of questions. He'd record the interviews, and if we needed follow-ups, they could go through him. Oonishi got to keep us his dirty little secret, and none of us had to go back to the hospital. Except Kim.

We got back to the condo in the last gloom of twilight. Lake Michigan spread out before us. With the storm clouds blown off, it was a darkness scattered with the lights from boats still on the water. Ex threw himself onto the couch. Chogyi Jake shrugged out of his jacket and went to the kitchen, followed quickly by the beep of the microwave and the smell of green tea. Aubrey and Kim and I sat at the dining room table, our chairs turned so that we could see Ex in the next room. When Chogyi Jake returned, cup of too-hot tea held gingerly before him, he was shaking his head.

'This place still feels small.'

'All right,' Ex said. 'Thoughts and opinions?'

Aubrey was the first to speak.

'I don't think he has much to tell. Apart from the data we've already gotten, he doesn't know much. He's resistant to actually working with us. I think he's going to do as little as possible.'

'He did call us in,' I said. 'That's something.'

'It may have been a desperation move,' Chogyi Jake said. 'And I think he's regretting it.'

'Exactly,' Aubrey said. 'That's exactly the feeling I get.'

Kim cleared her throat, a small sound.

'I think you're all being too harsh,' she said. 'And what's more, you're missing the point.'

Aubrey stiffened like he'd been slapped.

'Well, you *are*,' Kim said. 'Oonishi's a scientist, but he's also human. He's stumbled into something outside his frame of reference. It throws everything he's ever done into question, so of course he's frightened and trying to make it all go away. As I recall, your first experience with Eric wasn't all that different.'

'*Mine?*' Aubrey said.

'You babbled for a week,' Kim said. 'You did everything you could to convince yourself it was all some kind of elaborate joke. At least he's not doing that. If you give him a year or two to get his head around the idea, he could be very useful. But, as I said, that isn't the point. Even if he's totally recalcitrant, something is happening at the hospital. And as of today, something with the potential for real violence. That makes it our responsibility.'

'Does it?' Aubrey said. 'I mean, does it *really?*'

'Yes,' Kim said.

Aubrey's laugh was short and exasperated. A vague unease grew in my gut, like I was six again and listening to my father chiding Mom: an intimate disagreement between people who knew each other very, very well. For the first time, I wondered how Kim had felt about Oonishi's joking suggestion of sexual impropriety. And whether Aubrey might be jealous.

'We do have some access to the dreamers,' Chogyi Jake said, and sipped his tea. 'And the sooner we get our questions together, the sooner we'll know what they said. It may be that nothing comes of it, or we might get lucky.'

'I'd like him to replay the dream for them,' Ex said.

'Before any of the questions are asked, I want to see how they react physically when they see the thing.'

For a long moment, Aubrey seemed caught between two conversations: the argument with Kim and the planning session that Chogyi Jake and Ex were offering up to redirect it. Kim looked away, out the wide, dark windows. The angles of light and shadow made her look old. When Aubrey spoke, the effort in it showed.

'What kinds of questions do we want him to ask?'

For the next two hours, we built up a rough questionnaire and speculated on different kinds of riders, different flavors of magic. Kim and Aubrey relaxed slowly into the conversation, and my own unease faded even if it didn't go completely away. Ex and Aubrey went on a long side track about the causes of shared dreams, including one particularly unpleasant one we'd all had once when something very powerful was looking for us. Kim suggested taking Oonishi's dream data to someone who could do image enhancement, maybe put together the six versions of the dream to find more detail than we had in the raw feed. I had my laptop out and was typing up the instructions to my lawyer almost before Kim was done pitching the idea. It was nearly ten o'clock when, between one breath and the next, my BLT wore off. We hadn't done anything sensible like grocery shop, but I found a late night sushi bar that delivered.

By the time the five boxes of nigiri sushi and assorted hand rolls appeared, Kim and Ex were sitting on the floor together, going over the wording on our final list of questions, while Chogyi Jake and Aubrey and I watched the data files from Oonishi for what must have been the hundredth time.

It was like the air we were breathing had changed. Working together, all of us prodding at the same problem, exploring the same terra incognita, took all the history and baggage and awkwardness away, and left me with this small family I'd made for myself. We fought some; we pushed each other's buttons sometimes. That was what family meant.

There was a moment just before Kim left at midnight when I stood back and let myself watch us all like we were on television. The way Ex sat, leaning forward, pushing back the lock of hair that had escaped his ponytail. Kim's pinched, serious expression, and the dark circles under her eyes. The windows behind us all, night making them into mirrors so that the boat lights seemed to blink and shift through Chogyi Jake's shoulder and past Aubrey's head. It was a moment of real peace.

My high-water mark.

7

Morning shouldered its way past the thick curtains, pressing in around the edges. Aubrey, on the other side of my bed, muttered and pulled the pillow over his eyes. I tried to convince myself that the muzzy feeling in my head meant I could still fall back asleep. Ex coughed once in the kitchen. His feet shifted softly on the tile. Sunlight streaked the ceiling above me. I was awake.

My brothers aside, I'd seen only four men naked, and one of those had been a wholly awkward fifteen seconds with my dorm mate and her boyfriend. Aubrey, half under our shared sheet, was the oldest man I'd ever slept with. I'd always thought he was beautiful. Sure, he had a little belly, and his hair stood up like a metalhead's from the eighties until he washed it down. I pulled on my robe quietly, watching him sleep. There were scars on his body, some of them the result of skirmishes against the possessed. There was damage I couldn't see too. Spells that Uncle Eric had taught him that had taken a toll. And maybe other things.

I pulled my hair back with one hand so it wouldn't brush against him, kissed the small of his back, and slipped out the door. The flood of sunlight didn't wake him. I walked into the kitchen and the smell of fresh coffee.

'You're looking thoughtful,' Ex said. 'Anything wrong?'

'No,' I said with a yawn. 'Just booting up. Where's Chogyi Jake?'

'Meditating. As always.'

'I probably should do that too. I'm feeling . . . I don't know. Restless,' I said, sitting at the small kitchen table. The view of Lake Michigan in daylight was astounding. It was the kind of thing you paid an extra million for. I wondered idly how much the condo had actually cost. The clock said it was almost nine o'clock, and I wasn't sure if that felt too late or too early.

'You probably should,' Ex said. 'Good news is he went shopping first. Bacon and eggs?'

'Oh, Jesus, please,' I said. 'And tell me that's not just coffee incense or something sadistic like that.'

Ex grinned and found a cup, rinsing the dust out of it before he poured. My laptop was still in the living room. I'd left it turned on, and the battery was empty. I strung the power cord to an outlet in the kitchen and waited for the operating system to finish bitching at me while I drank my coffee. After a year together, we all knew one another's taste, and Ex made my coffee with just enough sugar and no milk.

'No word from Kim yet,' he said. I felt a wash of confused emotion: pleasure that Kim wasn't there, shame at being pleased, and resentment for being made to feel shame. I knew I was being petty and stupid, but that didn't stop it from happening. I covered by taking another drink of coffee before I answered.

'Were we expecting her?' I asked.

'Not particularly. I'm a little concerned about her going back into the hospital alone, though. After what happened.'

'Whatever it was, I don't think it was after her,' I said.

'Yesterday, it wasn't. Today's a whole new ball game.'

'Always is, feels like. She'll do the right thing. She's a big girl.'

There was e-mail waiting from my lawyer. She had called an acquaintance who ran an image and video enhancement service for the State Department and who would be happy to spend a couple hours on my project. She gave me his e-mail address and a link he'd provided for uploading the data files to him. As I started the transfer—about twenty minutes remaining, even with the high-speed connection—the pop and sizzle of frying bacon brought me back to the room. I sighed and stretched. Ex was reading through a thick file of papers even as he cooked. I recognized the study logs Oonishi had brought us.

'Anything interesting?' I asked.

'Some background on the subjects. We should think about contacting them directly.'

'If we need to,' I said.

He looked over at me. Half silhouetted by a wide stretch of water and sky, he looked softer than usual.

'It might upset the client,' he said.

'That would suck,' I said casually.

'Might upset Kim. This is her colleague we're working for, after all.'

'Then we won't do it unless we need to,' I said. 'But if it's piss someone off or don't figure this out, there's some feelings going to get bruised.'

Ex grinned and turned back to the bacon. I spooled through my other e-mail. Spam. A note from Trevor in Montana about processing a refund for the extra, unused training time. A note from my little brother, Curtis. I opened my brother's e-mail. He was back for his senior year in high school, which made me feel old all by itself. He had a girlfriend that Mom and Dad were doing their best to ignore. Jay, my older brother, was living in Orlando, and had just gotten engaged. Curtis speculated irreverently about whether Jay had gotten her knocked up. I wouldn't have said it to anyone, but that was my guess too. I started to reply to him, then dropped the message into the drafts folder. I needed to think a little before I wrote back. Maybe after I'd gotten a little more blood sugar.

I had never told the rest of the family what happened after I'd left ASU. As far as they knew, I was still the standard college dropout, wandering the face of the earth in search of permanent employment. Or possibly whoring myself out for drug money. My parents didn't have a good opinion of anyone's moral character unless they went to our church. I'd always thought of them as prudish, self-righteous, and narrow. Only the stories Eric had told Aubrey about my mother's affair gave evidence of clay feet, and I wasn't about to tell Curtis any of that. Maybe once he was safely out of the house too. Until then, I was playing everything close to the vest with the family, even the ones I liked. I didn't know what any of them would have made of my traveling companions, my chosen work, or my million-dollar view of the lake. If it really was a million-dollar view.

I connected to our private wiki and looked for the list of properties. I found the condo easily. It was actually a seven-million-dollar view with an entry that read like a real estate ad: North Lake Drive, 5bdrm, 3bth, and the obscure notations Eric had made, YNTH and DC1. I lingered over the notations as Ex put a plate in front of me. The Los Angeles DC1 house had held some of the most useful, interesting documents we'd found so far. But this place was so free from occult anything, it was like a rental. There wasn't even a copy of *Fortean Times* in the bathroom. I scooped up my fork and took a bite of the eggs.

'Mmm,' I said. 'Nice.'

'Thanks,' Ex said.

'You know,' I said around a mouthful of breakfast. 'I understand in my head how much money Eric left me, but it makes me a little dizzy sometimes.'

Ex sat down across from me with his own plate and cup of coffee. He ate with a seriousness that made it seem like a chore.

'It surprises me too,' he said. 'The things we don't know about Eric would . . . Jayné? What's the matter?'

A small tapping sound caught my attention. It was me, my left hand fidgeting at the keyboard. Something shifted in the back of my head, an idea I hadn't quite had yet. Aubrey yawned in the bedroom, and Chogyi Jake walked into the kitchen behind me with catlike near silence. The penny dropped.

I said something obscene.

'Did something happen?' Chogyi Jake said. Ex stared at me. The bedroom door opened, but I didn't look back. I was pointing at the wiki page.

'You were *right*,' I said. 'You kept saying it, but I didn't snap until just now. The place *is* too small.'

'What's going on?' Aubrey said behind me.

'Eric's condo has five bedrooms,' I said. 'We're in the wrong place.'

It took me five minutes to find the manila envelope Harlan Jeffers had given me the day before; it was under the couch, and his card was still in it. An hour later, we all headed down to the building management offices. Chogyi Jake had his point-man suit on, and the rest of us were also dressed to intimidate. Walking across the lobby, I felt like the opening sequence of *Reservoir Dogs*, only with wider ties. Harlan stood in the office doorway, face pale and eyes a little too round. I could see white all the way around his irises.

'S-so,' he said, as he waved us in. 'Is there something—'

'I'm having my lawyer fax you a copy of the paperwork from when my uncle bought this property,' I said. 'I have some questions.'

'I don't think this is something that I can—' he began, then lost himself and started over. 'Without having, um, counsel present, I'm not sure—'

Chogyi Jake put a hand on the man's arm and smiled.

'It may be a little early to build a legal defense,' Chogyi Jake said. 'Why don't we go in and talk.'

Harlan's gaze shifted from him to me and back. His nod was a sharp, small movement. Tiny drops of sweat beaded his upper lip.

The office smelled like burned coffee. A low black slate desk held the center of the room, trying to look expensive. On the walls, clean-lined modernistic frames held documents outlining Harlan's rise through business schools and professional societies, the times he'd shaken hands with important people or famous ones. There was one with a tired-looking Stephen King letting Harlan put an arm around him. On the desk, a smaller frame showed a chubby-cheeked three-year-old of uncertain gender that couldn't have looked more like Harlan if it had worn his clothes.

'All right,' I said once the door was closed behind us. 'Let's just go over the problem here so we're all on the same page. The place my uncle bought had five bedrooms. The one I'm in right now has three. So. What the fuck?'

Harlan sat down, his chair hissing as it took his weight.

'I understand your anger. And your confusion. We should have . . . I should have addressed this issue directly, but it was only after Mr. Heller passed that I became aware of it.'

Ex crossed his arms, scowling down at the man like the instrument of an angry god. He was good at that.

'Why did you put us in the wrong condominium?' Ex said. 'And where is Eric's real place?'

'What? No, 1904 is Mr. Heller's property. It's the one he bought.'

'It doesn't match the description we have of it,' Chogyi Jake said.

'It doesn't,' Harlan said. 'Look, I came on here three years ago. I never met Mr. Heller. I don't even know for certain that he ever came here. I mean, maybe he did. I don't know. We had very strict instructions not to go into his condominium. If there was a problem, I could call him or his lawyer, and that was it. A water line broke on the floor above? We couldn't even go in to repair the damage to his kitchen. I called, and he sent his own people. Until he died, I swear I never went in there once.'

'But after he died, you did?' Aubrey said. I sat down. My head felt like it was stuffed with cotton ticking, like I was wrestling an idea that wasn't ready to be thought.

'It was a tax issue.' Harlan stared at the far wall as he spoke, like he was confessing something. 'We had auditors breathing down our necks. It was the IRS, you know? When those guys start thinking you're hiding something, they get . . . It was a walkthrough. In and out, five minutes at most. No one took anything, no one touched anything. No one sat down on a chair. Nothing.'

'And?' I said, but I knew. Harlan had freaked out. The records said it was a bigger place than was there. When he'd come back and seen what Uncle Eric had paid for, it matched the paperwork, but not the floor plan. He drew the conclusion that they'd overcharged him.

To Harlan, it looked, at best, like a million-dollar oopsy. At worst, it was real estate fraud. Oonishi was right. People see what they expect to see.

'The statute of limitations for a contract in Illinois is ten years,' Harlan said the same way I imagined war prisoners giving name, rank, and serial number. 'I'm not saying we don't want to make this right, I'm only saying that litigation won't help anyone.'

'I don't think we need to go there,' I said.

He was like a prisoner whose guard had just opened the gate. His gaze shifted between the four of us in quick, bird-like movements. His voice squeaked a little.

'We don't?'

'Windows are on the east,' Aubrey said, already running down the same road with me. 'Hallway's on the west, so that means north or south.'

'Bathroom and the master bedroom pretty much eat the south walls,' I said. 'No place to put doors or a hallway. I'm betting north.'

Ex pursed his lips.

'Works for me,' he said.

I stood up, and we headed out together. Chogyi Jake paused in the doorway, looking back at the confused Harlan.

'Mr. Jeffers,' he said, 'I assume there's a super on site? A handyman for simple jobs?'

'Yes. Sure.'

'I don't suppose we could borrow a sledgehammer?'

It turns out—I'm not making this up—there's a construction tool called a stud finder. Had I known about these during my brief run as a college coed, I'm pretty sure my dorm mate would have been carrying one around the Northern Lounge, holding it up to guys, and saying *Nope, not you*. Instead, my first experience with one involved Ex slowly going over the southern wall of the living and dining rooms, marking the white plaster in thick pencil, while Aubrey, Chogyi Jake, and I moved all the furniture into the kitchen and three bedrooms. Empty, the living room took on the smallest echo. Our footsteps and voices had a new, unfamiliar depth. Just behind where the cow-skin couch had been, the marks made the unmistakable shape of a door frame.

In the absence of dust masks, Aubrey sacrificed one of the sheets, ripping strips from it with a sound like paper tearing. We all tied squares of five-hundred-count white percale over our mouths and noses. We looked like angelic bank robbers. Ex hefted the borrowed sledgehammer.

'We could just go through the walls,' I said.

'If we're right, I assume Eric protected that as well. Besides, I don't know where the wiring is,' Ex said.

'You don't *know* that doorway isn't trapped,' Aubrey pointed out.

Ex shrugged and slowly bounced the handle of the sledgehammer against his open hand in anticipation of the architectural violence ahead.

'How likely is it that we're about to introduce ourselves to the neighbors?' I asked.

'We could wait,' Chogyi Jake said. 'If whoever lives next door would let us in, it wouldn't be hard to take the dimensions of their rooms and see if there's the expected gap.'

I was tempted, but not because I had any doubt about what we'd find. The truth was, plastering over whole rooms so that they didn't seem to exist felt like exactly the kind of thing Eric would have done. I hoped whatever we found would shed some light on the incidents at Grace Memorial. And still, there was some small, quiet part of my mind that hesitated. Ex lifted his pale brows as if asking a question. Or permission.

'Let's do this,' I said.

The first blow cracked the wall, a spiderweb appearing out of nothing. Ex swung again. Fine dust rose in the air. It smelled hot to me. The room itself shuddered, and bits of Sheetrock fell away, hanging on by a thin membrane of old wallpaper and tape. With the morning sun still spilling through the windows, the white wall seemed to glow, the darkness beyond it as thick as ink. Ex kept swinging, debris piling up around his ankles, as the doorway came free. One swing went in farther than the ones before, passing through the wall and into whatever lay beyond. The unmistakable crash of metal stopped him. We came close. Aubrey had his cell phone out, the dim glow from the screen pushing into the blackness.

Recessed behind the wall just enough so that the drywall could cover it, a black iron-mesh security door blocked a short hallway with a door on either side beyond it. Ex pulled away a hank of Sheetrock, and I could see where the security door's frame had been screwed into the flesh of the building with round-topped bolts that defied removal. The hinges were on the far side where we couldn't reach them. Even with the relatively little training and awareness I'd picked up in the last year, I could feel the wards and protections burning off the metal like heat. The two dead bolts were covered in thin black-etched symbols. I'd seen only one thing like it before. Eric's place in Los Angeles. The other DC1 property.

'Bingo,' I said.

8

When I was about fifteen years old, I found a Rubik's Cube. You remember those? Hottest-selling toy of the 1980s? It's a cube with different colors on all six sides, with each side divided into nine squares. The whole thing's set up so you can rotate bits of it, scramble up the colors, and then—if you're really smart and patient—put it back the way it was before you messed things up. A sort of molded-plastic metaphor for everything else in life. I figured the best thing to do was steam off the colored stickers and put them back so that it looked solved. My older brother thought I was cheating. He solved it the old-fashioned way, by looking up the solution online. Even so, it took him three days the first time he solved it. He got to where he could do it in half an hour with only a little confusion and cursing. Once he understood what he was doing, it was easier. Not do-it-with-your-eyes-closed, but easier.

Breaking into Eric's secret fortress was like that too. It wasn't only that we'd been through defenses very much like it before. We were getting familiar with how Eric's mind had worked. Were there two obvious strategies to get past something? Look for a third. Stuck five layers into a problem? Go back two or three steps and see if the mistake wasn't that far back.

'Wait!' Aubrey said, and Ex and Chogyi Jake stopped chanting like someone had hit the pause button. Aubrey leaned in close to the iron-mesh door and shook his head. 'It's not working.'

'It is,' Ex said. 'You're just reacting to the aversions.'

'I'm not,' Aubrey said.

'You're open to them,' Ex said. 'In the last year, you've used the Oath of the Abyss. You've been ridden. Twice. You have to expect that you're going to be more vulnerable to things like this.'

'Ex. *Look* at it,' Aubrey said.

Ex stepped out of the protective circle of red chalk drawn on the carpet, squinted at the runes and figures on the lock, and said something crude.

'Perhaps we should reconsider our approach,' Chogyi Jake said. 'What if we began with the Itiru meditations, and then invoked the Mark of Lavavoth?'

'Not Lavavoth. South-southwest is a red herring,' Ex said. 'I just don't know what it's distracting us *from*.'

It was a little after three in the afternoon, and the condo was trashed. Ex had stripped back as much of the drywall out of the hidden doorway as he could, and it left everything covered in a thin plaster dust. Everything smelled like it. The air tasted of it. On the plus side, we'd made more progress in the last three hours than we had in the first three days in Los Angeles. On the minus, the strain was telling. Tempers were starting to wear thin, my own included.

While I let the three of them work it out, I went to my bedroom. The black electronic key to the minivan sat on the table beside Aubrey's wallet and cell phone. I picked it up, tossed it twice in the air, and headed back into the occult construction site.

'I'm heading out for a while,' I said. 'Anyone need anything?'

'Green tea,' Chogyi Jake said at the same time Aubrey called out 'Cleaning supplies.' Ex only looked sour and stared at the sigils on the locks. I scooped up my backpack and my laptop case, and I left.

As the elevator sank down to the garage level, I let myself sag. I felt frustrated. I felt tired and on edge. I felt like some part of me that I couldn't quite control was pacing in the back of my head like a tiger in a cage. I stepped into the semiopen air of the parking garage, muggy air pressing at my face and the back of my neck. My footsteps echoed, and I realized I half expected someone to jump out of the shadows and attack. Or maybe a bunch of people, all breathing together. More than that, I sort of wished they would.

I got into the minivan with something like disappointment and realized I didn't actually know where I was going. I had the general intention of shopping or seeing the sights or doing something to burn off some of the growing energy, but I hadn't Googled directions to anyplace. I hadn't even asked Harlan where the best local deli was. My options were to go back in or go forward without a clear idea where I was headed.

Or call the local expert.

Kim answered on the fourth ring, and for a few seconds I thought she was her voice-mail message. By the time I regained my conversational footing, Kim was already delivering a status report.

'I e-mailed Oonishi the questions,' Kim said. 'Honestly, though, I don't know how long it will be before we get the results. The others are right. He's starting to regret calling you in.'

'Nothing like getting what you asked for,' I said. 'Where are you right now?'

'I'm on campus. I just finished my lecture.'

'Lecture? You're taking classes?'

'I'm teaching them. You don't think they'd pay a mere PhD to do full-time research, do you?' she said, and the bitterness in her voice made it clear that wasn't how it worked.

'Parasitology?'

'I wish. Cell biology. *Introductory* cell biology. There's only enough interest for a real parasites section every two years or so, and so far I've had to co-teach with an MD from infectious diseases. It's not really the same thing, but having a chaperone keeps me in my place. Why? Is something the matter?'

'No,' I said. 'I just thought you'd be at Grace.'

'After yesterday? Not a chance. When we know what's going on, I'll consider it.'

'Can you do that? I mean just stop showing up there and not get fired or something?'

'No, I'll get fired eventually. Unemployed is better than beaten to death.'

I laughed. I didn't expect to, it just happened. Kim might have had the coldest, least sentimental mind I'd ever met. After a solid year of Ex's weird paternalism, Chogyi Jake's studied compassion, and my little romantic roller coaster with Aubrey, just talking to her was like seeing the world through new eyes. Of course she wasn't going in. I'd assumed she was because she wasn't at the condo. I didn't know why I'd fallen so easily into the idea that on one side there was Grace Memorial, and on the other there was me and the guys with room for nothing else.

'Well, if you're ditching work and have a few spare hours, I could use some help.'

'Did something happen?' she asked.

'No. Well, yes actually. But what I really need is to get out from underfoot while the guys work through something. I'll tell you all about it when I pick you up. But the thing is I don't know the city. Where to get a vacuum cleaner. Like that. And anyway, I could use the company. If you're up to it.'

'All right,' she said. 'Come get me.'

She gave me the address of a coffee shop. I gave it to the GPS and told her it would take me fifteen minutes to get there. She told me to expect thirty with traffic. I started the car, turned up the ramp, and headed out onto the streets of Chicago with only a reassuring, fake-British computer voice to guide me. Haze grayed the blue of the sky, softening the sunlight and bringing the infinite bowl of air a little closer. Traffic on the gentle left-then-right curves of the Kennedy Expressway was thick, but not as suicidally impolite as Los Angeles had been. Still, I found myself watching the other drivers carefully while the GPS told me where to go.

It almost worked. If it weren't for Bell Avenue ending about twenty feet before it hit Taylor Street and making my last turn impossible, it would have been twenty minutes. I parked on Bell and walked the rest of the way. All the buildings were brick, two stories at the least, three at the most, and crowded up against the sidewalk. A busker with a ukulele sang a Tom Waits tune as I walked past. The breeze that cooled my cheeks and brushed back my hair smelled like car exhaust.

The Bump & Grind Café didn't live up to its lurid name; it was all fresh coffee and baking apples. A flat-screen television was showing an art film that I remembered having heard about but had never actually seen. A few computers sat around, apparently for the free use of anyone who bought a coffee and wasn't surfing for porn. And Kim sat at a table by the window. Half of a latte rested in front of her, the film of milk on the glass matching the hazy sky. Her purse was tucked under the chair, her head bent over a book.

For the space of a heartbeat, she didn't see me, and I caught a glimpse of who she was when she thought no one was watching. Her clothes belonged on an older woman, neat, professional earth tones. Her pale hair gave the impression of being touched by gray, though I was pretty sure it wasn't. Her gaze was focused, intent, closed. The softness at her jaw and the first, faint wrinkles at her neck reminded me of how my mother had looked when I was still a girl. And there was something else too; she had the same air of waiting for something she knew wasn't going to come.

She looked up and nodded, and the impression vanished. She was once again my familiar, hard-edged Kim.

'So what's happened and why do we need a vacuum cleaner?' she asked instead of saying hello.

While we walked back to the minivan, I brought her up to date, not just on the discovery of the secret rooms but on Los Angeles and the Lisbon notations—DC1 and YNTH— with our assumption that the first meant high security and the second being anyone's guess. She listened with her head canted forward, like she was leaning into my words.

'What about the image enhancement on Oonishi's data set?' she asked when I was done.

'Already uploaded.'

'Do we have an estimate of the time it's going to take?'

'No,' I said, pulling out onto Polk. 'We'll know when we know.'

She nodded once, but she didn't look pleased. I felt a little tightness at the back of my throat, like I'd gotten a bad grade on a paper that I'd been proud of. Maybe hanging out with her hadn't been a good idea.

'Problem?' I asked, my tone carefully neutral.

'We've got too many tests and not enough data,' she said. 'I wish we'd gotten into Eric's secret rooms before we did the work for Oonishi. If there's anything useful in there at all, it's going to change the questionnaire.'

'It isn't like Eric left us directions.'

'God forbid,' Kim said. 'That man never let anything by if he could help it.'

'Did you love him?' I asked. I hadn't meant to. I hadn't even wondered until I saw her there in the café, waiting for something. 'I mean, I know you and Eric—'

Kim took a quick breath, shrugged, and answered just as if I'd had any business asking.

'No, I didn't. I don't know why I did what I did. At first, I thought it was only that we were confined in the same cabin for too long, and humans act like that. But then after, when it kept . . . happening. Well, I didn't love him. He didn't particularly like me. The sex wasn't very pleasant. It was just something we did. I rationalize it now. I say that I was lashing out at Aubrey or I just don't have a very healthy attitude toward men or it was a self-destructive moment, but I honestly don't know why I was with him.'

'You never told Aubrey,' I said.

'No.'

I turned the minivan up onto the Eisenhower Expressway, gunning the engine to bring us to speed.

'I didn't either,' I said.

'Thank you.'

The traffic slowed, the first deadening congestion of the coming rush hour. Kim leaned forward, looking up into the empty sky.

'You still in love with him?' I asked.

'I miss him. But I know why we aren't together. I don't have to like it, but I'm all right. I'm glad the two of you are together.'

100

'I'm sorry,' I said.

Her smile was fast and genuine and sad.

'You are too kind, Jayné,' she said. 'Really. It's a vice.'

'I'll try to be more of a shit,' I said. 'Any idea where we can find that vacuum?'

But before she could answer, Eric intruded.

'Hey. You've got a call.'

Kim flinched at the voice, and I pretended not to notice. I rooted through my pack one-handed, keeping the minivan in its lane with the other, trying to answer the call before Eric spoke again. The call was from Aubrey's number. I took it.

'Jayné,' he said. 'Where are you?'

'Fifteen minutes from you, if the traffic would get moving,' I said.

'Push them out of the way and get over here,' he said. I could hear him grinning.

'You got through?'

'Chogyi Jake had this flash of freaking genius about the whole Enochian directionality thing. I'll tell you about it when you get here.'

My heart raced. I bent toward the wheel, as if I could clear a path for us by force of will.

'The rooms,' I said. 'Did you get into the rooms? What's in there?'

'Come home, sweetheart,' he said. 'See for yourself.'

The hidden rooms didn't look the way I expected. Secret rooms should be dark, with cobwebs and wrought iron fixtures and probably creepy organ music. And rats. These looked almost normal. Almost. The door on the east side of the hallway opened onto a simple officelike space. A cheap desk with the wood-grain laminate starting to peel at the sides, a landline telephone in a style twenty years out of date, two four-drawer filing cabinets, and a bookshelf half-filled with folders, books, and boxes. The drapes were chocolate brown bleached almost beige by the sun. In fairness, there were a couple of cobwebs.

The western door opened to a smallish bedroom actually decked out to sleep in. A steel-frame single bed with a thin mattress, a little bedside table, and that was about it. It had its own stripped-down powder room with stainless steel fixtures and no towels. If I hadn't been walking in Eric's footsteps for the past year, I might not even have noticed that the light fixtures were of unbreakable security glass and mesh, that the bed and table were bolted down, or that the solid-core door was fitted with a double dead bolt and hung with industrial-grade hinges. A cell. So that was interesting. There weren't any restraints on the bed, but slapping on a couple of handcuffs would have been easy.

Kim, behind me, was drawing the same conclusion.

'He must have expected somebody to be possessed,' she said. 'And that it would take a fair amount of time to get the rider out of them.'

'Seems like,' I said, tapping the walls absently as I walked through the empty space.

Ex, Aubrey, and Chogyi Jake had apparently given up all pretense of keeping order in the condo. The couch and coffee table had been pulled back from the bedroom and were now pale with dust. A pile of photographs and maps sat on one corner, a fragile-looking roll of blueprints lay open in the center, and five leather-bound books were on top of them. A glance was enough to show me that the blueprints were of Grace Memorial, and that the extra markings and symbols on them weren't from the general contractor.

'What have we got?' I asked.

'A lot of what, and very little why,' Chogyi Jake said. 'But we haven't had time to go through it yet.'

'Two boxes of surveillance and background on someone named David Souder,' Aubrey said. 'Runs a roofing company in Waukegan and seems totally innocuous.'

'Name rings a bell, though,' I said. 'Is he in the wiki?'

Aubrey shook his head.

'All right,' I said. 'Anything that does make sense?'

'There was a very serious binding on the winter solstice, 1951,' Ex said, holding up a weathered-looking three-ring binder stuffed with handwritten pages. I recognized my uncle's script. 'So, not quite sixty years ago.'

'I'm shocked, shocked,' I said dryly. 'And it happened at the hospital, right?'

'That's not as clear as you'd think,' Aubrey said. A patch of white dust smeared his temple like badly applied stage makeup. 'Eric was trying to find the site when he died. He'd narrowed it down to a few likely suspects. Grace Memorial was one of them, but he wasn't certain. All this? He put it here just in case Grace turned out to be the site.'

I sat on the floor, legs crossed and elbows on the table. The top photograph on the pile shifted with a hiss as soft as whispering.

'Do we know *what* got bound?' I asked.

'Working on that,' Aubrey said. 'Eric's notes refer to it as Rahabiel and Daevanam Daeva, but until we can dig out some actual details, we might as well call it Shirley. But I haven't even started looking at the books yet.'

'We also may be able to infer something about it from the manner in which it was bound,' Chogyi Jake said. 'We do have an outline of that, and it was fairly impressive. Interment, just as the dreams suggested, but there were at least two more layers on top of that. One that kept the site obscured and the residual effects of the rider difficult to recognize, and then another secondary containment.'

'Okay,' I said.

Chogyi Jake shook his head.

'Too technical?' he asked.

'A little jargony,' I said. 'Retry?'

Kim, behind me, was the one to answer. She stood in the doorway, her arms crossed and a flush in her cheeks. She looked excited and engaged. Almost happy. I remembered what she'd said about having no one to talk to about things like this.

'They buried it first,' she said. 'And then they did something that would keep anyone from hearing it pounding on the coffin. And then they built a prison around it, so that even if it got out, it wouldn't get free.'

'Yes,' Chogyi Jake said.

'And the prison?' Ex said. 'It's Grace Memorial.'

'Any idea why it would want to jump on my head?' I asked.

'We don't even know that it did,' Ex said. 'The attack could have been whatever was bound trying to reach out, or it might have been a particularly vicious kind of aversion built into the binding.'

'Might have been the prisoner, might have been the prison,' Aubrey said.

'How do you bury a rider?' I asked at the same moment Kim said 'Why the uptick in activity?'

'Interment bindings traditionally involve a sacrifice,' Chogyi Jake said, answering me first. 'It's not unlike normal possession, only instead of the rider taking control of a person through its own will, the spirit is driven into someone. Usually someone who has offered themselves up, but unwilling sacrifices have also been made. And then, the horse and rider are—'

He gestured apologetically.

'Buried alive,' I said.

'It's not a popular technique,' Chogyi Jake said. 'But why the activity increased in the last year turns out to be a very interesting question. Of course, there hasn't actually been an increase in the thing's reach. It's pounding on the coffin just as loud. Only now people can hear it.'

'You're saying things like that mob attack have been happening at Grace for the past fifty-odd years, and just no one noticed?' I said.

'Yes,' Chogyi Jake said. 'Until last year, when the second

layer of the binding was broken. After that, it became psychologically possible for people to be aware that something odd was going on.'

'Even people like Oonishi,' Ex said. He could really pack contempt in his voice when he tried.

'The increase in people leaving the hospital against medical advice,' Kim said. 'They see things. They get scared.'

'That's the assumption we're working with,' Chogyi Jake said.

'All right. That's better than something's eating them, right?' I said. 'And what broke that keep-it-quiet spell?'

'Us,' Aubrey said. 'Or, specifically, you. Back in Denver.'

I didn't get it. And then I did.

'*The Invisible College?*' I said. '*They* did this?'

'Thought you'd find that interesting,' Ex said.

9

For a split second, I wanted to punch Ex hard enough to break something. His nose, my hand. Whatever. I tried to take a deep breath and force myself to calm down, but the best I could manage was to slow my panting a little. My body felt like a high-voltage wire. I started pacing because I couldn't be still and I didn't want to start shrieking. Aubrey's eyebrows had the little angle to them that meant he was worried. He was right to be.

'Jesus Christ,' I said. Then I repeated it under my breath twenty or thirty times, just for the sensation of speaking.

'This is what Eric was doing in Denver,' Kim said. She at least sounded rational. 'He wanted to find this Rahabiel, whatever it is, and breaking the Invisible College was how he could do it.'

'Only they found out what he was up to,' Aubrey said, 'and . . . well, stopped him.'

'Why?' I said, a little too loudly. 'Why did he want to know? What was he going to do with it? This is crap. This is just *crap*. What the hell am I supposed to do with this?'

'We've only been looking for half an hour,' Aubrey said. Ex looked up as if seeing me for the first time.

'Is there a problem?' he said.

I laughed, but there wasn't any mirth in it.

'Yes, there's a problem,' I said. 'The people who killed Eric are behind whatever the hell is going on in Grace Memorial.'

'And?'

'And we don't know what they did or why Eric was trying to find this buried rider thing or generally speaking what the hell we're in the middle of.'

Ex's gaze was steady and impatient and a little amused. The first trickle of embarrassment started to ooze past my panic and rage.

'That's all true,' Ex said. 'And?'

'And that's a problem,' I said. 'That's a real first-class, industrial-grade problem.'

'And we're investigating it,' Ex said. 'Is there any action you'd like to take differently from what we're already doing?'

I wasn't sure what it said about Ex that he was enjoying the moment quite so much. Maybe his father had been the stern sarcastic type and he was getting off on the opportunity to revisit his childhood. Maybe six months of Aubrey and me in the same shower had bothered him more than any of us admitted. Whatever the impulse behind it, it pulled the plug on my outrage. I crossed my arms, scowling so hard my cheeks ached a little, but the monkey bouncing around in my brain got a little quieter. Ex nodded once, then turned back to the notebook.

'All right, then,' he said.

'Why is it still bound?' Kim said. 'That doesn't make sense.'

'Why not?' Aubrey asked.

'When Jayné broke the Invisible College's power, it lifted all the spells,' Kim said. 'We know for certain it lifted this don't-notice-me thing at Grace. But the interment is still holding.'

'So it follows that someone else must have done the actual interment ceremony,' Chogyi Jake said.

'Who?' I asked. 'And why?'

'I don't know,' Chogyi Jake said. 'But it may be in here. Somewhere.'

Kim shrugged in my peripheral vision.

'Okay,' I said. 'What should I start looking through?'

'Your pile's there, right behind Kim's,' Aubrey said.

In the year I'd spent doing weird occult work, I'd come to think of it as being a lot like crime. I spent time finding guns and getaway motorcycles. I bought a house in New Orleans in part because the storage shed out back could be turned into a prison strong enough to hold a kidnapped teenage girl. I'd gotten a policeman to steal a car in order to cover my tracks. I'd killed . . . not a man, but the thing living in his body.

As I sat at the dining room table and watched the high-rise shadows creep out across the water, everything seemed different. I had thought all this time—weeks, months—that Chogyi Jake and Ex and Aubrey and I had been investigating. Going from property to property, place to place, gathering information. As I read through articles my uncle had clipped from newspapers and magazines, I got a glimpse of how wrong I'd been. Jetting across the world to add new entries into the wiki, to list more obscure book titles, to inventory arcane objects and magic items hadn't been investigating. It had been cataloging. We had put together a tremendous wealth of data, but I'd never had time to make any real knowledge from it.

It was the student nightmare. I'd spent all semester studying the wrong things, and now the test was here. I held a note in fading ink on brittle, yellowed paper. Eric's handwriting. *HH biter or bit? Ask Rosental next Wednesday. If bit, need to find ally groups before Red Rite.* I stared at it, despair and panic growing in the back of my head like the thickening of air before a storm. I didn't know if it was the clue that would crack every mystery open or a random bit of gibberish, Eric's version of doodling. I spread the notes and pages out on the table, my gaze skipping from one to another, waiting for a pattern to emerge. Nothing came. An article about German artists immigrating to America in the thirties. A street map of the area around Grace Memorial. A detailed woodcut of a double-bladed axe. It was all supposed to mean something. It had all been important enough for Eric to keep. To hide. And it meant nothing to me.

When I'd planned things before, there had been an objective. Kill someone. Abduct someone. Steal something. This time there was only the weight of figuring out what I was supposed to do. What Eric had been doing. It was detective work, and behind it lurked the terrible thought that whatever the answer was, my uncle had died for it. And now it was mine to screw up.

All the others were going through papers and boxes and books too. I moved to the couch for a while until Ex and Aubrey started talking about a file of papers in Hebrew they'd found and the relationship between the Sephirot and fractal geometry. Every time one of them said something I didn't quite follow, I felt stupider and more thoroughly out of my depth. The wind picked up just after sunset, muttering and thumping on the glass. Our reflections bounced and deformed as the air bent the windows. Aubrey and Kim ordered pizza. When it arrived, the smell of hot grease and garlic actually overpowered the dust. Chogyi Jake disappeared into the secret rooms, coming back half an hour later with all the books from the shelves arranged by language. I watched him place the stacks on the coffee table, one next to the other. I'd taken three semesters of French in high school. I could talk about my aunt's pen and closing the window. I had no business being here.

When he was done, I looked back down at the notebook I'd been reading. I couldn't remember anything from the last four pages. I set it down, went to the master bathroom, and sat on the toilet with my head in my hands for twenty solid minutes. Just before midnight, Kim asked for a ride back to her place. I jumped at the chance to get out of the condo and away from the books and files. Going down the elevator to the parking level, she looked as tired as I felt— gaunt at the cheek, her skin with an undertone of ash gray. Her lips were thin and bloodless.

'Fun night,' I said as the doors opened. She grunted in reply.

The wind was still blowing hard. On the expressway heading south, I could feel it in the steering wheel, urging me off to the left. When I glanced over at my passenger, she was pinching the bridge of her nose, her eyes closed.

'You okay?' I asked.

'I'm fine,' she said, but the weariness in her voice was unmistakable. 'It's just that being back in the middle of all this may be a little harder than I thought. I keep being reminded of the bad old days.'

Her apartment building was less impressive than I'd expected. Three stories of crenellated architecture that gave each apartment its own tiny patio, its own square foot of yard, and a few windows. I let her out on the street, then watched to make sure she got all the way to her door. It didn't seem like a neighborhood where a lot of women walked alone on the street at midnight. I pulled away wondering why I'd expected something grander.

Back at the condo, Ex had moved into the newly discovered study, the lamplight spilling down the hallway like a promise not to sleep until the world was made right. Chogyi Jake was putting the pizza boxes into wide black trash bags along with the detritus of the day's demolition efforts. His smile was as genuine and constant as ever, but his eyes seemed focused on something else, lost in thought or contemplation. I waved my good night and slipped into the bedroom.

Aubrey lay on the bed, his hands laced behind his head,

staring at the ceiling. The bedside lamp gave the room a soft, golden glow without being quite bright enough to read by. I sat down on my side of the bed, looking down at him. In the warm light, he looked younger. Softer.

'Yes?' he said, encouraging me as if I'd spoken.

'Yeah, well,' I said with a sigh. I rolled down onto the bed beside him, belly down, my head turned toward his. 'Did we figure anything out?'

'Some,' he said. 'There's still a lot left. Things that Eric knew, so why bother writing them down anywhere.'

'Great.'

'You want to talk about it?'

'No,' I said. I closed my eyes. My head felt thick and heavy against the pillow. Gravity had been turned up a notch, and the world itself and everything in it was pulling me into the mattress. I wanted to sleep not particularly because I was tired, but because it meant forgetting for a few hours. I felt ready to forget.

Aubrey shifted, the mattress bending toward him as he moved. His leg slid over me, his weight coming to rest not quite on my ass, but where you couldn't really call it thigh anymore. His hands rested on my shoulders, fingers pressing into the muscles. I didn't moan. It was more an appreciative grunt.

'You were looking pretty freaked out there,' he said. He pressed the heels of his palm along my spine, shifting gently. I could feel where a joint in my back wanted to crack, but I was still too tense for it to go. 'Feeling any better?'

'Yeah,' I said. And then, as my throat seemed to thicken, 'No.'

'You want to talk about it?' he asked again. His voice was softer this time.

'I just . . . I don't know. When it's just the four of us, it feels like I have a handle on things, you know? At least enough to fake it. And then something comes up that I feel like I ought to know, and I'm at sea again.'

He pulled up the bottom of my shirt, his hands against my skin now as he worked his way down my back. I felt the tightness in my muscles, the combination of tension and pressure that he kept just below the threshold of pain. I started to relax.

'I mean would a to-do list be too much to ask for?' I said.

'Yeah. Do the laundry. Take the car in for a tune-up. Defeat evil.'

'Maybe a little more detail than that.'

'Maybe a little,' he said. He'd gotten down to my sacrum and started his way back up. It felt wonderful. 'What about you? Doing all right?'

'Just as far out of my depth, but less worried about it. I've got an advantage. I'm just trying to figure out what's going on at Grace Memorial. I don't have to be Eric while I'm at it.'

'And I do?'

'You seem to think so,' he said.

I shrugged.

'What if the Invisible College was just one cult he was fighting against? Am I going to know that, or will it just be me walking along the street one day, and boom, some-one shoots me?'

'I don't think they will.'

'Or you,' I said. I was rolling now, and it was hard to stop. 'Or Ex or Chogyi Jake. Or Kim. What if something had happened at the hospital? What if my protections had given out?'

'They didn't,' he said.

'If we don't figure out how to prop them up, they will. Eventually.'

He got back up to the middle of my back, paused for a moment. The funny thing about a really good bra is that you don't really even notice it's there until your boyfriend unhooks it. He pressed his hands into me. I felt his splayed fingers all along the inner edges of my shoulder blades. His weight against me felt a little more intentional.

'Are you coming on to me?'

'Would that be a problem?'

'No,' I said.

A few minutes later, I was on my back, Aubrey's weight still on me. Then his shirt was gone. And then all our clothes. In the gold lamplight, our skins looked exactly the same color, like we were carved from the same stone. Between the feeling of his skin and the rush of blood under mine, I lost myself for a while, and I didn't miss me. Sometimes—the best times—sex with Aubrey felt like I was swimming in a wide, warm sea. He was bearing me up, carrying me, until I reached the shore spent. I never could figure out quite how he did that, but I loved it.

We lay in the near darkness, and I traced my fingers along his flank. My mind felt clear and calm. Nothing was going to break into my little corner of peace and contentment. Whatever was under the hospital, it wasn't here. I yawned, stretching my arms out above my head, and the joint in my spine cracked.

'The thing is,' I said, resting my head on Aubrey's side, 'I want to go back.'

There was a moment's silence.

'Back to Montana?' he asked.

'Back to Grace,' I said. 'I hate the idea of waiting and reading and poking around. What I want to do is head back in, find where this whatever it is lives, and face it down. I don't know if I could, or if that's what Eric would have done, or anything, really. But I want to go. I want to *do* something.'

'Fight it out,' Aubrey said. The amusement in his voice told me he'd understood.

'There are no problems that can't be solved by enough duct tape and a hammer,' I said.

'What a wonderful world it would be,' he half sang.

Classical conditioning. That's what Chogyi Jake had called it. It was true, everything I'd faced since Uncle Eric had passed his legacy on to me had eventually come down to violence. And even when I'd had the crap kicked out of me—and oh, I had had the crap kicked out of me—I'd wound up on top at the end. Evil vanquished, peace restored, nothing wrong that a few stitches, a couple handfuls of Tylenol, and a week's rest wouldn't cure. Something

116

in my hindbrain had learned from that. Maybe not the right lessons.

I heard Ex's footsteps in the kitchen, the clink and gurgle of coffee being poured into a cup. Aubrey snuggled into the bed, his breath growing deeper and slow. The red numbers on the clock said it was almost two in the morning. Sleep seemed like a distant rumor to me. My mind kept going back to Grace Memorial: the strange angles of its walls, the windows staring out into the street like they were looking for something. The maze of corridors and rooms, twisting in and back on each other. Stairways that skipped whole floors or led to nowhere. It reminded me of something I'd heard about when I was a kid. A mansion built by a rich, crazy woman with false halls, stairways that went up to nothing and ended blind. She lived in a labyrinth so that the evil spirits would get confused. Grace was the same thing, writ large. Only it was also a hospital. The place where people go to be born and to die and to linger in the weird halfway place in between.

And like a dog chasing a car, I wanted it.

I didn't think I could stand another day of going through Eric's cryptic notes to himself and apparently random articles about everything from Jews fleeing Germany in the thirties to the communication signals of Argentine ants. Not to mention the unlabeled pictures of men and women and rooms. And those boxes of surveillance reports on Declan Souder. Or, no. Not Declan. The guy's name was David. Why was I thinking Declan? Who was Declan Souder?

I started grinning before I knew why. My one, delighted cough of laughter roused Aubrey enough that he opened an eye. He grunted a wordless question.

'Declan Souder redesigned Grace Memorial in the 1940s,' I said. 'He *built* the place. And what do you want to bet David's his son?'

10

I would have lost the bet. David was his grandson.

Chogyi Jake sat on the kitchen counter, a cup of green tea steaming between his laced hands. Ex sat at the table, squinting against the blasting light of early morning. Aubrey and I were splitting a blueberry bagel with cream cheese. Outside, Lake Michigan had an eerie mother-of-pearl look to it: water and mist and sunlight.

'Nice work,' Ex said. He sounded almost disappointed. His all-night study session had also borne fruit. Looking through Eric's Lisbon notes, he'd Googled every YNTH notation. Every city listed had a building or natural structure that might have worked as a second-stage prison, like Grace: ancient catacombs in Italy, a network of natural and constructed smuggler's tunnels under a port town in Maine, the Winchester Mystery House in San José. Good, solid research that tended to confirm our view of what was going on, but no breakthroughs. My flash of postcoital insight rankled him a little, and the mere fact that it did made me want to tease him a little.

'Really?' I said, my eyes wide. 'Did I do good?'

Ex rolled his eyes.

'It is suggestive, at least,' Chogyi Jake said. 'Declan died at the end of '51. Daedalus-as-sacrifice has some very strong resonances, and it would tie the two layers of imprisonment together.'

I took the last bite of bagel and raised my hand.

'Too jargony?' Chogyi Jake asked.

'Kind of, yeah.'

'Two of the three things they did in '51 are bindings,' Aubrey said. 'The buried-alive part being the first, and the . . . the maze. The hospital itself. That's the second. If this guy was the sacrifice that went into the coffin, it would help those two spells reinforce each other. There'd be a connection.'

'It's not proof,' Ex said. 'But as circumstantial evidence goes, it's not bad. And then there's the fact that Eric was interested in his bloodline.'

'Which he'd need,' I said, 'if the point was to break whatever's under Grace out, right? So we can start working with the assumption that Eric was looking to undo everything the Invisible College and their buddies did here. Crack the thing free.'

'Very good, grasshopper,' Ex said, actually managing a smile. 'Soon you will be able to take the pebble from my hand.'

I looked at him blankly. Instead of explaining himself, he shook his head.

'We don't know why, though,' Aubrey said. 'Or even what exactly Rahabiel is. Why it would attack Jayné.'

'If it even did,' I said. 'I'm starting to like the idea that it was the hospital that got pissed off at me. Allergic reaction to other magic, maybe.'

'I don't see what Eric planned to lock up in the cell he built,' Ex said.

I pulled back my shoulders and refused to be discouraged. I had a lead, by God, and one I'd figured out for myself. If it hadn't cracked the whole case open wide, that mattered less than the feeling of making some actual progress. That I could follow up on it without braving Grace Memorial itself only made it better.

'Okay,' I said. 'So what's the plan for the day?'

Ex spoke first.

'I have a meeting with the hospital chaplain at noon,' he said.

'You're going back there?'

'No,' Ex said. 'Meeting him at a bookstore well off the hospital property. I won't need backup.'

'I was going to read and organize more of Eric's notes,' Chogyi Jake said. 'We still have two drawers we haven't looked through. And I believe Kim was planning to call in sick and come help with that.'

'Cool,' I said.

'And you?' asked Aubrey.

'I was going to take you and the laptop up to Waukegan and meet David Souder,' I said.

'Saw that coming,' Ex said.

'But before we go,' I said, 'I want to make a couple phone calls.'

Aubrey hoisted an eyebrow.

'I want to see if they've cleaned up Oonishi's dream data yet,' I said. 'I'm wondering if there's something in there our man Souder might recognize.'

* * *

It was a two-hour drive, and we didn't get on the road until almost ten. Aubrey drove, and I sat in the passenger's seat, my laptop open, replaying the cleaned-up dream file over and over. It wasn't, I'd been assured, the absolute final version, but it was pretty great compared with the originals. The six feeds of Oonishi's data had been put together, cleaned, sharpened, averaged, and then tweaked so that whichever one had the greatest level of detail in any single frame was given greater weight. The man I'd talked to was going through now and making the same adjustment within frames, so that if one subject had better resolution in the upper left and another in the lower right of any given frame, the relative weight of the image could be split between them.

All in all, it wasn't more than thirty seconds, but now I could see the soil sliding and shifting as the black coffin split open and the light poured out. The digital-imaging man had also sent an e-mail with four frames set apart from the flow of images. The details in the stills were as clear as photographs. The eye caught in a flash of light, clearly human only with an uncanny elongated pupil like a goat's. The splayed hand, its palm out toward me, the fingers just too long to be right. A detail (he'd noted that it was the clearest single image in all the data streams, and it had only been *really* clear in two of them) of thin, pointed teeth like some kind of deep-sea fish. And then one thing I hadn't noticed before; as the coffin split, in the instant between the fine-lined cracks and the whiteout of arcing light, there was a moment when the side of the coffin was lit and showed carved letters. In the moving image, they were just a moment of uneven texture. In the still image—captured, manipulated, sharpened—they were readable.

Nomen mihi Legio est, quia multi sumus.

The Bibles I grew up reading were all in English, but I didn't need to Google this one to place it. *My name is Legion, for we are many*. Seeing the words there made the hair on my arms stand up and a vague, electric sense of vertigo swim at the back of my head. Bible stories were what I grew up with instead of comic books. Jesus casting the unclean spirits into a herd of swine and driving them over the cliff was for me like the Kiefer Sutherland version of *The Three Musketeers* had been for my college boyfriend: something that had seemed thrilling and mysterious when you were eight and seriously cheesy when you were twenty.

It didn't seem as cheesy now.

'You okay?' Aubrey asked.

'Yeah,' I said, closing the laptop. 'Just ducky.'

The streets sliding by outside the car seemed too normal to be true. Pizza Hut and Burger King didn't belong in the same world with the thing I'd just been watching. When we stopped at the corner of Sunset and Northern, a blue Corvette with tinted windows pulled up next to us, pushing out a bass line loud enough to sterilize anyone inside. An old man with skin the color of weathered wood and white hair as short as his beard crossed in front of us with an air of utter superiority. I took a deep breath and tried to calm myself down. It wasn't going to make things easier if I went into this freaking myself out.

Souder Roof and Tile was tucked between a Payless shoe store and a three-bay car service joint called Merlin's. The sign was jauntier and more optimistic than the building. There were only two cars in the parking lot, and neither of them had been made in the last ten years. Aubrey pulled into the space nearest the glass-paneled office door as the faux-British GPS voice told us we had arrived. He killed the engine. We sat for a few seconds, looking at the place.

'Any idea what you're going to tell this guy?' Aubrey asked.

'Nope,' I said. 'Figured I'd wing it.'

'Sounds like a plan,' he said.

Sounds like one of *my* plans, I thought, but I popped open the car door, and we headed in. The interior wasn't much more inspiring than the outside had been. The cool air smelled a little bit like dampness and old fish. Carpet patterned in beige and brown almost hid a few old stains. The white walls were hung with pictures of houses sporting new roofs. The lone desk was topped with bright glass, an Apple computer, and a pile of three-ring binders advertising products like coal tar pitch, polyiso roof insulation, and waterproof caulk. The woman sitting at the desk looked up at us with bare surprise in her expression. The door closed behind us.

'Hi,' I said. 'I'm looking for David Souder. Is he . . . ?'

I pointed at a door behind the woman with a plastic Staff Only sign tacked to it and started walking toward it as if the sign clearly couldn't apply to me.

'Oh, I'm sorry,' the woman said, shaking her head. 'Big

Dave's not in the office today. Was there something I could help you with?'

I smiled and tried to decide whether I believed her. Maybe forty-five, maybe fifty, she seemed like the kind of woman I'd grown up around: careful makeup lightly applied, bright blouse and skirt in a lemony yellow that didn't quite suit her. An empty cross hung from the silver chain around her neck. Her concerned and helpful expression was so practiced that I couldn't tell whether she was lying or not.

'I'm sorry,' I said. 'It's not a business thing. I just need to talk to him.'

Her hands gave her away. I'd just let her off the hook, told her that whatever this intrusion into her world was about, it at least wasn't her problem. Her hands should have relaxed, even if just a little.

They tensed.

'I'm really sorry,' she said. 'I can leave him a message if you want.'

'Cell phone number?' I said.

The woman laughed, but there wasn't much mirth in the sound. Instead there was something rueful. I glanced back at Aubrey. The slight pursing of his lips and the carefully blank expression told me he was seeing the same things I was.

'More than that. I've even got his cell phone,' she said. 'Big Dave leaves it in the office when he's not on-site somewhere.'

'Oh,' I said. 'Well, could I get his home address, then? I can swing by there.'

'I'm sorry. We can't give that out. There's a policy. But if you want to leave a message, I'll get it to him as soon as he comes in,' she said. 'I don't know when exactly that'll be, but I'll make sure he calls you back.'

Calls you back. Not *he'll see it.* Not *that he knows you came by.* She was promising to make him act on it. I was pretty sure by now that she wasn't lying. The way she held herself, the way she spoke, reminded me of my mother talking about someone from church. Someone who wasn't doing well.

There was probably a graceful way to do this. Something subtle and clever. The right words. But since I didn't know what they were, I went for blunt.

'He's in trouble,' I said. 'You *know* he's in trouble, right?'

Her smile didn't vanish, but the air went out of it. She swallowed once, and when she spoke her voice had lost its cheerfulness.

'Big Dave's doing fine.'

'Something's been wrong with him, though,' I said. 'Acting strange. Missing work. Maybe he doesn't look as good as he used to. Like he's not sleeping?'

'Well, I don't know that—'

'It started about a year ago,' I said. And then, 'It's getting worse.'

The smile collapsed like a mask falling away. With the concern and fear clear on her face, she looked more genuine. When she spoke, it was like hearing her for the first time.

'How do you know him?' she asked.

It would have been easy to lie, but I had the sense that

the woman was watching me very closely. I shook my head.

'My uncle knew a lot about him,' I said. 'I'd never heard of him until yesterday. But if there's something eating him, I know what it is. And I can help.'

She looked down at the table. Her jaw was set firmly. The computer chirped once and the screen changed. In my peripheral vision, Aubrey leaned against the wall, his arms folded.

'If I'm right,' I said softly, 'I may be the *only* one who can help.'

'Can you tell me what's the matter?' she said. 'Is it drugs?'

'It's not drugs. And it's not gambling. And it's not women. But it is important.'

'Can't you just tell me?'

I could, but it would blow my chances of holding her trust. I didn't say anything, and let the silence drag. The woman sighed, leaned back, and pulled the thin top drawer of the desk open. She didn't look at me as she picked out a business card and a pen. She wrote with small, fast strokes, like someone brushing away sand. When she did look up, she seemed almost angry.

'We love Big Dave,' she said. 'We need him back.'

'I'm on it,' I said, taking the card. She'd written a street address on it. I put it in my pocket, turned to catch Aubrey's gaze, and then nodded to the door.

'I'm trusting you,' she said as we walked out.

I didn't know how to answer that, so I didn't try.

*　　*　　*

We pulled up at the place. Two stories, windows obscured by cream-colored drapes, a tree in the front yard with a tire swing on an ancient, untrustworthy rope. The green grass lawn got a little patchy at the edges, and the black fake-iron house numbers by the front door had chipped. A dog was barking somewhere nearby in a lazy, conversational way.

Aubrey walked just ahead of me up the thin concrete path, and I had a small cascade of memories—Trevor chiding Aubrey for putting himself in harm's way to protect me, another house we'd walked to about a year ago when a *haugtrold* had nearly killed us both, Chogyi Jake warning me not to push the wards and protections that kept me safe. And then I was at the door. I fidgeted with my backpack and took a deep breath.

'I hate this part,' I said.

Aubrey nodded.

'Hi,' he said, 'can I talk to you about your relationship to immaterial, abstract parasites? Does kind of make the Jehovah's Witnesses seem plausible by comparison, doesn't it?'

'And yet,' I said, 'it's what we do.'

I rang the doorbell. The dog, wherever it was, took note and stepped up its color commentary. We waited. I knocked.

'Not home?' Aubrey said.

'Maybe not.'

The doorknob felt surprisingly cool. The door wasn't locked, and the hinges were silent. I looked at Aubrey looking at me, and then I swung the door wide.

'Hello?' I called as we stepped into the living room. 'Anybody here? David?'

Piles of paper littered the room—magazines, newspapers, printed websites, sketchbooks. The smell of rotting food was faint but distinct, almost more taste than odor. A worn leather couch dominated the room, a wide, low coffee table before it. An open doorway showed a small kitchen, and a dark hallway ran beside and behind a flight of carpeted stairs. The art on the walls mixed old-time ads for coffee brands and soda crackers that I'd never heard of with amateur photographs. David's work, I assumed. A flat-screen television hung on one wall, an incongruous line of Post-it notes fluttering beside it. I walked to them carefully, trying not to disturb anything. I wondered whether it counted as breaking and entering if I didn't have to break anything. Someone—David, I guessed—had drawn simple pictures on each little yellow sheet. Little architectural cartoons by someone who knew something about architecture. They were all slightly different, but since I'd seen Grace Memorial so recently and paid so much attention to it, I could see it in each of them.

'He doesn't know it,' I said, 'but he sort of does.'

'Hmm?'

Aubrey was standing by the coffee table, looking down at the papers and printouts. I gestured toward the drawings.

'Grace,' I said. 'But not. Close, but never quite right.'

Aubrey nodded and pointed to the table before him.

'He's been reading up too,' he said.

'On?'

'Schizophrenia. Dementia. Compulsive personality disorders.' Aubrey cocked his head, reading the title of a book. 'Dream interpretation.'

The kitchen was a mess. Piles of old dishes teetered by the sink. The smell of spoiled food thickened. Dark brown beer bottles stood in uneven ranks on the countertop. A few had the labels picked off. One was broken. Out the back window, a small yard had been neatly kept not too long ago. I didn't see anyone back there. In the living room, Aubrey whistled low. When I got back, he was holding up an old-looking leather-bound book. The title on the spine was worked-gold Gothic lettering and looked German to me.

'I've heard about this book, but I've never seen a copy,' Aubrey said. I stood beside him. The title page sported a woodcut print that looked at first glance like a human form, until I noticed that all the parts—arms, legs, improbably oversized penis—were also drawings of buildings and people, like one of those optical illusions where you could see something as either a face or a collection of objects. The title was *Der Körper und der Geist*, and below that, in smaller, bright red letters: *Ein Versuch auf dem verklemmten Leviathan*.

'It belonged to the grandfather,' Aubrey said. 'His name's on the flyleaf.'

'Any idea what it says?'

'The title translates to "Body and Spirit," but the sub-title's new to me. *Versuch* is experiment or trial, but I think it can also mean essay. So, I guess an essay or an experiment of the something-or-other Leviathan?'

'Look at its hands,' I said. The woodcut was rough, the printing old. If I hadn't seen them in a different context earlier in the day, I would have thought the strange, almost disjointed fingers were just bad technique.

'Good call,' he said, his voice grim.

I was about to reach for my cell phone with the idea of getting Ex and Chogyi Jake up to speed when a sound came from behind us, familiar from a dozen action flicks: the slick and clatter of a round being racked in a shotgun.

11

My body dove forward, pushing Aubrey down, almost before I knew I was doing it. By the time my conscious mind caught up, I was crouching between coffee table and couch. My weight was on my fingertips and the balls of my feet. Aubrey lay half behind the couch, his breath ragged. I wanted to look at him to make sure it was just surprise and caution, that I hadn't hurt him, but my head wouldn't turn.

In the dark frame of the hallway, the man with the shotgun stood. He was broad across the shoulders and belly with a neck as wide as his head. His eyes seemed to tremble in their sockets, and his face was flushed the deep red of rage. His bathrobe and T-shirt were stained by grease and time. As I watched, he took another step into the room, growling like a dog. He swung the shotgun toward me, the barrel deep as a well. I flipped the coffee table up between us and dropped low as the blast reduced it to splinters. Then, against all common sense and instinct, I leaped forward.

His eyes widened, and he took half a step back. He'd started racking a second round, but I had the barrel in my hand, the heat searing my skin like I'd grabbed a skillet. He was easily one and a half of me, but I twisted, pointing the barrel at the ceiling. I drove my knee up toward his crotch, but I didn't have the leverage to put any power into the blow. We were both holding the shotgun now, fighting for it. I tried to push him back, but he rose up over me, pressing down until my wrists ached. His breath stank of whiskey. His eyes were bloodshot.

He charged with a roar, bulling me forward into the ruins of the coffee table. I kept hold of the shotgun and let myself fall back, the force of his attack and my weight both pulling him forward. As he fell on top of me, I tried the knee again with much more satisfying results. We were locked together on the floor so close that I felt his gasp of pain against my cheek. I twisted my body, pulling my arms in between us and digging a straight-fingered hand in under his ribs. I heard Aubrey someplace to my right and felt a shudder as something hit my assailant's back. It didn't matter. He'd flinched back from my hand strike, and I could squirm out from beneath him. Small, younger, fueled by magic, I was on my knees before he could get his hands under him. I dropped an elbow onto his left kidney twice, then pulled the shotgun away from him.

When he could finally roll over, it was too late. I had a fresh round racked, and the barrel digging into the flesh of his throat. The fight was over, and I felt myself starting to tremble and pant in its aftermath. He sneered up at me, his lips in a squared gape of defiance and rage. And there was something else. The knowledge that his death was a finger's twitch away. Something that looked like relief.

'David Souder?' I said between pants.

He nodded, the movement translating itself to my hand along the length of the gun.

'I'm Jayné. Hi. We're here to help.'

I hadn't gotten out of it totally unscathed. A splinter of coffee table had gouged a deep red stripe down my back, and the fall had driven a small finishing nail into my shoulder deep enough that only the small silver head showed, like something equal parts body piercing and Home Depot. We got it out with a pair of pliers. The palm of my right hand was cooked red. I sat at the kitchen table, holding a Ziploc bag of ice cubes. My T-shirt was blood-soaked and torn. David, once he'd calmed down a little, had offered me an old gray University of Michigan sweatshirt that was too small to have ever been his.

The good news was I'd had several tetanus shots within the last year, didn't seem to have soaked up any of the shotgun pellets, and wouldn't have to go to a hospital to have little bits of metal spooned out of my flesh. Go me.

'That was incredible,' David Souder said as Aubrey applied a square bandage to the circular burn on the man's neck. 'The way you threw that table. And when you jumped? I mean you are goddamn fast. Are you a black belt or something?'

'It's a long story,' I said.

'Stop moving,' Aubrey said.

'Sorry,' David said.

'The short version,' I said, 'is that we're working on a problem, and we have pretty good reason to think it involved your grandfather. And because of him, you.'

'Who put you up to—'

'Stop moving.'

Aubrey stepped back. He didn't look happy.

'All right,' he said. 'Move. That's the best I can do.'

David put a hand to the bandage. I had the feeling he was less checking how it felt than whether it really existed.

'Who put you up to this?' he asked. 'Was it Alexis?'

'No one put us up to it,' I said. 'We were looking at something else. It involves a building your grandfather designed right before he died. We had some reason to think you were involved, even if you didn't directly know you were.'

David looked from me to Aubrey and then back. With his fear and anger gone, he looked much less dangerous. His bulk made him look like a young Winston Churchill. His eyes were puffy and red-rimmed, and the way he held himself spoke of a profound exhaustion. He brushed at his robe with a wide hand, as if he could erase the stains with his palm.

'You're really not . . . I'm sorry. But I can't believe this is really happening.'

'I know. It's weird,' I said. 'How long has it been since you slept?'

'Three days this time. I've made it four or five before, but I was just starting to fade when I heard the two of you talking. You really know what's going on? What's wrong with me?'

Aubrey looked at me, his expression a question. *How much do we tell him?*

'We're putting it together,' I said. 'How about you tell us a little about what's been going on with you. Compare notes.'

'I can get you something to drink,' Aubrey said.

'I'll make some coffee,' David said, hauling himself up. 'You two take decaf?'

We both agreed it would be fine. He lumbered over to the stove and started a kettle to boil, his brows knotted. He was silent for so long, I felt like I had to prompt him.

'It started about a year ago,' I said.

'Yeah. It did. It was about eight months after the last part of the divorce. Alexis moved down to Dallas. We didn't have any kids, and I never really liked her dog. It had been a long time coming, and with her gone I thought it was just some kind of delayed stress thing. Bad stuff happens and you seem all right for a while, but then it comes back up? I did that a lot when I was a kid. I was half expecting it. So when I started having the nightmares, I didn't really think much about it.'

His voice was calm enough, and steady, but I felt like he was leaving out bits and pieces. Dropping half thoughts out through the cracks between words. I'd been that tired a few times, but only a few, and not for long.

'Somewhere August, September?' I said.

'I don't know. Somewhere in there, yeah. It started off just being a sense of waking up trapped. Like the blankets were too heavy, and I couldn't open my eyes. But I knew where I was. I knew who I was. I figured it was a kind of metaphor. You know, you feel trapped and smothered in a relationship, and so you dream about being trapped and smothered. Pretty straightforward.'

He opened one of the cabinets and took down two mugs. There were other dishes, but none of them clean. He picked up a third mug off the table and rinsed it out.

'I was just using this one,' he said. 'It hasn't been sitting here like the others.'

'Okay,' I said. His embarrassment was touching in a weird way. For someone who'd tried to kill me less than an hour before, he seemed vulnerable and more than a little lost.

'So,' he said. 'Well, I figured it was a phase. I could tough it out. But they kept getting worse. Going on longer. Sometimes I'd wake up in the middle of the night screaming. I wasn't just stuck in bed anymore. I was buried. Like something out of a Poe story. I was in a coffin and I could hear the dirt hitting the lid. The more I had the dreams, the less I could rest, and the less I could rest, the worse they seemed to get.'

'Did you hear any voices in the dreams? Words, maybe?'

'No,' David said. 'Just this sense of being buried alive. But then it got worse. I wasn't alone in the coffin anymore. There were other things. Bugs or spiders or something. I don't know. And then I wasn't me anymore.'

He stopped to rinse out a gravity funnel and stick a fresh filter cone in it. He put it on top of one of the mugs. Not his.

'I haven't told anyone about this stuff,' he said. 'I probably shouldn't be telling you.'

'Do it anyway?' I asked, and I got a smile out of him.

'I knew what it meant when I started dreaming I was Grandpa Del,' he said, pouring fresh coffee grounds into the funnel. He sounded angry, but I knew better. I knew shame when I heard it. 'There's a . . . there's a history of mental illness. In the family. Okay?'

'Mine too,' I said. It was mostly a lie, depending on how pious someone has to be before you start looking at them funny. But it was a small one, and David seemed to unwind a notch.

'Well, you know then,' he said. 'Dad only talked about it when he was drunk. About keeping the great architect from letting it show. All the crazy things he did. Grandpa thought there were demons. Real demons. That they were always trying to get inside of you and make you do or think things. That they could make people into werewolves and vampires and all that. It wasn't a metaphor for him. He really thought it was true.'

David shook his head and gave a little half grin. *How crazy is that, right?* I smiled back.

'When I started dreaming, I knew what my subconscious was trying to tell me,' he said. The smile was gone. His voice was gray as slate. 'It was happening to me. I was going crazy too.'

'You never thought maybe your grandfather was right?' Aubrey asked.

'Sure I did. For hours at a time,' David said. 'After a really bad dream, I'd think it was all stone-cold true for three, maybe four hours. That's how I knew. That I was next. And the dreams were getting violent. The thing in the box with me wasn't bugs anymore. It was some kind of . . . I don't know. Something huge. And it was mad at me. I mean really mad.'

The kettle whistled, and we all jumped a little. David turned off the heat, picking up the kettle's black handle with a fold of his robe. He poured a little water into the funnel, steam wafting up over his hands.

'I started missing work. There was this woman I was going out with, and I broke things off with her. I didn't want her involved in this. Wasn't fair to her.'

'Did you go to a doctor?' Aubrey asked.

'No. I felt like if I didn't tell anyone, maybe it would all go away. Stupid, I know, but . . .'

He shrugged. The truth was doctors probably would have thought the same things he did.

'What happened next?' I asked.

David shrugged, then switched the funnel to the second cup, dribbling a small line of coffee across the table between them.

'It got worse,' he said. He wiped the spill with a sleeve. 'I started getting this constant feeling that I should go . . . somewhere. Like I was being called. The thing in the coffin wanted me to go somewhere and do something.

It didn't seem angry anymore. Not exactly. More command-ing. That's normal with schizophrenia, you know. Command hallucinations. Something outside of you telling you what to do.'

He added more water to the top of the funnel and then handed me the first mug. When I took it, a little stab of pain went through my shoulder where the nail had been, but I tried not to show it. The coffee was surprisingly good, especially for decaf. Not at all bitter, and with a smoky undertone that caught my attention. He must have seen my reaction because he smiled a little.

'Do you know what it wanted you to do?' Aubrey asked.

'No. It was trying to tell me, I think, but mostly I just knew I was supposed to come. To be there, wherever *there* is. I started constructing it in my mind. I had this sense of the place, you know. There were days I'd go into work, and instead of doing anything, I'd just draw this vision in my head over and over. Trying to get it right.'

'And the book?' I said.

'Which book?'

'Your grandfather's book. The one in German.'

A look of chagrin passed over David's face as he switched the funnel to the last mug. He added more water. I had to think the coffee grounds were getting pretty much used up by now.

'I had this idea,' he said. 'If I understood the way my grandfather went crazy, maybe I'd at least get a little insight into what was coming next. How it would all go. I had some boxes in the attic. That was in them. I don't know any German, though, so it didn't help.'

'Here's the thing,' I said. 'You're not crazy. Neither was your grandfather. The place you're drawing? It's Grace Memorial Hospital. Your uncle . . . sorry, your *grandfather* redesigned the place back in the forties. And there really is something weird and powerful that's buried there. And it's alive.'

David sighed.

'No,' he said. 'Thank you, but no. That won't work.'

'I can get you pictures of Grace Memorial,' I said. 'Or don't trust me. Google Maps is going to have a street view. Go look for yourself.'

'What if it is? What does that prove? That as my brain started breaking down, it grabbed anything related to Grandpa Del. Including some building of his I'd seen and half forgotten.'

'You're pretty rational for someone in the throes of a schizophrenic break,' Aubrey said.

'I think I am,' David said. 'But I would, wouldn't I?'

I leaned back in my chair, coffee mug in both hands. The movement sent little sparkles of pain through my back and shoulder. I ignored them.

I'd been where David was now. I knew what it felt like to fall down the rabbit hole. Only I'd been lucky. Aubrey had been there to help me, and through him Ex and Chogyi Jake. There'd also been a truly ugly vampire named Midian Clark whose company I still missed. He was one of the bad guys, but we'd still been friends, just for a while.

David, though, hadn't had anyone. The weird hidden world had washed into him, and he'd made the only sense of it he could. He saw what he was prepared to see: a slow, creeping madness. And over months, he'd turned in on himself and made it almost true. I couldn't help wondering what I would have done in his place. Proving to myself that riders existed had almost gotten me killed, and I'd had guides and allies. If I'd been on my own, I might have come to the truth. Or else my doubts and disbelief might have gone septic too.

'We can agree that you haven't told anyone else about what's been going on? At least not in specifics?'

He nodded.

'Cool. Hang here,' I said, and put the coffee mug on the table with a thump.

Stepping outside, I was astonished by how late it was. The sky was already crawling toward a steel blue twilight. The air smelled damp, like it had rained when I wasn't watching. The conversational barker had gone away or been put in a house, and the distant throb of outsized car speakers rose and fell in its place. I went to the car, popped open the passenger-side door, and took out my laptop carrier. I opened the computer as I walked back through David's house, stepping carefully over the scattered papers and the fragments of coffee table. I had the file pulled up and ready to play when I got to the kitchen.

I didn't talk or explain. I just put the laptop on the table in front of him, scooted the cursor over to the play button, and clicked. Oonishi's dream sequence played out in silence, and I wasn't watching it. David started off guarded, maybe even amused. And then his face went bloodless, and he sat forward. I could see the pulse pushing the bandage on his neck. When the recording was done, he played it again. And again. By the fourth time through, silent tears were running down his face.

'That's it,' he said, his voice soft and choked. 'That's the thing in my dream.'

'Yeah,' I said. 'Other people have seen it too.'

'Oh,' he said. 'Oh, thank God.'

12

'Well, you two look smug,' Kim said as Aubrey and I came in. 'What's with the new shirt?'

'Bled all over the old one,' I said. 'Where's Ex?'

'We just got him to take a nap,' Chogyi Jake said, coming in from the kitchen. 'I told him I'd get him up as soon as the lasagna was ready.'

The condo had changed in our absence. The night pressing in at the windows was the same, but the smell of dust had been replaced by the reassuring scents of garlic and hot butter. And instead of a ragged hole in the wall, fresh pale wood made a clean, unpainted door frame. The iron security door was gone too. The scum of white that had covered everything had been cleaned up, and a squat red shop vacuum lurked in the corner beside the couch. Aubrey put the box of Declan Souder's belongings borrowed from David's attic on the coffee table, and I told the story. Kim and Chogyi Jake sat, listening to the whole thing.

Kim picked up the *Der Körper und der Geist*, paging through it with a frown. Chogyi Jake looked through the other contents of the box—a couple of books on architects named Speer and Troost whom I'd never heard of, a notebook of sketches, and a moth-eaten blue suit. In return for it, I'd left David my number, an offer to call him if I found out anything important, and stern instructions to start carrying his cell phone instead of leaving it at the office. If I'd asked for his car, I think he'd have given it to me.

'Poor bastard,' Kim said. 'He must have been in pretty bad shape.'

'Worse than Kelly after his gels went bad,' Aubrey said in a tone of agreement. 'This guy's been trying not to sleep for months.'

'Kelly?' I said.

'Sorry,' Aubrey said. 'Guy we used to know. I just meant that David was messed up. I did a couple small cantrips to lessen influences and help him sleep. Hopefully, they'll give him a little cover. At least until we can get whatever this is resolved.'

'Speaking of,' I said. 'What did we miss? And who's the carpenter?'

Chogyi Jake tilted his head, unsure what I meant, and then followed my gaze to the new door frame and grinned.

'Harlan seems to have been taken by a generous impulse,' he said. 'I think he's still relieved that he's not being sued. He sent building maintenance just after you left. I had them take out the security door too. I hope that's all right?'

'Kicks all the ass,' I said.

'Other than that, we've been hitting the books,' Kim said. 'Dividing up the material into piles. Division of labor and all that. No word from Oonishi yet, but I left him a voice mail. And I have more details on the interment ceremony. It does look like it would take someone of the same bloodline to open it.'

'Which fits in with the idea that Eric was looking to pop this thing loose,' I said. 'He was keeping tabs on David on the theory that if Grace Memorial was the prison, then Declan Souder was the one the Invisible College sacrificed. Big Dave's the key that opens the coffin.'

'It begins to look that way,' Chogyi Jake said.

Ex came in as Kim and I were setting the table, his face still marked by the pillowcase. He insisted that the whole story of David and Grandpa Del be retold, and then ignored dinner in favor of sitting alone in the living room with the German book. Aubrey rolled his eyes, but other than that, we let him be. The lasagna was out of the frozen section, but it tasted wonderful. Kim had brought a couple bottles of red wine that went with it beautifully. I relaxed in my chair. The conversation wandered off the subject of riders and magic quickly, turning to things like the story of Kim's sister accidentally running over their mother's leg with a truck and Aubrey and Chogyi Jake debating when exactly Quentin Tarantino had jumped the shark. It was as if we'd all tacitly agreed to step back, take a breath, and just have a quiet dinner among friends.

I went along with it, talking movies and books and politics, but it was playing a role. I wanted to relax into a simple, uncomplicated dinner. I could act like I was, but inside, I felt like I was lined up for a race and waiting for the starting gun.

After dinner, Chogyi Jake and Kim cleaned up while

Aubrey brewed some distinctly nondecaf coffee. I headed back out to the living room where the blueprints of Grace Memorial still lay unfurled. Ex nodded to me, but didn't speak. I sat cross-legged on the floor and let my fingers trace the curves and lines of the hospital. Even at this level of abstraction, it looked overpacked and organic. I found myself thinking of dissections in high school biology. Frogs and fetal pigs. The blueprints had the same feel. Here was something that had been hidden, brought to light.

And just like with the frogs, I wasn't quite sure what I was looking at.

Sleep didn't come easy that night. I'd expected it to. I was tired enough, but also restless. The tension that dinner had tried to dispel was seeping back. Every time I closed my eyes, images popped up like a slideshow—Grace Memorial glowering out at the street through the huge compound eye of its windows, the face of the red-haired man who'd attacked me, the coffin opening. And every time I opened my eyes, the darkness pressing in at the bed made me think about being buried alive. The interment ceremony. Some poor bastard having the unreal force of a rider driven into him, and then the coffin closed. I told myself that I couldn't imagine how horrible that would be, but the truth was I could almost feel it: the painful, electric rush of the spirit entering my flesh; the constriction of the coffin; the air growing thick even before the sound of earth being shoveled over it had faded. I stared at the distant, dark ceiling above me and wondered how long Declan

Souder had been alive. A normal person, it might have been hours. With the support of a rider, anything was possible. For all I knew, the man was still alive, down there in the darkness.

Aubrey muttered in his sleep, turning his back to me and pulling a pillow over his head. His back rose and fell with slow, soft breath. My hand tapped at my leg, and I noticed that I was humming a song. It was a kid's gospel song I'd sung in church group about a million times. *I've got the joy, joy, joy, joy down in my heart, down in my heart, down in my heart.* But the voice I heard singing in my head was a man's and the words had changed themselves.

> *I've got the boy, boy, boy, boy down in the dark*
> *Down in the dark*
> *Down in the dark*
> *I've got the boy, boy, boy, boy down in the dark*
> *Down in the dark he'll stay*

My skin felt like it wanted to crawl off. I sat up. It didn't matter how tired I was, I wasn't sleeping. Even if it was only because I didn't want to know what kind of dreams bubbled up out of a mind that was writing songs like that for itself. I got up, fumbled into my bathrobe as quietly as I could, and stepped out of the bedroom. The glow of light from the living room was a relief.

Ex was still on the couch, hunched over *Der Körper und der Geist,* one hand holding back his long, pale hair, one on the page. He was smiling like a wolf that's just scented a rabbit. The west wall had been stripped of art. Instead, it had about twenty wide, yellow Post-it notes with bits of information on them, and half a dozen pictures stuck to the wall with thumbtacks. A picture of David taken from Eric's big box o' surveillance was posted by the door just under an image of his grandfather that I recognized from the Wikipedia article. One of the Post-it notes written in Chogyi Jake's hand read *CCU/fMRI suite—ley line connection?* Another one beside it said CIVIL DEFENSE WARD in block letters I didn't recognize and assumed were Kim's. The whole thing reminded me of a homicide board out of a murder mystery.

'You all right?' Ex asked without looking up.

'Can't sleep,' I said. 'Creeped myself out. I'll try crashing again in a little bit. Did Kim take off?'

'No. She's in the new guest room. I loaned her a T-shirt and a towel. I assume that's all right?'

'Sure, of course. How's she holding up?'

'She's a professional,' Ex said. His tone made it a high compliment. I wanted to follow up, dig more. How did she seem when I wasn't in the room? Did she talk about Aubrey at all, and what did she say? I couldn't think of a way to ask that didn't seem weird and petty. I let it drop.

'Hey,' I said, 'I didn't ask how things went with the chaplain. Did you meet up with him?'

'Did,' Ex said. 'Nice guy. Totally out of his depth. He's aware that something's happening at the hospital, but he's spending his time and energy ministering to the patients and praying for guidance.'

'Doesn't sound like you have much use for that,' I said. 'I thought you were a big prayer kind of guy.'

Ex sat back. His eyes were narrow and intense. With his unbound hair spilling down his face, he looked softer, but it was deceptive. From the first time I'd met him, Ex had never seemed anything less than driven. Wrongheaded sometimes, condescending and paternalistic. Frightened sometimes. Even brokenhearted. But never soft. For a moment it seemed significant that he and I were the only ones awake.

'I am a big prayer kind of guy,' he said. 'But I have a more nuanced idea of prayer than Father Gilmore. For him, it's a way to not take responsibility. When he gives a problem over to God, he thinks he's done, you know? Yesterday, he wanted guidance. Today, I showed up. Tomorrow, he's still going to be asking for guidance. I don't have a lot of patience with that.'

'Sounds like you didn't think much of him,' I said. A stack of files sat, ignored, at Ex's side. I picked them up just to have room to sit.

'I love everybody,' he said. 'Doesn't mean I have to like them. What about you?'

'Me?'

'You're the one being mobbed and shot at,' Ex said. 'Might throw some people off stride.'

'No. I'm fine,' I said. And then, 'I guess maybe it's a little weird that I'm fine, but I am. It's just business, you know?'

'And you can handle yourself.'

'What? Skeptical?'

His smile started and stopped in the corners of his eyes.

'No, I think you can handle yourself. This is good, by the way,' he said, holding up the German book. 'This is very good. And it's *big*. I think you may have gotten the key to the whole thing, right here.'

'Yeah? What are we looking at?'

'Well, we know it's something that affects people without having actually possessed them individually. We know it had to be driven into someone for the interment. And we know it's powerful enough that even that didn't entirely silence it. It's looking like some kind of *haugsvarmr*. Given the subtitle, probably a *leyiathan*.'

'Taxonomy's always a bitch,' I said. 'And what exactly is a hog-swarmer?'

'*Haugsvarmr.*'

'Whatever.'

Ex waved an impatient hand, his hair drooping down over his eyes. While he talked, I paged through the files on my lap. One was labeled as security personnel for Grace Memorial as of three years before. Another had a list of the contractors who'd bid for the new emergency room five years ago, and records of their workman's comp filings.

'It's a level up,' Ex said. 'It's . . . Okay. Look. Riders possess people. That's how they work. Someone who's being ridden doesn't have the demon in their finger or their liver or even their brain. When a rider takes over, it takes over the whole human system. It controls the hands and the feet and the muscles. It can use them in ways a normal, unpossessed person can't. But it isn't those parts.'

'A possessed guy isn't a guy with a possessed gall bladder. It's the whole guy. Got it,' I said.

I spotted a file with Kim's name on it. I shot a look at Ex. I was pretty sure he wasn't paying attention, so I shifted it into the pile set aside for her to look at. Better that the boys not find out about Kim and Eric's affair that way. Hell, better they never found out at all.

'The *haugsvarmr* are riders that possess larger structures,' Ex said.

'So like haunted houses?' I asked, thinking of Declan Souder's architectural dissections. Ex shook his head.

'Social structures. Like political parties or nations.'

I stopped looking through the files. I could feel my eyes getting wide, and I fought a sense of growing vertigo.

'Hold on. What?' I said.

'It hasn't happened often, but it's not unheard of,' Ex said. 'Rosh, Meshech, and Tubal are probably the first recorded examples. Hitler's Germany was the most recent.'

'Okay, time-out,' I said. 'World War Two was about riders? Germany was *possessed*?'

'Well, the apparatus of the Nazi Party was. And maybe the nation as a whole. Why does that seem weird?'

'I just . . . I mean . . .'

Ex cocked his head. The expression on his face left me feeling dim and obvious, like I'd just blurted out my amazement that politicians don't always tell the truth. A little burn of resentment lit in my chest.

'You know your problem?' he said.

'I think you're going to tell me.'

'You and Aubrey and Kim,' he said as if I hadn't spoken. 'Even Chogyi Jake? Do you know why all of you can't quite make sense of all this? You live in a morally neutral world. You don't like the idea of evil, and so you don't look for the patterns. Riders are just another kind of insect or amoeba to you. Parasites.'

'And for you?' I said.

'They're demons,' he said. 'The Second World War was a battle between a flawed, struggling human resistance and a force of pure evil. It's the same struggle that's going on right now. Whether you choose to acknowledge it or not, it's the job you've taken on. It doesn't matter whether you think of Hitler and Goering and all the rest as evil men or evil spirits in human form. They're still evil, so they're the enemy. Whether they're *nosferatu* or *noppera-bo* or *haugtrold* only matter when we start planning tactics.'

'What about angels?'

'Never met one.'

The way he said it closed the subject. I backtracked.

'But the Nazis knew about this? Riders. Magic.'

Ex relaxed a little, back on safe ground. I made a mental note to ask Aubrey why angels were one of Ex's buttons.

'There's still a lot of debate about what exactly Himmler was up to when he founded the Ahnenerbe,' Ex said with a shrug, 'but we know for a fact that he was deeply into riders. We know that part of what happened at Dachau was ritual death magic.'

'You're talking about Indiana Jones digging up the Ark of the Covenant?' I said, trying to make a joke out of it.

'Well, all right,' Ex said and grinned. '*That* they made up. But more generally, yes, Nazi occultism isn't a big secret. Part of the national policy from 1939 on was to harness riders for the cause. Karl Wiligut spent most of the war in a project to make pacts with the riders, and enslave the ones that wouldn't play. They certainly bound Wotan Irisi and the Black Sun. They worked with the Graveyard Child, but it's not clear whether that was a free pact or a binding. There were dozens of *asatro* in the hierarchy of the German military, and more *loupine* than you could count.'

'*Loupine*,' I said.

'There was a reason the Nazi resistance to Allied occupation were called werewolves,' Ex said. 'Whatever's happened at Grace Memorial, it's involved with the sort of thing the Nazis were looking at. Or the kind of thing that was looking at them, depending whether you think Hitler was the chicken or the egg. And'—he tapped the book in his hands twice, hard, sharp sounds—'a *haugsvarmr*. Probably a *leyiathan*.'

I knew I wasn't thinking straight. It had been a hard, long, exhausting day that had involved four hours' driving and being shot at in the middle part. I could feel that I was missing something here, some question or piece of information that would reframe the whole thing. Pull everything into focus. The best I could manage was a protest.

'But Eric was looking to get it loose,' I said. 'His whole project was to *free* it.'

'And if we knew why, we'd know a lot more,' Ex said.

'Could he need it for an ally?' I said. 'The Invisible College was part of tying it down. Maybe he was looking for something that would help him against them, and—'

'Eric planned to break the Invisible College as *part* of digging this thing loose,' Ex said. 'Not as something to do afterward. No, I've been looking at that angle, and I don't know what ends Eric could have been aiming at. *Haugsvarmr* aren't usually aware of individual humans, at least not in the way we're used to. They need a reason to care that we even exist. Eric would have needed a plan for getting its attention. Something that would make it notice him in the first place.'

'Any idea what?'

'Best guess? Access to David. If Eric could make himself a middleman between those two, he'd have been in a good position to bargain.'

'For what?'

'I don't know. I assume he wasn't looking to re-create the Nazi Party, though.'

'Are we a hundred percent that the hog-swarmer was what got bound? Could it have been something else?'

Ex shrugged.

'Not a hundred, but high nineties.'

'Any chance they could have been working with a hog-swarmer to tie something else down? A common enemy?'

'Possible,' Ex allowed. 'Politics in the Pleroma aren't something any of us understand.'

A tapping sound caught my attention; it was my own

fingers dancing nervously on the file with Kim's name. I forced myself to stop. Ex watched me, his pale eyes gentle and challenging at the same time.

'Well, I don't know either,' I said.

'We'll find it,' Ex said. 'There's a plan in here somewhere. All we need to do is find it.'

The tone of his voice was ambiguous, but I was pretty sure he was talking about God as much as Eric. I'd lost faith in religion before I'd ever met Ex or Aubrey, but whether God had a plan for all things or not didn't matter. Ex was still right. There *was* a plan, because Eric had made it. I could tell myself that the hard part was done. Once I knew what to do, doing it was easy. The thought was almost enough for me.

Almost.

'Hey,' I said. 'Once we figure what Eric was up to, we're going to have to talk to this thing. Strike some kind of deal.'

'Looks like, yeah.'

'So it's probably not all that bad, right? You're not scared of it?'

Ex actually grinned. I waited for him to say *No* or *We can do anything* or even just *God is with us*. Something motivational and upbeat that I could half believe.

'Petrified,' he said.

13

I expected that, when I finally did fall asleep a little after three in the morning, I would be troubled by nightmares. Or at least disturbing, unpleasant dreams. As it happened, the only dream I could remember involved trying to get the right dog out of an Italian groomer's that was also a public library. I kept getting the wrong dog and having to go back in and try to explain the mistake in Italian without raising my voice. I woke up late and tense. Aubrey had already gotten up, but the bed had a small depression where his body had been. My back felt tight, wounded muscles bracing themselves as if bunching up would keep the pain away. I checked the clock—nine thirty—and made my way to the bathroom and a long, hot shower.

The whine of the pipes and the splash of the water drowned out any other sounds, and for the few minutes I stayed there, I could almost pretend I was alone in the condo. My mind unfocused, I wondered what it would be like to live by myself the way David Souder did. The way Kim did.

I'd never tried it, going from home and the family to the dorms to my traveling occult circus without any real gaps in between. I couldn't quite imagine waking up without having anyone to wake up to. I thought of David going quietly insane in his house. Would that still have happened if there'd been someone there to see it? Not even a lover, necessarily. A roommate. A friend. That was an extreme example, maybe, but other things could happen. Slip in the shower. Get a really bad round of the flu. Being alone that way didn't make the chances of something bad happening any better or worse, but it made recovering from them harder. More dangerous.

When I finally did kill the water, I could hear Kim laughing out in the kitchen. I patted myself dry with a big, fluffy white towel, the cut on my back leaving a little red on the nap. I put a fresh bandage over the little puncture where the nail had gone in. The flesh around it didn't look red or feel hot. I was going to get away with my little IKEA vaccination after all. My seared palm didn't hurt as much as I'd expected either. By the time I was dressed and my hair mostly dry, it was after ten.

'Hey, boss,' Aubrey said as I came out into the kitchen.

'Hey,' I said. 'There's still some coffee, right?'

Kim poured a fresh mug for me. She was swimming in one of Chogyi Jake's shirts. I always forgot that I was taller than her. Ex was in the living room, almost in the same place he'd been when I went to sleep. His skin had a waxy look and there were dark smudges under his eyes, but he looked content as he read, so maybe the abuse made him happy. Chogyi Jake himself sat at the table between Aubrey and Kim, fresh as if he'd just woken up too, though he'd probably been up for hours.

'Calling in sick again?' I asked Kim as I took the coffee from her.

'It's Saturday,' she said. 'They do let me off for the weekends.'

'Guess days kind of run together when you don't have that work structure thing,' I said. 'Do we have a plan?'

'David called for you,' Chogyi Jake said. 'We told him you'd call back after you woke up.'

'Did he sound all right?' I asked.

'He did to me,' Aubrey said. 'Better than yesterday, anyhow.'

'Right,' I said. 'Besides that?'

'We are going to get through these files,' Ex said, making it sound like a death march.

'I've tracked down a couple of the walk-aways,' Kim said. 'Huge privacy violation, but they've agreed to be interviewed, so a couple of us should do that. And I was trying to find someone else who had heard one of the people coming up post-op speaking in tongues. A recording's too much to hope, but the hospital's a pretty cosmopolitan place. Lots of multilingual staff. Someone might have recognized something.'

'Good thought,' I said.

'Declan Souder left his personal papers to the Illinois Institute of Technology,' Aubrey said. 'I was going to go take a peek at them. See if there was anything useful.'

'More obscure books of German magic?' I said.

'For instance.'

'So two interviews, a research visit, and everything Eric left,' I said. 'Doesn't leave much time for shopping?'

'Doesn't,' Ex said, failing to appreciate the joke.

'How about we split up, then,' I said. 'Kim and I can take the walk-aways. Aubrey does the Souder recon. Ex and Chogyi plow through as much of the local stuff as possible. Plan?'

'I can drop Aubrey at the institute,' Kim said. 'I know where it is, and one of the people who agreed to talk lives in Bronzeville.'

That shouldn't have given me pause, so I hid it.

'Great,' I said. 'Gimme the other guy's address, and we'll hit it.'

'Don't forget to call David,' Chogyi Jake said, which was good since he'd already slipped my mind. I took my phone to the new room to keep the background chatter of the other four planning to a minimum. While the phone rang, I wrote my name in the dust on the window.

'Jayné!' he said. 'Thank you. Thank you for calling. I slept last night. I really slept.'

'No dreams?'

'Nothing like before,' he said, 'but I was thinking. Maybe I should go down there. To the hospital you were talking about. That's where this is all coming from. If I go down close to it, knowing what I know now, maybe I can find out something more.'

'Bad idea right now,' I said. 'We're making some real progress, but you shouldn't jump the gun until we have a better idea what we're looking at. Just hang tight, and I swear I'll let you know as soon as we've got something solid.'

'I want to be part of it,' he said, and the happy tone of voice seemed a little strained. 'I mean, you're not just breezing in here and then I never hear from you again, right? This was my Grandpa Del. Whatever's going on, I'm part of it.'

I closed my eyes and pinched the bridge of my nose. I wanted to tell him to sit tight, stay quiet, and hope that whatever we needed wouldn't require him to do more than let us draw a little blood with a nice sterile needle someplace as far away from Grace Memorial as possible. There was no point. When I'd stumbled into the secret world of riders and magic, that wouldn't have worked for me. No reason to think it would work on David now.

'You're absolutely part of it,' I said. 'What we're doing now is background work. The stuff you gave us was really useful. I think we're on the edge of cracking it open, but for right now, just hang tight.'

'Okay. All right. But if there's anything I can do—'

'You'll be the first to know,' I said. 'Promise.'

I dropped the call. Kim, beside me, spoke.

'Are you really going to get him involved?'

'He is involved,' I said. 'I'm just going to try to keep him out of trouble.'

We broke up a little before noon. As I pulled the minivan up out of the parking structure, it occurred to me again that I still didn't have an actual vacuum cleaner apart from the borrowed Shop-Vac or a good idea where to get one. Just another little loose end to bug me while I worked on the big stuff, I supposed.

I'd heard songs and stories all my life about the south side of Chicago, starting with 'Bad, Bad Leroy Brown' and ending up with Moby singing about having weapons in hand as he went for a ride. I was ready for a war zone, but it wasn't bad at all. There were plenty of soccer-mom mini-vans parked on the street. Leticia Cook answered the door. At a guess, she was in her early fifties, graying hair pulled back from her face. She wore clean blue sweats that made me think of what my own mom would have worn on a quiet day.

'You're the girl who wanted to talk about that hospital?' she said after I introduced myself.

'I am.'

She raised her eyebrows, looking me quickly up and down, then motioned me in. The town house was neatly kept. A couch with understated floral upholstery domin-ated the front room without being particularly large. The walls were filled with pictures of her and her family. Three children, two boys and a girl, getting older and then younger again, depending on where I looked. Leticia leaned up a narrow stairway and shouted.

'We've got company down here. Make yourself decent before you come down.'

A muffled 'Yes, dear' was answer enough. She waved me into the front room and onto the couch. She pointed to another picture on the living room wall. A tall black man with a sly expression beamed out at us.

'That's my son, Jimmy. He's a lawyer. Works out in San Francisco. Made partner last year.'

'Really?' I said. 'He looks young for that.'

Leticia laughed, and at first I wasn't sure if it was with me or at me.

'Keep that up and we'll get along just fine. Now, what was it you wanted to know about that place?'

I started carefully, asking how she wound up at Grace Memorial, what her doctors had told her about the hospital, things like that. She'd been in after she'd fainted at the grocery store. When she came to, she was in Grace with eighteen kinds of monitors glued to her skin and a saline drip feeding into her arm. Heart attack, and from the test results, not her first one.

'Now they've got me sucking down Lipitor and aspirin every day. Walking.' She shrugged. 'I should have been exercising my whole life, but who has time?'

'You left before they released you,' I said. 'What can you tell me about that?'

The warmth in her eyes drained away as if it hadn't been there.

'You probably don't believe in God,' she said.

'I don't,' I said. Maybe I should have lied, but this didn't seem like the place for it. I had the feeling she would have known. 'If it helps, though, I believe that I don't know much.'

That got a half smile out of her.

'I believe in our Lord and Savior, Christ Jesus. And that's the reason I left that place even though the cardiologists told me not to. I was in more danger staying.'

'Did you see something? Hear something?'

'Felt it,' she said. 'I felt it moving in the air and the walls of that place.'

I leaned forward, the couch shifting under my weight.

'Have you sensed spirits before?' I asked.

'Is this a psychological evaluation?' she asked. 'Because we can skip to the end, and I'll tell you I don't hear voices.'

'It's not. I just want to understand what's happening at Grace.'

'Nothing good,' she said.

I stayed for another half hour, but she'd become evasive. I supposed I should have been glad I got as much of her time as I did. Before I left, she went upstairs and came back with a small silver cross hanging from a delicate chain. As I stood on her doorstep, she pressed it into my hands.

'If you're going back there, you should have this,' she said. 'The devil is in that place.'

I looked at it. Two bits of metal set at right angles. The primary symbol of most of my life. From the time I was old enough to understand it I'd gone to sleep with a cross above my bed, saying my prayers at mealtime, asking God what His will was for me. Part of me resented the years when the cross had been more than two bits of metal at right angles. Part of me missed it. I handed it back to Leticia, shaking my head.

'If you've got it in your heart, you don't need it,' I said. 'If you don't, it's not going to help.'

Back at the apartment, Ex and Chogyi Jake had spread their maps and notes and documents across the floor, and were locked in a serious debate over the relationship of architecture to sigil work. I dropped my backpack on the cow-skin couch and lay back, letting their voices wash over me. I didn't realize I was falling asleep until it was an hour later, and Kim and Aubrey came in with three plastic shopping bags filled with five kinds of Thai food.

After the dinner plates were cleared—my turn this time—and water set to boil for coffee and tea, we all retired to the living room. Aubrey and Chogyi Jake sat on straight-backed wooden chairs taken from the living room. Kim sat on the couch, looking through a small stack of files with a scowl, and Ex sat beside her. To my surprise, he had a beer in his hand. I sat cross-legged on the floor, the coffee table before me and the Post-it notes on the wall behind my left shoulder.

'Well,' I said. 'I guess I call the meeting to order. I talked to one of the walk-aways, but I didn't get much. How about you guys?'

Ex started.

'I think we can take as a given that we're looking at a *leyiathan*. All the circumstantial evidence points there. It also seems safe to say Eric was searching for it and for the way to free it, but with strings attached. He wanted something in return.'

'What kinds of things could you get from it?' I said. 'And specifically what could you get from it that you couldn't get someplace else?'

We were all silent for a moment. Ex took a drink of his beer.

'What if there's another one already loose,' Aubrey said.

'We know Eric allied with riders when there was a common enemy that made them the lesser evil.'

'Doesn't wash,' Ex said. 'It's like allying yourself with a nuclear bomb because someone else has one.'

'Perhaps,' Chogyi Jake said, 'it isn't something here. If there was something he wanted to happen in the Pleroma . . .'

'Next Door?' Aubrey said.

'Sure,' I said. 'That's good. The interment doesn't just keep the thing out of our world, it keeps it out of the riders' world too, right? It's stuck in the box. Physically and spiritually cut off.'

I've got the boy, boy, boy, boy down in the dark, my head muttered. *Down in the dark he'll stay.*

'That seems more plausible than trying to use it for something in the human world,' Chogyi Jake said.

'New theory,' I said. 'Are we sure it's a bad guy?'

There was a moment's silence. I saw Kim stiffen, as if she was about to speak, but her eyes were on the file in her hands. Aubrey was frowning, Chogyi Jake waiting patiently, and Ex slowly shook his head. I put my hands flat on the table before me.

'Maybe we're looking at this the wrong way,' I said. 'I know that we always think of riders as being bad by definition, but whatever's down there, Eric was going to set it free. And the Invisible College tied it down. If the thing in the box is the good guy, then it's Grace Memorial that we need to be fighting, right?'

Ex steepled his fingers.

'What if it's an angel?' I said, a little surprised by the hesitance in my own voice.

'Son of a *bitch*!'

The change in Kim's face convinced me for a moment that Grace had somehow reached out and taken her over again. Her skin was bloodless white except for two bright splotches on her cheeks, like she'd been slapped. She rose up from the couch with a fluidity borne of violence. She had a file in her hand. It was the one with her name on it. The one I'd put in her stack for her.

'Did you see this?' she shouted. Her eyes were locked on mine. 'Did you *read* it?'

'No,' I said. 'Kim? What's—'

Rage buzzed in her body so loud I could hear it. Her breath came in a shaking staccato. Aubrey was on his feet, looking from Kim to me and back like he didn't know whether he was about to break up a fight. Her head trembled. Her whole body trembled.

'Kim,' Chogyi Jake said. 'I'm seeing that you're angry. But I don't understand why, and I feel alarmed by it.'

Her laugh came short and hard and deeper than a bark, like something that was being torn out of her.

'If you knew about this, Jayné . . . if you were part of this—'

'Part of what?' I said.

'He put me here. Eric put me at Grace Memorial. *I* was part of his plan.'

14

'Kim,' Aubrey said. 'Take a breath.'

She stopped like her shoes had been nailed to the floor. Her gaze locked on Aubrey, and her mouth opened a little, then shut. The desolation in her eyes went past tears into something else. I felt something at the back of my neck pulling my skin tighter. My rib cage might have been empty, except for the sparrow-sized heart beating itself to death against my bones. Kim held up the file.

'He put me here,' she said, and her voice had lost its frenzy. 'He wanted a canary for his coal mine. Someone who would see things getting strange and call him for help. He planned to have me working at Grace Memorial. From before the *wendigo*. Almost from the first time we met him.'

'That doesn't work,' Aubrey said gently. 'You're reading it wrong.'

'I'm not. He stage-managed all of it. My job interview. The research projects. All of it.'

'He couldn't have known you'd be leaving Denver,' Aubrey said. 'We weren't even having trouble back then.'

I closed my eyes. This wasn't how he should find out. I should have told him a year ago, just so that it wouldn't happen this way and now. I forced myself to breathe, to look. Kim had gone gray. Less than gray. Colorless. Her shoulders slumped forward, her body turning in on itself like she was bracing for a blow.

'Eric *was* the trouble between us. After him, it was impossible for me to stay there. In Denver. In my life. He ruined us.'

'Kim—'

'I was sleeping with Eric, Aubrey. Before I left. Almost before we were having trouble. I didn't even really know why until . . .'

She lifted the papers in her hand. I watched Aubrey understand, like I was seeing something delicate fall just too far away for me to catch it. Ex and Chogyi Jake and I weren't even in the room with him.

'I thought there was something wrong with me,' Kim said. 'Even after he died, I knew I couldn't come back to you because whatever was broken in me would still be just as broken. Do you see?'

Ex looked between Kim and Aubrey, his face a mask of confusion and distress. Chogyi Jake leaned close to him and murmured something that made Ex's eyes go wide. Tears were finally starting to gather in Kim's eyes. I didn't want to watch this. Carefully, Kim put the file down on the coffee table, half covering the blueprints of Grace. She walked down the hallway, into the secret bedroom, coming out a moment later with her purse in her hand. No one moved as she walked out the door. The sound of the latch clicking home was deep and final. Ex cleared his throat.

'Shouldn't someone go after—'

'Leave her alone,' Aubrey said, and that closed the issue. He leaned forward and picked up the file. His face was empty. 'I need to look at this.'

'Aubrey,' I said, but he didn't look at me. He put the file in his lap, smoothed the pages, licked the tip of his index finger, and opened to the first page. Ex, Chogyi Jake, and I sat in silence for a few seconds. Aubrey turned the page. The hiss of the paper seemed unnaturally loud. I stood up quietly and walked to the kitchen like Aubrey was my father in a foul mood, and anything might set him off. Chogyi Jake and Ex followed me a few seconds later. Chogyi Jake brewed tea, and Ex stared out at the moon and the stars, the lights of the city and the darkness of the lake, with blank amazement.

'He didn't do it,' I said. 'Whatever Kim thinks she saw, she's wrong. Eric was a good man.'

'I always thought so too,' Chogyi Jake said, and I wanted to yell at him for being so diplomatic. It wouldn't have killed him to just say yes, that Kim was wrong.

'Still,' Ex said softly, 'I would like a look at that file.'

'Hey,' Eric said from my bedroom. 'You've got a call.'

With a thin, whispered string of obscenities, I walked to the bedroom, scooped up the cell phone, and turned off the ringer. It was David's number, and I couldn't talk to him right now. I let it roll to voice mail, promising myself I'd call him back if the message sounded too freaky. When I took the chance of peeking around the door frame and looking at Aubrey, he hadn't moved from his high-backed chair. He turned another page. The air felt thick as a thunderstorm. I stepped back into the kitchen just as the voice mail icon appeared on the phone.

'Jayné,' David's recorded voice said. 'I wanted to see how things were going. You know, if you'd found something. If there's anything I can do. I know you said I shouldn't go to the hospital, but I really think we should talk about that some more. So if you could give me a call back. Anytime. Don't worry about waking me up. Okay. Thanks.'

I deleted the message. If he wasn't on the highway south to Chicago at that moment, he wasn't my top priority. Chogyi Jake passed me a cup of green tea still hot enough to scald my tongue. The steam smelled like cut grass. I stopped drinking it. Out on the lake, a huge yacht made its slow way across the water, its hull outlined in white and yellow lights brighter than stars.

'I can't stand this,' I said, and went back into the front room.

Aubrey didn't look up until I took the pile of papers he'd already read out of the left side of the file. Rage bubbled just under the surface of his expression, but I kept myself from looking away. For a heartbeat, a breath, we were like two wolves fighting for dominance. I didn't like the feeling. Aubrey looked away. I sat.

The first five pages were a background report on Kim, but not the one I knew. It was who she had been when Eric met her. Born in Elizabeth City, North Carolina. Moved to Reno when she was four, and then to Oakland when she was eight. Her parents were divorced. Her mother died of an accidental overdose of prescription painkillers the year Kim went to college. Her father and sister lived in Houston, but didn't appear to be close. There was a reported sexual assault during her second year as an undergraduate, but no charges had been filed, and whoever had put the file together hadn't been able to get a copy of the original campus police report. Her medical records showed evidence of a broken arm in childhood, a slightly enlarged left ovary, and extensive adolescent orthodontic work, but no major health conditions. The report did note that Kim had admitted to occasional bouts of bulimia when she was a graduate student, but there was no other mention of eating disorders. It outlined her work at the Medical Center, listed Aubrey as her husband, and gave both their salaries as a joint household income. The section ended with a blank page.

It wasn't the first of its kind I'd ever seen. I'd had my lawyer build things like it several times before. On Randolph Coin, the head of the Invisible College, shortly before I killed him. On Karen Black, when I first started working with her. Never on someone I knew. Never on someone I liked. Knowing that Karen Black had been treated for chlamydia or that Coin suffered gastric reflux hadn't made me uncomfortable. Now, in five pages, I knew about Kim's mother, a possible rape, eating disorders. I knew about her ovaries. This time felt different. This time I felt like I was violating something, and it made me wonder a little about all the times before when it hadn't troubled me at all.

After the skipped page, the notes became Eric's. They

were typed, but I didn't need handwriting to recognize his almost telegraphic style.

Smart. Skeptical, but not dismissive. Dedicated to Aubrey. I wonder how needy she is underneath it all.

A sketch and description of the apartment Kim and Aubrey had been living in. I'd never seen it. Aubrey was living in a one-bedroom apartment by the time we'd met, but I imagined how it would have felt for Aubrey to revisit that part of his life this way. Eric's notes on the place were tactical—exits, lines of sight, defensibility. Nothing in it reflected a nefarious plan. Or the entanglement I knew was coming. Instead, there were entries for each time they had met, copies of the e-mails they'd exchanged about the life cycles of parasites, about the logic of host-parasite interactions, about the idea of nonphysical intelligence. Eric annotated these with his own thoughts afterward. And then, slowly, I saw hints of the collapse.

Eric's notes started mentioning Grace Memorial and whether Kim would fit there. A second report detailed Kim's research work in much more detail, including the names of her collaborators and their allies within the academic community, a sort of six-degrees-of-Grace-Memorial taking shape like the first few strands of a web. There was more speculation about Kim's character, her relationship with Aubrey. A few pages before the end of my stack, I saw the first reference to a *wendigo*. Kim had told me that the first time she and Eric had slept together, they'd been trapped in a cabin waiting for a *wendigo* to dissipate. There was a short description of something called the Mark of Naxos that, from the context, looked like some kind of love spell. I remembered what Kim had said the first time she'd told me about the affair. How she'd found herself driving to Eric's place without knowing she meant to. A love spell.

Three pages before the end of my stack, I found a two-word entry that made my chest ache and my mouth tighten.

Fucked her.

In my life to date, I'd had sex with three men. I'd kissed four. I knew I wasn't the world's most experienced woman when it came to love or sex, but I also knew cold when I saw it. No hint of guilt about the betrayal of Aubrey. No regret. And what was almost worse, no pleasure. Some part of me had expected the affair to have been the kind of thing I'd seen in movies. Two people drawn to each other, even though they knew it was wrong. Good intentions washed away by passion. I'd never expected that he'd be singing her praises and beating his breast like in some kind of Gothic romance, but I hadn't been prepared for the clinical chill of those two words.

He hadn't even been bragging.

I took another pile of papers from Aubrey. He was almost finished. He looked sick.

Eric cataloged the death of Kim's marriage, the fights she'd had with Eric, the reports he'd heard from Aubrey of the fights they'd had. The times she'd told Eric that she would never come to him again, and then later the times that she did. Twice he noted that Aubrey seemed suspicious, but nothing more. And then Eric's notes went back to the web of relationships and Grace Memorial. An entry noted that the assistant to a personnel director at UIC had an unsupportable credit card debt. Eric listed the man's contact information. A study touching on the cystic extent of *T. gondii* infections lost its funding at UCLA and found a place to continue crunching its numbers at Grace Memorial. A few coincidences reminded a Chicago-based friend of Kim's of her. They got back in touch. Things in Denver got worse. And then the break. Kim hadn't talked to Eric, so all the entries were reports from Aubrey. Kim had moved out. She'd asked for a divorce. She'd put in for work elsewhere.

Aubrey handed me the last pages and walked back toward the bedroom without speaking.

A flurry of fresh entries, tracking each of Kim's applications, and one by one, sinking them. The money for the NIH study went to AIDS research instead. The interviewer at LSU heard a rumor through the grapevine that Kim had an alcohol problem. The promising young researcher stopped his fieldwork in Panama a few months early, edging her out for a position in England.

And so, Kim came to live in Chicago and work at Grace.

The record ended, I assumed, when the hidden rooms were sealed. There might have been more. There could have been moments through the years when Kim had thought of leaving Chicago and Grace. If there were, Eric hadn't listed them here. I took all of the pages, squaring the edges neatly on the coffee table just to give my hands something to do.

My head felt like someone had blown a wind through it,

my thoughts scattered and powerless as sparrows in a storm. And underneath the confusion and emptiness, a raw, red anger started to grow. None of it—none of it—had anything to do with me. I'd been trying to read all the way through *The Grapes of Wrath* for my high school English class when all that had been going on, and how dare Kim and Aubrey leave me feeling like I was supposed to apologize for something?

I was drowning, grasping at anything that floated through my head. I was totally out of line, and what was worse I knew it. I just couldn't stop.

Aubrey was sitting on the bed, his hands laced on one knee.

'So,' he said. 'Just one question.'

I stood in the doorway, arms crossed.

'You knew,' he said. 'About Kim and Eric. You knew, right?'

'She told me,' I said.

'You didn't tell me,' he said.

'I asked if you'd want to know whether she'd been sleeping with someone, and you said it didn't matter now. That you didn't want to know. That's what you *said*.'

I was whining. I was starting to cry. I felt the crushing weight of having done something unforgivable and also the monstrous injustice of not even knowing exactly what it was.

'I came to help you do Eric's work,' Aubrey said. His voice was calm and soft and implacable as the sea. 'Kim aside, Eric's betrayal would have been germane.'

'You wouldn't have come?' I said. It came out as a challenge. *Tell me that you wouldn't have stayed with me.*

'If you'd given me all the information and let me make my choice,' he said softly, 'probably I would have joined up. But I can't know now, can I? You told me as much as you saw fit, and I did what you wanted. Worked out fine.'

His gentleness was a mask. It was a fake. I could feel the pain coming off him like heat from a fire. I could feel his need to hurt something. Someone. Me.

'You're like him,' he said, looking at his hands. 'You're a lot like Eric.'

I coughed out a breath, something between a laugh and a gut-punch gasp. He had picked his words well. They stung.

'Yesterday that would have been a compliment,' I said.

'It isn't yesterday,' he said. And then, a long moment later, 'I can't do this.'

'Can't do what?'

'I should leave now.'

'What can't you do? Where are you going?' I said as he walked past me. 'Aubrey, where are you going? Aubrey!'

He didn't look back at me. The front door closed behind him.

15

When I woke up on Sunday morning, it took a few glorious, floating seconds to remember why Aubrey wasn't in the bed beside me. Then, like someone pressing a hand on my sternum, it all came back. I rolled over, pressing the pillows over my head. I didn't want to get up. I didn't want to go out. I wanted to sleep my way backward in time to when the worst thing I had to face was a rider buried alive under its own prison. It seemed vaguely monstrous that my wounds from David's house hadn't healed yet. It was only two days ago. It was forever.

Eventually my bladder forced me out of bed, and by the time I was done in the bathroom I was too awake to even pretend sleep. Instead, I sat in bed and checked my e-mail. Curtis, my younger brother, reported that my older brother, Jay, had indeed gotten his girlfriend pregnant and had set the wedding date for before she started showing. Our mother was 'hip deep in wedding magazines.' My lawyer had sent a financial report with a note that I shouldn't panic, the downturn was temporary and my holdings safely diversified. I checked my former friends' blogs. I cruised a few of the paranormal sites; I Googled *haugsvarmr* and *leyiathan* and got all the same links I'd found before; I wasted time. It would have felt like goofing off except for the dread that seemed to hang in the air like dust motes. Aubrey's bags were still in the room. I tried to take comfort in that.

When I couldn't put it off any longer, I closed the laptop, steeled myself, and went out to the living room. A scrim of thin clouds stretched to the horizon, turning the blue to white. The green-gray lake stuttered and trembled, tiny whitecaps stippling it. Chogyi Jake sat at the table.

'Hey,' I said.

He turned to me, smiling the same as always. It was just my imagination that put the weariness around his eyes and the gray cast to his skin. I pulled myself up to sit on the countertop.

'Bad night,' I said.

'Difficult,' he agreed.

'You read the thing?'

'Ex and I both. It wasn't pleasant.'

'Yeah, no,' I said. 'Ex around?'

'Out at the store. We're low on toothpaste and toilet paper.'

'And Aubrey . . . ?'

'Came in just before dawn and slept in the new bedroom for a little while,' Chogyi Jake said. 'He went out an hour ago.'

I nodded, caught between relief that he'd come back at all and a twisting rage that he'd left again without at least the courtesy of speaking to me. Of course if I hadn't been sulking in my room, he would have had to. The thought didn't make me feel any better.

'Did he say where he was going?'

'No, but he didn't take the car keys.'

'Okay,' I said. That meant he was nearby. Or using taxis and public transport. Or Kim was driving. I hated how much I didn't like that last option. 'All right.'

'He's hurting,' Chogyi Jake said. 'The information in that file is causing him a lot of pain.'

'That's deeply stupid,' I said, knowing as I said it that I was out of line. I couldn't help it.

'You're hurting too. We all are.'

'Then we're all stupid,' I said. 'We don't have any idea what the context of that file was. Okay, it looks lousy, but we don't know what would have happened if Eric had done something else, right? I mean, maybe he knew that Kim would get killed if she stayed in Denver. Or with Aubrey. Magic does that sometimes, right? Tells you what's going to happen.'

'It can,' Chogyi Jake said.

'So how is Aubrey so sure that wasn't how it started? How do we even know for sure that it's not a fake that someone snuck in here to mess with our heads? I'm just amazed, you know? We find one thing that looks weird, and he just loses faith in Eric. He's just . . . folding.'

Chogyi Jake looked at me in silence for what seemed like an hour and probably took fewer than ten seconds. He lifted his eyebrows and looked down at the floor. *Back me up on this*, I thought. I already knew that he wouldn't.

'I hear what you're saying,' Chogyi Jake said, picking his way through the syllables like they might explode. 'And I understand what Aubrey is thinking too.'

The refrigerator hum dominated the room. My mouth tasted like ashes. A flock of pigeons wheeled past the window, gray wings skimming so close to the glass I could have reached out a hand and plucked them out of the sky.

'But you can't be sure, right? We don't know why he decided to do that. And even if Eric did break Aubrey and Kim up and put her here, he might have had a reason.'

'You can never prove a negative,' Chogyi Jake said. 'There always might be some letter or notebook or simple fact that changes everything. Makes it not what it appears to be. Always. Even if we go through every drawer and box in every property Eric owned, we can't know that something new won't show up. Only that it hasn't yet.'

'And if it's not true at all?'

Chogyi Jake didn't answer. For a few seconds, I thought the countertop had started shaking. Then I realized it was me. I was trembling. My fingers were digging deep into my thighs. I was losing control of my own body, only unlike when I got into a fight, there was no uncanny competence rising up to save me. And the strange thing was that this feeling of waking up from a good dream into a tragic life was familiar. It was like I'd done this all before.

Because, of course, I had.

'I can't do this again,' I said.

'Again?'

I took a deep breath.

'So here's the thing. I went to a secular college,' I said, fighting to keep my voice steady, 'despite what my father wanted. Big fight. Ugly. Don't darken my doorstep stuff.

He thought Arizona State was the first step on the road to hell, and I went anyway. I got this little scholarship and some financial aid. Work-study. That kind of thing. Anyway, I moved out there, and I didn't know anyone. And I didn't have anyone back at home who could talk to me. I think my mother would have, but with Dad doing the patriarchal shunning thing, I don't think she had the option.'

Chogyi Jake was looking at me. Bearing witness. It was what he did. I went on.

'I made some friends, right? Around Thanksgiving break when I didn't have a family to go home to, my roommate in the dorm sort of took me under her wing. She got me into her circle. They were just a bunch of college rowdies, but they were tight-knit. There was one girl who was the center. She had a house of her own near campus with her fiancé and another guy, and we all used to hang out there. Make dinner for the group. My roommate and her boyfriend. And then my boyfriend too. And this girl. The one with the house and the fiancé? We really clicked. We were best friends.'

As if the word were magic, a flood of memories came back to me. Her almond-shaped eyes and weird orthodontist-defying eyeteeth. The way her house had always smelled like sandalwood and patchouli. Sitting in a circle in her living room, playing card games and drinking too much beer. The time the neighbor's cat had come in the back door and demanded love from each of us in turn. Scenes from a different and better life, made painful only because I knew how it all came out. I took a deep breath, let it out slowly.

'We were best friends,' I said again, 'until about a month before the end of the spring term.'

'What happened?'

'I don't know,' I said. 'I couldn't stay in the dorms over the summer, and the other guy who lived at her place was going to Nova Scotia with a bunch of his friends, so I was going to sublet his room. And then one day she said that it wasn't going to work. She stopped calling me. They all stopped calling me. My boyfriend, Cary, hung around longer than the others. Every time I asked him what was going on, he pretended not to know what I was talking about, and then he'd pick a fight about something else. Eventually we called it off, and then there was no one. And it messed me up. I missed some of the financial aid deadlines. I dropped out.'

'I understand,' he said.

I hated talking about it. The confusion and betrayal and sense of being suddenly, unexpectedly lost back then folded itself into today. Aubrey walking out and my college friends turning cold, Cary pretending nothing was wrong and Eric's manipulations of Kim's life. They weren't the same. And they were. I'd lost two families already. I couldn't lose another one. Chogyi Jake's usually placid brow furrowed.

'I can't do that again.'

'Nothing lasts forever. Everything changes, all the time,' he said. 'And that's all right. We all came together last year, and if some part of that changes, it's because it's time that it change. We've all lost families and lovers and things that were precious to us, and we've all survived.'

It felt like he'd punched me. I couldn't take a breath. He wasn't looking at me. I wanted him to stop talking. I wanted his eyes to meet mine. I wanted to know if he was telling me that everything was going to be all right no matter what happened, or if he was giving me his justification for leaving too, but I was afraid of what he'd say. My arms wrapped around my rib cage, and I found that I was hugging myself and crying.

'We make a picture,' he said, 'of how we want the world to be, and most of the time it isn't like that. Holding on to that image causes the suffering. Not the world, not the truth. Our disappointment is what makes us hurt.'

'Aubrey's not going to stay, is he?'

'He's in a difficult place,' Chogyi Jake said. 'I think he feels that whatever he does will involve being disloyal to someone. You or Kim. And he isn't comfortable with that.'

'But I didn't do anything wrong,' I said, choking on the last word. 'This isn't my fault.'

'It isn't,' Chogyi Jake said. 'And it isn't fair. To you or to Aubrey or to Kim. Or to me. But this isn't about fault or judgment or righteousness. Those are all traps. This just is what it is.'

My cell phone went off, Eric's voice coming from the bedroom, muffled and mechanical and distant. I pushed myself off the counter and walked away, still crying and trying to stop. The phone was in the pocket of yesterday's jeans. Because it had almost rolled to voice mail by the time I wrestled it out, I didn't pause to check the incoming number. I just accepted the connection and said hello while I wiped my tears away with the heel of my palm.

'Jayné! It's David. David Souder. I'm in Chicago.'

'You're what?'

'I'm here. In Chicago. I had this idea last night about Grandpa Del. I know you said not to go to the hospital, but I think the reason I've been having all these dreams is that he's still *there*. You know?'

'David—'

'No, listen. The dreams weren't just nightmares. They were trying to say something. To ask for help.'

'Just tell me where you are,' I didn't quite yell. The pause wasn't longer than a heartbeat, but when he spoke again, he sounded a little taken aback.

'I'm at a Starbucks. It's on Franklin and Chicago. Right by the El.'

'Okay, listen to me. I want you to hang up, go to the counter, and ask them for a very big cup of coffee. Decaf. When you get it, I want you to find a nice comfortable chair, sit down, and then don't even think about moving until I get there. All right?'

'I didn't mean to—'

'Don't. Move. All right?'

'All right,' he said, and I dropped the connection. Chogyi Jake stood in the doorway while I pulled on a light jacket and the backpack.

'That was David. It's calling to him,' I said. 'And he's going.'

'That might not be wise,' Chogyi Jake said.

'Y'think?' I said, checking for my wallet. It was in my pocket. 'The car's not here. Right?'

'Ex took it shopping.'

'Fine. I'll get a cab.'

'Should I come?'

Of course I wanted him to. Everything from the back of my throat to my stomach was the solid, stretching ache of wanting someone I could count on. But he had just finished telling me that I couldn't rely on him or anyone else. That families fall apart and get lost.

Holding on. That's what causes suffering.

'I'm good,' I said. 'I'll be fine.'

I saw him hesitate, but I left before he could talk about it anymore. When the elevator doors closed on me, I almost started crying again. But only almost.

The Starbucks was indeed right by the El. The hazy white sky didn't cast clear shadows, so the darkness under the orange-brown supports and dark webworked steel didn't have a clear border. It just seeped in. The gray stone of the building looked like a cross between a storage facility and a mausoleum. The building just down the street was taller redbrick with ornamented windows at the front and a billboard on the side, and it made the coffee shop's two stories look squat. I pushed my way in, stepping out of the real world and into customer service land. The smell of fresh coffee filled the air, and Pink Martini's 'Tempo Perdido' was playing softly from hidden speakers. I felt vaguely betrayed that my favorite band had been here without me.

Sunday afternoon left the place sparsely populated.

David was sitting on a soft couch, a large cup of coffee looking small in his hand. With clean clothes and a better night's sleep than I'd had, he looked more like a retired NFL player. The round burn of the shotgun on his neck looked better too. When he caught sight of me, he smiled and rose. I walked over. His smile faltered.

'Hey,' he said. 'Are you all right?'

'Peachy,' I said.

'Do you want anything?'

I sat down in the chair across from his couch, then waited, looking up at him until he took his seat too.

'All right,' I said. 'I'm here. Tell me what you've got.'

'Well, I don't have anything solid,' he said. 'It's more a feeling. I was thinking about all the—'

He stopped, looked around uneasily, and hunched in close before he went on.

'All the dreams. They're horrible. All of them, but it's not like they did me any damage.'

I shrugged, unconvinced. Maybe he didn't remember what he'd looked like on Friday. *Undamaged* wasn't the first word that came to mind.

'When I was dreaming that I was Grandpa Del, maybe it was because he was trying to reach out to me. And he can only do it through dreams,' he said. He was getting excited now. I could see the enthusiasm in the smile that flirted with his lips, the way his broad, thick hands patted at the air. I wondered if this had been what it was like for Eric, watching Aubrey and Kim discover the secret world of riders and magic. The idea depressed me.

'And so he's sending you a year's worth of soul-destroying nightmares? Wouldn't a couple *"Hey, Dave, could you get me out of this box"* dreams be a little more likely to keep you from killing yourself before you could help out?'

'That bothered me too. But there was this movie I saw when I was a kid. I don't know the name, but it was all about this guy who was in a coma. Trapped between life and death. And he kept pulling other people into his dreams. What if it's like that? What if Grandpa Del is trying to reach out, only he's dreaming too?'

'So you're thinking that maybe he's been kicking the crap out of you because . . . ?'

The door swung open and two surprisingly lovely women came in. One was blond, the other a redhead with a complexion that said the color hadn't come from a bottle. They had the kind of looks that made men lose their car keys. David glanced at them, dismissed them, and turned back to me.

'You swim much?' he asked. 'You know not to go in after someone who's drowning. Throw them something or get them a stick, and you're fine. But if they get ahold of you, they'll try to climb up you, and you both drown. I think Grandpa Del is flailing like that.'

I could feel my mind wrapping around the idea even as my head shook its own decisive *no*. There was something about it I liked. That I wanted to be true. That maybe the thing under Grace was scared, alone, and thrashing in its sleep. Maybe it was one of the good guys, and so maybe Eric was too. I had to put it aside now and focus on David.

'Listen to yourself,' I said. 'You don't go after someone who's drowning. Because you might get hurt or worse, and you sure can't help that way. Right?'

'Right.'

'And what's your plan? Go to Grace Memorial?'

David opened his mouth. At the counter, one of the beautiful women broke out in a peal of laughter. She wasn't paying attention to us, but it still had the feel of the universe mocking us. David blushed and shook his head. His face could have been put in a dictionary beside *chagrin*.

'I'm going in after the drowning guy,' he said. 'Because I'm an idiot.'

'You're being called,' I said. 'You're trying to answer. That's not dumb. But it is dangerous.'

'You want me to go home,' he said. His voice was sour.

'I do. I want you to wait until we know what we're looking at. And I swear as soon as I know something, I will tell you.'

He sighed, staring into the black surface of the coffee. The espresso machine hissed and spat. Pink Martini gave way to some modern big-band swing. I took his hand. It was warmer than I expected, and when his fingers squeezed mine, I made myself smile.

'Trust me,' I said.

In my imagination, a vampire I'd known once took a drag on his cigarette, smiled with ruined lips, and said *Being new to the game makes you an easy mark, kid. Happens to everyone.* It would have been simple to use David now. It was almost harder not to. He wanted me to ask him for something. I could tell him to write me a check for his whole savings, and he would. I could tell him to go to Grace Memorial just to see if the hospital attacked him.

Or I could keep him safe. Give him a real life and the chance to live it. Push him away and tell him to run like the devil was after him. It probably was. And that was the one thing I could say that he wouldn't listen to.

'I trust you,' he said. 'Just don't leave me out.'

'Promise,' I lied.

16

I sat at the table for a while after David left, then went up and bought myself a latte I didn't want so that I could keep sitting. The music moved on, landing on eighties nostalgia, some guy telling me it was always mesh and lace and offering to stop the world and melt with me. But the coffee wasn't bad if I put enough sugar in it, and the emotional equivalent of a loose scab was forming in my heart. I knew the grief and anger and fear were there, but if I didn't jar myself or scratch at it, I could ignore them. I wasn't, for instance, in tears. That was a start. I could almost think *Aubrey might leave me* without breaking down.

The Sunday afternoon crowd stayed light. Behind the counter, a nice-looking blond guy and a hatchet-faced woman who seemed too old to be steaming milk for a living talked about television while they cleaned the wood-grained laminate and straightened stacks of prepackaged biscotti. The beautiful girls were joined by two equally beautiful guys. They laughed and flirted and raised arch eyebrows. The trains of the El came by now and then, the clatter of their passage competing with the music. I remembered Kim sitting at the Bump & Grind Café with a latte and heartache of her own. I even remembered feeling sorry for her.

The scab shifted a little, threatening to slip off and expose the wound. I looked out the window, forcing myself back to the here and now. Either it was later than I'd expected or the clouds were thickening. The darkness had spread from under the El and was loitering in the street. I considered calling Ex or Chogyi Jake. Or a cab. I wanted to talk to Aubrey. I wanted to talk to Uncle Eric.

This was the moment when I needed a best friend. Sad and sobering, but I didn't seem to have one who wasn't already hip-deep in the problems I wanted to get away from. I pulled my cell phone out of my backpack and stared at it. There were almost two hundred contacts in the phone book, most of them put there by Eric. A few that were particularly mine. None of them felt right. All those numbers and no one to talk to.

Except.

My heart sped up just a little as the whole plan popped into my head. It wasn't like thinking of it so much as remembering something I'd already planned. I picked up my cell phone and went back to the counter, digging through my backpack as I walked. The blond guy trotted up with a professional, practiced smile.

'Get you something else?'

'Yeah,' I said. 'Stay there for a minute. Here.'

I still had the same wallet I'd had at ASU. The fake leather was cracked and the fabric underneath showed through. I opened it, pulled out a hundred, and put it on the counter.

'I need a little favor,' I said. I started dialing my old

phone number. The shape of the digits on the number pad were familiar and alien at the same time. 'Just ask for Curt.'

'Curt?' the guy said.

The phone on the far end started ringing. I passed my cell across the counter.

'Curt,' I said. 'You know him from school.'

The blond guy mouthed *School?* and then I heard the click and a compressed, distant voice saying hello.

'Hi,' the blond guy said. 'Is Curt there? This is John. From school.'

The voice on the other end muttered something. The blond guy widened his eyes and pursed his lips in a little mock-naughty *oh*, enjoying the game of it. A new voice came on. Younger. Male. Questioning.

'Curt?' the blond guy said. 'Great. Hang on.'

He handed the phone back to me. I pushed him the hundred. He looked at me like I was being silly and pushed it back.

'Hey, little brother,' I said. 'How's the Bible belt treating you?'

There wasn't even a moment of shocked silence.

'Sure, I've got the syllabus in my notebook,' Curt said. 'Let me just get to my room, okay?'

He sounded so much older than when I'd left home. There was gravel in his voice now. I supposed he was probably shaving. It broke my head. While he bumped and clattered down the hall to his room, I made my way back to my table. A long way away, a door shut.

'Hey,' he said softly. 'What's up? What are you doing?'

'I've been traveling with some friends. We're in Chicago.'

'Wicked.'

'Yeah,' I said. 'It got a little weird. I just needed to hear a friendly voice.'

'Well,' Curt said, 'everything here is a fucking opera production. Jay's thinking Carla—that's the fiancée—got knocked up on purpose so he'd have to marry her. And it turns out her mother's Mexican, and Mom is dead set on making sure no one at church knows about it. Dad is saying that Jay should have thought about all that before he sinned, which effectively puts him on the same side as Carla and our new Latino branch of the family. Oh it is high, high drama.'

'Yeah?' I said, leaning back. 'Tell me all.'

For almost an hour, Curt poured out gossip and trivia and the family's dirty laundry. He never asked how I was doing. He never asked what was going on with me or if I had a boyfriend or if I was happy or what I was planning to do next. He was the perfect self-involved teenage boy, and I loved him for it. When at last my father's distant bellow demanded to know who Curt was talking to and why it was taking so long, Curt signed off with 'Call me back and I'll tell you the rest.' I put my phone back in my pack. I'd run the batteries down below half their charge on that call alone, but it had been worth it. I didn't know if it was the reminder of a life larger and broader than my own occult minicabal and our very real problems or only the glimpse of the world I'd escaped, but I felt calmer. Still angry. Still hurt. But calmer.

I got another latte with a slice of pound cake this time, and tried to put the situation in order. I knew that I needed to deal with the *haugsvarmr* one way or the other. I also knew that I couldn't do it while I freaked out about all my friends leaving me, so I needed to find Aubrey. And after him, Chogyi Jake and Ex. If I was on my own, it would crush me. But Chogyi Jake was right; I'd been crushed before. Hadn't killed me. The ache in my chest came back, just to remind me how bad it had been. How bad it would be this time. It didn't matter. Before I could do anything else, I had to know where I stood.

I tried calling Aubrey's cell and got voice mail. Either something was up with his cell phone or he wasn't taking my calls. That was all right. He'd just found out that his marriage had ended because of something about a thousand times more complex than he'd thought. With that kind of unfinished business hanging loose, I figured I knew where to find him. On my way out the door, I waved to the blond guy behind the counter and bowed my head a little. *Thank you.* He rolled his eyes and waved back. *It was nothing.* The small complicity was nice, and I tried to hold the feeling as I hailed a cab and gave the driver Kim's address.

A stiff wind had picked up by the time I reached Kim's place. The air was heavy and muggy, with the ozone smell of impending rain. The blue skies were gone; the storms were coming back. I pulled my jacket tight around my shoulders. Steel and concrete stairs rang under my footsteps. I kept telling myself it would be okay and at the same time imagined ringing the bell and having Aubrey open it wearing a sheet. The fake iron apartment numbers were cracked. The pale door had a long scratch in it. Clouds had muffled the late afternoon light. I waited for what seemed a long time to see if I would press the doorbell. Then I did.

Kim answered the door wearing old gray sweatpants and a white T-shirt. Her hair hung in limp, sweaty lines, and her eyes were bloodshot and rimmed red from crying or sleeplessness or both. Her gaze tracked up and down slowly, judging me.

'You look like shit,' she said.

'Is he here?'

'Did you expect him to be?'

'Kind of, yeah.'

'I don't know if that makes you an optimist or a pessimist,' Kim said. She walked into the apartment, leaving the door open as if she expected me to follow, so I did.

For a moment, I thought the little apartment's disarray came from yesterday's revelation, but the clutter was too deep for one day's work. Piles of magazines lurked at the edge of a patterned beige couch. An exercise bike lurked in the corner, dry cleaning bags hanging from its handles. Cobwebs haunted the corners of ceiling and wall. A plastic laundry basket commanded the dining room table, and I couldn't tell if the clothes in it were dirty or clean. The air smelled like old pizza. It was the kind of place I might have lived in without the windfall of Eric's fortune. Kim glanced around, seeing it because I was there. She shrugged.

'It's home,' she said, almost apologetically. 'You want a drink?'

'I don't want to intrude,' I said.

'Stop being so fucking formal. How about rum and Coke? I don't have the vodka for screwdrivers.'

'Um. Sure.'

I had never seen her like this. The aggressive intelligence was still there, but not so tightly controlled. Her hypercompetence had slipped, and the despair behind it showed. I sat on the arm of her couch and watched her over the breakfast bar. The kitchen was tiny, so she just spun slowly in place, reaching up for a glass, turning to pluck a bottle of Captain Morgan out of a cabinet, and then opening the refrigerator for a red and silver can. She didn't have to move her feet.

'Aubrey took off, then?' she asked.

'Most of last night. And again this morning,' I said. 'I figured he'd come here.'

'Haven't heard a word from him. Why would he be here anyway? I just told him I'd been sleeping around on him. I don't think men usually find that endearing.' She pushed a glass across the bar, the soda still fizzing, and started another one for herself.

'But the Mark of Naxos. The love spell . . .'

Kim waved her hand, pushing the words away.

'So what if he used magic to get me into bed? I'm still the one who chose not to tell Aubrey about it. I'm still the one who chose to take off instead of trying to figure things through. Did you think sleeping with Eric was the only way I betrayed Aubrey?'

'But . . .' I started. My head felt like it was full of cotton ticking. I felt like I'd tricked myself into arguing against Eric, and I wasn't sure exactly how it had happened. Kim drank half her rum and Coke in two swallows, then coughed. She wiped her mouth with the back of her hand.

'I think I owe you an apology,' she said.

I had imagined a thousand scenarios in coming to Kim's apartment. Aubrey absent, Kim apologetic, and rum and Coke hadn't figured into them.

'I threw a fit,' she said. 'I was embarrassed and . . . No. I was humiliated. I *am* humiliated. I don't like my private business being thrown around in front of everyone. When I saw that file, and how he had played me, and that all of you were going to have to know too . . .' She paused. Her chuckle dripped with self-loathing.

She took a sip from her glass, and I mirrored her, then looked down at the drink. She mixed them strong. I wondered how many she'd already had. How many it would take to wipe away what had been in that file. She shook her head.

'Anyway,' she said. 'I could have done that better. Sorry. For what it's worth, I've been looking at it, and I think we can put something like the Invisible College's spells back in place.'

She must have seen the confusion in my expression. She put up a hand, palm out, in a gesture that asked for my silence.

'I'm not saying it's easy,' she said. She walked out from

the kitchen to lean against the dining room table. 'They're riders. What they did was one big thing. Poof. Done. Using dinky little human spells and cantrips, it'll take maybe six months. A year. And the *haugsvarmr* will probably be pushing back pretty hard that whole time.'

'Okay,' I said. 'Hold on. You've been figuring out how to put the lid back *on* Grace Memorial?'

Now it was her turn to look surprised.

'Well, yes,' she said. 'You aren't still thinking about letting it loose, are you?'

'I don't know,' I said. 'I hadn't exactly been thinking about it at all.'

'What *have* you been thinking about?'

'Whether Eric's having'—I stumbled a little, and then recovered—'done what he did to you and Aubrey meant that all my friends would ditch me. If Aubrey is going to break up with me and go back to you. If Chogyi Jake and Ex would decide that anything Eric touched is too tainted to be around. Whether doing one deeply shitty thing really means Eric was a bad person, or just that he did one really shitty thing. Like that. Oh, and talking David Souder out of going to Grace Memorial.'

'He was going to the hospital?' she asked sharply. 'Why?'

'It's calling him,' I said. 'He thinks his grandfather's still alive in that coffin and wants out.'

'We have to keep him away from there,' Kim said sharply. 'Between being inside the labyrinth and the connection to his grandfather, he probably wouldn't be able to resist it. Even if he didn't want to, it could force him to break the interment. What did you tell him?'

I recounted David's call, our meeting, the outlines of our conversation. But even while I looked for the right words, I was amazed by how totally she'd ignored everything else I'd said. Aubrey, Chogyi Jake, Ex. Even Eric. It was eerie, and then it was perfectly clear. Eric's file on her had pulled the rug out from under both of us. I was obsessing over my fears and grabbing for anything consistent and solid in my life. Kim was focusing on the things she could control and ignoring anything that she couldn't. She was pretending that everything she'd lost didn't matter. Seen from that perspective, it wasn't so weird.

But it wasn't what I needed.

'That's got to be why Eric had the secret rooms fitted out with the cell,' Kim said. 'If he was going to have Souder as a negotiating point, he'd need to control him.'

'Kim. Stop it. Okay?'

The light from the kitchen put half her face in dim shadow. Annoyance tightened the corners of her eyes. She crossed her arms.

'Stop what?'

'Can we just put the riders and magic and all that away for a minute? We need to talk. About Aubrey.'

'No we don't,' Kim said. 'What would we say about him?'

I blinked. He was my lover and her husband. Their marriage had been torpedoed by my guardian angel. Of course Aubrey was the axis that everything turned on. At least, I'd thought he was. And yet standing there under Kim's gaze, I couldn't think what exactly I'd intended to say. I took a stab at it.

'You love him,' I said.

'So what?' Kim said, a rattle in her voice like a car engine going bad. 'You think Aubrey's the worst thing Eric did to me? Do you know what it would have meant to get the position at LSU? Or, God, the England job? I would have been working with the best people in my field. I would have had the money and resources to do real work. Something basic. Something the field could really build on.'

'You aren't doing real work here?'

Her cheeks flushed red and her nostrils flared. A line of bloodless white appeared around her lips.

'I am third researcher behind two people I helped *train*,' Kim said, her voice getting louder. 'I am teaching undergraduate cell biology. I'm a PhD in a medical center. All these MDs look at me like I'm some kind of trained chimp. Eric Heller didn't just take away my marriage. He sabotaged my career. He ate my life.'

'I'm sorry,' I said softly.

'Why?' Kim demanded. 'Did *you* tell him to do it?'

'No, but—'

'You were off getting drunk at senior prom or something. You were taking your SATs. Do you know how old I am?'

'Thirty-seven.'

'Thirty-seven,' Kim said, pointing at me accusingly. 'And I've published in goddamn *Nature*. So yeah, you're sleeping with the man I love. So what? What do you want me to do about it?'

'Forgive me,' I said. 'I want you to forgive me.'

The rage drained out of her. She seemed to shrink into herself. She coughed out a last, empty laugh and drank the rest of her rum and Coke.

'You're not Eric,' she said. 'You didn't do anything wrong.'

'My life got better because yours got ruined,' I said, 'and I like you.'

She looked at her glass, the brown-stained ice rattling in it like stones. A gust of wind pressed at the windows, making the cheap curtains shudder and shift. Kim shook her head.

'You want another one?' she asked. Her voice was smaller.

'Probably not. I'm kind of a lightweight.'

'You don't mind if I do,' she said, taking the three steps back to the kitchen. 'I'm somewhat experienced. Does Aubrey make you laugh?'

I didn't answer. Maybe she didn't expect me to.

'He used to be the only one who could really get me going,' she said. 'He'd do that Bill Clinton imitation, and I'd just start losing it. You know the one?'

'Yeah,' I said, even though I didn't. 'He's great.'

'He is.'

Kim poured herself another rum and Coke. I watched

how much rum she was putting in this time. I was amazed she had any left in the bottle. She drank it fast, and then looked at me solemnly.

'I'm drunk,' she said.

'Yeah, I know.'

'I didn't mean to be.'

'Oh, I think you had it coming,' I said. 'I'll go. Let you rest up.'

'Okay.' And then, as I reached her door, 'You don't need my forgiveness.'

Outside, a soft rain glowed in the streetlights and darkened the sidewalks. I wondered where Aubrey had gone if not to Kim. On one hand, the relief that he hadn't been there was like someone taking a stone off my belly. On the other hand, the clarity I'd been looking for was just as far away. Worse. Before, I'd had to figure out why Eric wanted the thing under Grace set free and what he wanted from it in exchange. Now I also had the option of muffling it again, taking back what I'd done. I could do anything, but I couldn't do everything. And if I sat on my hands and waited, David would eventually be drawn to the hospital. The rider would get free, and I didn't even know for sure whether that would be a bad thing.

The only thing the rider had done that I knew about was confuse David and give Oonishi's dreamers their shared nightmare. But what if David had been right and the thing under the hospital really was just thrashing in its sleep? It might not have meant any harm. If the Invisible College had bound something good, something that we could work with to make the world safer or better, then maybe everything Eric had done made sense. Maybe Eric had been viciously ruthless, but not evil. What if the rider was really some kind of angel? Confusion and despair, and a weird anger for Aubrey and Kim and me swirled together like the weather. If there was just some way to *know* . . .

Standing at the curb, looking for a taxi to flag down, I surprised myself with a frustrated cry.

'Fine,' I heard myself say. 'If that's what it takes, then *fine*.'

With the same near-disembodied sense I had during a fight, I pulled my cell phone out of my pack, looked up my recent call history, and found the number I wanted. Standing in the rain, my hair getting slowly heavier, I listened to the distant ring. I didn't know what I was going to say, but my body carried me forward.

'Hello?'

'Dr. Oonishi,' I said. 'This is Jayné Heller.'

'Chogyi Jake's assistant?'

I felt myself smile.

'Yes,' I said.

'I haven't had a chance to finish the interviews you wanted,' he said.

'That's fine. I was wondering if you were running your sleep study tonight?'

'No,' he said. 'We have three sessions a week. But I could have you observe tomorrow night, if you'd like.'

'Actually,' I said, 'I want you to let me in when there isn't anyone around.'

Jesus, I thought, *I do?* And then, a heartbeat later, *Wow. I really do.*

'I suppose . . . I mean . . .' he said, and then sighed heavily. 'Is this really necessary?'

'Yes,' I said. My voice sounded so convinced, I started believing it myself.

'Fine.'

'Can you meet me there?'

'It will take me half an hour,' he said. 'We can meet at the emergency room waiting area. I'll take you in from there.'

'Perfect,' I said. 'Thank you.'

I dropped the connection, then stood staring at my own hand for almost a full minute. The sense of dislocation was gone, and in its place the warm glow of anticipation. I didn't have David locked in the condo, but I knew where to find him. I was in as good a negotiating position as Eric would have been. From the time we'd left, part of me had wanted to go back to Grace Memorial and face this thing down. Eric had planned to do it, and apparently without help from Ex or Chogyi Jake or Aubrey. And if he could, so could I.

'Right. Enough screwing around,' I said, as if there was someone to agree with. Eric, maybe. The Eric I'd known and trusted. The part of me that was him. The one I'd aspired to be.

Rahabiel. *Haugsvarmr*. Daevanam Daeva. *Leyiathan*. Legion. I didn't care anymore. Grace Memorial had already hurt my people and threatened my little created family. I wanted answers. I wanted to know what the rider could tell me. I wanted to kick some unreal ass and make the universe take back all the hurt that my coming to Chicago had done. And anyway, the fear felt like exhilaration.

I was going back to Grace.

17

The taxi dropped me off across the street from the hospital. I wanted the rain to be a torrent, water pounding down on the streets like the assault of an atmospheric fire hose, but the tiny drops only drifted. The street shone wet-asphalt black and streetlight orange. Traffic hissed by in a cloud of car exhaust and ozone. My hair clung to my head, cold and damp without quite reaching soaked. Grace Memorial rose up toward the low, gray sky.

We stood for almost a minute, the hospital and I, looking at each other. I watched a man in pale green scrubs emerge from the dark front doors with a bicycle. An ambulance lumbered in under the emergency room's long concrete canopy, its siren beating at my ears and its flasher blinding me for half seconds at a time. Above me, the hospital windows glowed in the bright gray night, emotionless as a boxer the moment before the bell. Darkness didn't make the buildings any less awkward or ugly. I knew now that it had been designed as a prison, but that wasn't what it looked like either. Instead of institutional, strong lines and threatening, solid walls, it looked like something half formed. A chrysalis cracked open too early.

I hitched my pack high on my back, waited for a break in the stream of cars, and crossed the street. Then under the canopy toward the greenish, bulletproof glass doors, and inside. I stopped in the entrance hallway. At an admission desk to my left, a professionally unimpressed nurse was asking formulaic questions from a gray-skinned old man. Two sets of double doors at the hall's end had stern warnings against anyone besides hospital staff trying to pass through them; security bars and magnetic locks drove the point home. A thick-shouldered woman in a janitorial uniform mopped the pale linoleum, the water she left still pink with someone's blood. The sounds of a television crept in from the waiting room to my right: animal screaming followed by a narrator's somber and instructing voice. I wondered what genius had decided that Animal Planet was a good distraction for people in medical distress. Seemed like a lousy call to me.

I waited for the lights to dim or for nurse and janitor and patient to start breathing in time, turn toward me with murder in their eyes, but nothing happened. Only the sense of being watched. Even if none of the people knew me, the building itself seemed aware of who I was and what I had come here for. I felt a trickle of adrenaline in my bloodstream, tensing me and brightening everything.

It was easy to see how someone could get paranoid.

'Can I help you?'

The nurse was a wide-faced man, his hairline receding. He held a clipboard in his arm like it had grown there.

'Are you all right, miss?'

'Fine,' I said. 'I'm meeting someone.'

'You have their name? I can look them up on the computer.'

'No,' I said, turning toward the waiting room. There were maybe a dozen people on plastic-upholstered couches. Two of them were thick, muscular men, but one of those was holding his elbow and tight-jawed with pain. If the hospital set them on me the way it had in the cardiac unit, I was pretty sure I could hold my own. As long as Eric's protections held.

'No name?'

'Sorry,' I said. 'It's not a patient. I'm meeting a doctor. He knows I'm here.'

The nurse shrugged and walked past me to an older woman coming into the hall behind me.

'Can I help you?'

'Can't . . . breathe . . .'

'Come right along here with me, ma'am. We'll get you a seat.'

I went into the waiting room. Animal Planet broke to commercial and the bicyclist-killing mountain lion was replaced by a CGI-enhanced puppy asking for a particular brand of canned food. Dull eyes looked up at me. Some looked away, some just got glassy and distant. None seemed an immediate threat. The air smelled of old vomit and alcohol. I took a seat near the door, my back against the wall where no one could get behind me.

I didn't know when I'd started thinking tactically, but clearly I had. I spent a few minutes judging whether, in the event, the skinny guy in the Christian Academy Crusaders T-shirt was more likely to reach me before the red-haired girl with her head on her knees. In the hall, a stretcher came through the high-security double doors and a couple of large men lifted the can't-breathe lady onto it. Animal Planet came back, promising more tales of mutilation and death. I thought about walking back out, but if I slipped now, I wasn't sure I'd have the nerve to come back in. I gritted my teeth and waited. I checked the time, willing Oonishi to get there.

And then, as if I'd summoned him, he appeared. He saw me, nodding as I stood up. He wore a pale gray button-down shirt starched to within an inch of its life and black slacks. I wondered if I'd gotten him out of some late church service. He was dressed for Sunday. He came close, bending down toward me as if four fewer inches of air would give us some kind of privacy.

'Where's Chogyi?' he asked.

'Not here,' I said. 'He has other lines he's investigating. I'm just doing a little legwork.'

Oonishi frowned. Over his shoulder, I could see Nurse Receding Hairline watching us with interest.

'If you're going to be in my lab, I'd prefer that he come himself,' Oonishi said. 'It looks a little strange, taking unaccompanied women in when there's no actual work going on.'

I smiled.

'If they ask, I'll tell 'em you're trying to bang me, but you haven't had any luck,' I said.

To give the man credit, he had the grace to look abashed. I pulled my backpack onto one shoulder.

'Okay,' I said, 'let's—'

'Hey.'

The voice was weak and miserable. I turned back. The red-haired girl was looking up at me. She was pale, and her skin had a yellow, waxy look to it. I was pretty sure there was vomit caked on the ends of her hair. Her focus seemed to come in and out, seeing me then looking past into nothing, and coming back again.

'Be careful,' she said. 'It knows you're here.'

'That's all right,' I said. 'I know *it's* here. Keeps us even.'

The girl nodded deliberately and let her head sink back to her knees. Oonishi stared at me, his mouth actually open.

'What?' I asked.

'You know her?'

'Never seen her in my life.'

'And you told her about this?'

'Of course not.'

'How does . . .' He stopped, looked around, bent in for another inch of false privacy. 'How does she know, then?'

'Spirits,' I said. 'You should take me to your lab now.'

On the television, a bear began savaging a bunch of campers as the waiting patients looked on, drifting in and out of their misery. Oonishi looked at them all. His pock-marked skin and carefully cut hair weren't enough to keep him from seeming lost and out of his depth. Welcome to my world, I thought.

'I hate this,' Oonishi said, digging in his pocket. He came out with an ID tag clipped to a blue nylon lanyard like the ones Kim and Aubrey had. He pointed to a small blue door marked Staff Only. 'This way.'

Leaving the emergency department for the hospital proper was like stepping into a different world. Dim corridors passed empty, darkened clinics. Our footsteps echoed back on us, leaving me with the sense that someone else was walking just ahead of us or else just behind. Instead of simple, straight passages, the hallway bent, looping back on itself like something grown instead of built. The walls stepped in closer to one another, squeezing us together until I was almost walking behind him, and then just as suddenly they spat us out into a huge courtyard with couches and tables and a clear roof three stories above us. I paused, watching the almost invisible waves of rain sluicing down the glass. I had the sudden, brief sensation of terrible pressure, like I was forty feet underwater and looking up toward the air.

'Over here,' Oonishi said. 'It's a little hard finding the way.'

I trotted after him. We passed the chapel: a length of wood-paneled wall with the holy symbols of half a dozen faiths worked in bronze. An empty cafeteria opened out behind five sets of lowered bars. A bank of darkened windows showed desks glowing with the blue almost-light of computer monitors that hadn't turned off. Oonishi stopped at an alcove, swiped his ID card at a weirdly narrow elevator door, and gave me a polite, uncomfortable smile.

There had been years when the prospect of being alone in an elevator with a strange man—especially in territory I didn't know and he did—would have scared me. My mother had always drilled into me that, my father excepted, men weren't trustworthy; that just because you didn't see the demons of lust and violence in a man's eyes didn't mean they weren't there. In retrospect, it was a little surprising I'd ever risked kissing a boy. Getting into the narrow elevator with its white plastic walls and recessed fluorescent lights, I had only the vague echo of unease. Oonishi seemed to pick up my thoughts; I noticed him being careful not to stand too close to me or look at me for too long.

'The lab is actually on this first floor, but you can't get there without going up one level or down two,' Oonishi said. 'It's a terrible design.'

The elevator's panel buttons counted down from thirty to one, and then fell into letters. G. L. B. B2. SB1. SB2. SB3. R. It was like reading the legend off a map in an unknown language. I tried to remember how many floors there were underground. If I had the blueprints from the condo, I could look it up. A lot, anyway.

> *I've got the boy, boy, boy, boy down in the dark*
> *Down in the dark, he'll stay*

The elevator chimed. The door slid open. We stepped out into a waiting area just wide enough to turn a gurney around in. Oonishi headed right. I followed him through a set of double doors that warned us only authorized personnel were allowed. The long, cool hallway had doors like a hotel. Some were open, the two beds beyond them occupied by men and women, curtains and flickering televisions with the sound turned down. In one, the patient was a young man with the darkest skin I'd ever seen and an open, bloodless belly wound with what looked like a clear plastic vacuum sucking at it. Another had a woman lying perfectly flat, not even a pillow under her head, and arms at her sides, palms up. An old man in a dark suit stood by her side and looked up as we passed without saying anything. Someone nearby was groaning and calling for help in the tired, doomed voice of someone who knew no help would come. The high desk of the nurses' station glowed with the light of a little desk lamp, hidden away beneath it. It lit the night nurse's thick face from below like she was the bartender from *The Shining*.

'How's it going, Annie?' Oonishi asked as we walked by.

'Restless, Doc. No one's sleeping here tonight.'

'Bad weather,' Oonishi said over his shoulder. The night nurse looked me up and down, her eyes dead as a fish on a slab. I smiled sweetly and kept moving.

The next unit was Cardiac Care. I braced myself, waiting for the red-haired man who'd headed the first attack to pop out of a closet or from behind a desk. I didn't know if the growing feeling of being watched was the rider, the hospital, my own fear, or all three. After another set of double doors, the hallway split, Oonishi heading to the right and then left into a long hallway totally empty of doors or windows. Every fifth light was on, leaving long stretches of unrelieved darkness between the pools of gray. We turned a corner that wasn't quite a right angle, and the corridor split again in an intersection so like the ones we'd passed, I felt a rush of déjà vu. Oonishi went left, past a green steel door with a red exit sign above it, through the pale door beyond it, and to a bank of elevators. While we waited, I tried to think how I'd retrace our steps back to the emergency department. I was pretty sure I couldn't.

Oonishi's lab was tucked in the back of a much larger sleep disorders center. The door took not only Oonishi's card but also two separate keys in double dead bolt locks. He walked in and turned on the lights with the air of a man showing off a really nice bachelor's apartment.

'Here you go,' he said. 'Six separate imaging suites. One per subject. Once the study's done, they'll be available for other patients to use, but right now, they're all mine.'

I looked into one of the rooms. The round, white-and-gray machine dominated the space: a huge donut shape that went from floor to ceiling, with a platform big enough to lie down on that could slide a body into the donut hole. Looking at it, I couldn't imagine sleeping on the thing.

'It's been a bitch of a study,' Oonishi said. 'These things are really loud and uncomfortable. We have to strap the heads in tight. You can't let them move around. And we didn't want to sedate people if we could help it. It took us eight months to find six subjects. Got funding for all six machines, though.'

I had the feeling I was supposed to be impressed, but I didn't have the spare attention. I leaned over, looking into the dark tube of the fMRI, and shuddered. Being fed into it would have been like being buried alive.

'There was one woman we got as far as training, but she developed heart trouble. The pacemaker they put in wasn't MRI-safe.'

'Okay,' I said. 'What else have you got?'

A monitoring room with a server rack to show the data streams from all six suites and a wide white board hatched in green marker with names and dates listed in black and red and blue. A couple bathrooms where the test subjects could change into pajamas or whatever. A closet filled with cheap hospital blankets and plastic-wrapped pillows. Oonishi's own office. No couches, no cots. I sighed, dropping my backpack onto his desk.

'All right,' I said. 'I'm good. You can go if you want.'

'Go? You're staying here?'

'I'm sleeping here,' I said, walking back to the supply closet. If I laid out two or three of the blankets, it would be sort of like having a thin mattress.

'I'm not leaving anyone alone with my equipment,' he said. 'I don't care how much Kim and Chogyi trust you. This is my lab.'

'Then stay,' I said, 'but be quiet.'

I picked a stretch of floor behind his desk. Oonishi stood

in the doorway, caught between trying to kick me out or else staying all night in the lab. I put down a couple of the little pillows.

'Is this necessary?' he asked for the second time that night, and I knew he wasn't going to give me any trouble.

'Is,' I said. 'Don't turn out the light when you go, okay?'

He closed the door, and I shoved the filing cabinet over to block it. It wouldn't keep the door from opening if the hospital got a good mob going, but it would certainly make enough noise to wake me if the rider sent its influence into Oonishi or a night nurse or someone. I looked around the room one last time, then turned out the light.

The darkness almost made it impossible to navigate back to my little impromptu bed, but by the time I got there, my eyes had adjusted. The office door became a line of dim light. A soft, almost subliminal glow came from the screen on the wall. I lay down, took a deep breath, letting it out slowly, willing my shoulders to relax. The crackling of the pillow under my ear didn't quite drown out Oonishi's footsteps. Going to the monitoring room, I thought. The bulk of the hospital felt heavy above me, like an avalanche waiting for a single too-loud noise to start it, and me getting ready to shout.

I wanted to get up, to call Aubrey again. Or if not him, at least Chogyi Jake and Ex. Hell, even Kim. I wanted backup and friends and not to be alone in the darkness. I wanted someone to talk me out of being there. At this edge-of-the-diving-board moment, it wouldn't have been hard. Instead, I closed my eyes.

I told myself all the reasons this was going to be okay. The rider was bound and couldn't hurt me directly even if it wanted to. I was better protected than anyone else. Whatever had provoked the first attack, I'd beaten it once already. I had what the rider wanted safely tucked away in Waukegan. And most important, it had what Eric had been after: the power or knowledge or favor so critical that he'd betrayed Aubrey and Kim, that he'd risked death against the Invisible College and lost. Everything pointed toward this. A confrontation between human and *haugsvarmr*. A negotiation. A trade. I had to know what it could possibly offer that would justify all he'd done. Papers and note-books, grimoires and files: they were just more puzzles. There was only one thing that could answer the questions I had.

'Come on,' I said to the dark air. 'Talk to me. Whatever the hell you are, come talk to me.'

I forced myself to relax muscle by muscle. Feet, calf, knee, thigh, moving inch by inch up my body until all my attention was focused on my scalp. My mind started to fish-tail under me. I felt certain that Aubrey had left me a message on the phone, if I could just remember what the access code was. It had to do with yachts and something Kim had said. I roused just enough to recognize the surreal patterns of dream, but the part of me that watched all the rest saw it wasn't going to work. I was too anxious for a real, deep sleep; I could skate around in nothing more than a light doze until morning.

And then between one breath and the next, dream lifted a dark arm, took me by the throat, and pulled me down.

18

When I was about twelve, I had a long run of nightmares.
The recurring dreams didn't have the same action or even
the same people or things, but they did share locations. An
abandoned factory with hell underneath it was one. A
flooded school building. A network of tiny little crawlways
underground so cramped and tight that my legs would get
caught sometimes when I tried to squirm around a corner.

And then there was the desert.

Seeing it again now was like going back to my old grade
school: familiar and foreign at the same time. The wide,
dark horizon, the pale hardpack of stones and pebbles, the
drifts of sand. A gritty wind pressed against my skin, hot as
breath. I'd been here before, and it had always been with a
sense of awe and fear that I'd called a visit from the devil. I
was naked, and sitting down. The stones were smooth and
hard against my legs. I wanted badly to stand up. I tried,
strained, but the effort was infinite, and even though I felt
myself moving, I never rose up. The other me (my childhood nightmares often involved having two copies of
myself) wanted to sit, and no matter what I thought, it was
going to sit.

Above me, or possibly us, thin clouds skittered past

something that wasn't the sun or the moon: a pale disk that radiated something besides heat or light. Purification. The desert was pure. That was what made it terrible. It was also my home. I was waiting for something, holding the line. I was insisting that the devil visit me. With the logic of dream, I could also see myself as if from a great distance. A girl not more than thirteen with my black hair, but a serene expression that properly belonged to the other me. I tried to call to her, to tell her to run, that it was coming, but my voice didn't carry over the susurrus of wind and sand.

Something happened, deep and resonant as a church organ striking a chord. I didn't hear it as much as feel it, and the panic started me scampering. The body sitting on the sand didn't move, and I willed myself back into it, even though I'd also never left. The dark, luminous sky peeled back, and something inconceivably huge looked down at me. The enemy. The thing I'd been waiting for. I was standing now, and it was before me. It was two things at the same time. On one hand, it was a good-looking young man with razor-cut hair and dark eyes. He wore a suit cut like something from a forties movie and a fedora, and I knew that the fabric was made from raw silk and the dreams of mad children. His expression was amused and kind. And on the other hand, it was a monstrosity, translucent, vast, constantly in motion, and made up of millions of evil-looking beasts like those deep-sea fish that unlucky sailors sometimes pull up in their nets. These two different aspects of the thing didn't compete with each other; it was just both things at the same time. I knew when it smiled that I hated it. And what was more, I knew it hated me.

The desert was a vast, dark ocean now. The water pressed against me, crushing and cold. The rider smiled toward but not at me, its eyes unfocused. Slowly, it spread its long, weirdly jointed hands, as if it was asking me something. I wanted to answer, but I knew like I was remembering something that I couldn't speak first. It was a trap. I waited. The school of monstrous fish shuddered and spun in its cold ocean, annoyed that the trick had failed.

'I can't see you,' it said. 'But I know you're here. I can smell your skin. You were my slave once.' It took off its fedora, combed back a lock of hair with its strange fingers, and put the hat back on. 'You know what happens to bad slaves.'

'We haven't met,' both of my selves said together. It started at the sound of my voices, its fish-school body glittering silver and spinning wildly. It was trying to find me. *You're hard to see*, I told myself. *That's your protection. Try not to touch it.*

'Who are you?' it asked.

'I am my mother's daughter,' I said, but I meant that I was Eric's niece. The rider understood.

'Why are you here?' it asked. 'You wanted to see me now that the tables have turned? Is that it? You want to gloat?'

'I can set you free,' I said, and my voice seemed small and singular. The man looked at me, his gaze passing through me like a blind man's. The icy water surged invisibly around me, stroking my skin like an unwanted caress. 'I know where the blood is that will open the box. I am the only one who can release you. Or I can leave you where you are forever.'

'I'm listening,' it said.

'What can you offer me?' my small voice said. I sounded like a child pretending to negotiate with a pack of wolves.

'I can give you the world,' it said, as if the world were something it owned already and was willing to part with.

'Not enough,' I said.

Its laughter was the chittering of a million fish teeth.

'I can kill for you,' it said. 'I can bind for you. Enter into pact with me, daughter-thing, and I will bring you the Graveyard Child in a box and a bow. I will bring you the Angel Chesed. I will do again what once I did to your mother, and place you on the throne where I sat.'

Some part of me was tempted. I didn't know what its words meant, but I wanted what it offered like I wanted air and love and petty revenge against everyone who'd ever pissed me off. I almost reached out to it. I almost took its hand, but at the last moment, I pulled back.

'Who are you,' I said, 'to offer me these things?'

'I am the Beast Rahab.' Its voice was growing louder, deeper, ringing around me like a church bell and buzzing like a swarm of wasps. 'I am Legion, Ravens of the Burning God.'

The words were meaningless to me, but images rode on the syllables. A huge bull lying on its side in a barren field, screwfly maggots eating its living flesh. A blue-skinned baby held to a wailing mother's breast. A line of naked men with machetes and guns driving their powerless victims over a cliff. All temptation was gone, and in its place, a vast and intimate grief. Here was the thing I'd come to see, to talk with. Here was my unspoken question, answered.

If something was tempted by the rider, it wasn't me. The thing trapped under Grace Memorial was raw evil, and there was no cause noble enough to justify giving it freedom. My world collapsed quietly, no one aware of the fact except the two of me. My uncle Eric, whom I loved, who watched out for me, who gave me everything, couldn't have been negotiating with this thing and been the man I thought he was. The man I wanted him to have been.

And as soon as that was clear, everything else shifted. Oonishi said we see what we expect. The other thing is we ignore what we don't expect. Eric had worked with Midian Clark, the vampire. Carrefour, the body-hopping serial killer. He'd hidden who he really was and what he really did from everyone I trusted. He'd used magic to get Kim into bed. I'd pushed it aside or pretended it didn't matter because it didn't fit with what I expected to see, and I'd talked Aubrey, Chogyi Jake, and Ex into digging in to do Eric's work with me.

We were the bad guys.

'I,' the rider said, 'am Daevanam Daeva, Angel of Shells!'

'Yeah?' I said. 'Well, I'm Jayné Heller, and I think you *suck*.'

In an instant, all pretense of negotiation vanished. With a roar, the rider's fish-school body scattered, expanding out in all directions. Its human body, face distorted with rage, swung at me blindly. I drew back, my dream body moving with inhuman grace, but the rider's outstretched fingers brushed my arm. It knew where I was. I tried to push it away, but the long-fingered hands wrapped around me, pushing me back. I felt myself stumble. The pale, gape-mouthed fish were all around me, their collective mass hanging above me like a mountain. I pulled into myself, folding into fetal position while phantom teeth ripped at my back and shoulders, legs and thighs. The rider's will pushed at me, crushing me. Fear and grief and the terrible presentiment of my own death swirled in my mind. I started to scream, and the rider forced itself in, flooding my mouth and nose, filling my lungs. I was drowning in it. I tried to dig it out of my mouth with my fingers.

And then, in the middle of my panic, I became calm. I didn't try to breathe. Instead, I found my belly and concentrated on the feeling of warmth there. I drew my qi—the energy of life and magic—up my spine and into a burning sphere. I felt the rider shudder around me and pressed out, the dark sphere within me widening as I gave up my body. I became perfect, impenetrable. My qi boiled the dark water. The rider surrounded me, scrabbled teeth and claws against me, but found no purchase.

'You're weak,' I said. 'You have been cast into darkness, betrayer, as you deserve.'

I pushed out, and it screamed. For a moment, I saw something. A dark room, deep underground with a shut steel door. The vision retreated, snatched away.

It hadn't wanted me to see that. I chased after the other

thing's thoughts, shoving myself into the soft, viscous body. It flailed at me, bit, strangled. I caught another glimpse of something. A storage locker, maybe, with an ancient-looking tank of compressed gas, green paint bubbled and flaking off. The word *cyclopropane* popped into my mind, surreal and inappropriate as a pigeon in a fish bowl. The rider pulled away again. We were in the desert. *My* desert. The rider's silk-and-madness suit was ripped, and seawater blood poured from a cut in his forehead. He grinned, and his mouth was filled with pale, cruel dagger-teeth. His eyes were the empty silver-and-black of fish.

'I am weak,' it said, 'but you are young, and I will be strong before you're old. I am already half free, and you cannot stop me.'

The despair, the grief, the fear and panic and even the calm all shifted. Rage leaped up in their place, and hatred for the thing lying on the desert floor before me. The thing that had taken Eric from me. The thing that had taken Aubrey and broken my little family. Even before I spoke, the rider's eyes widened, and it jerked its head from side to side as if it was hearing something vast and threatening that it couldn't quite locate.

'You think I can't take you?' I screamed. I could actually feel the air rattling in my throat. 'You think I can't *break* you?'

I leaped for it, my hands bent like burning claws. It shrieked and pulled back when I touched it, but I was in my place now. No more frigid oceans for me. Oh no. I cut into it, and a dozen demonic fish shattered into luminous bone and blood. I swung my fist, rolling through the shoulder, and felt the bridge of its nose shatter under my knuckles. It screamed, and there were words in the cry.

Hurry, she's killing me.

I hesitated, and in that moment, the rider lashed out, stinging me across the eyes. I yelled, pulled back. I was on the ground, something soft constricting me like a web. My balance was off, and the desert around me suddenly small. I had the hazy sense that the rider was pulling me into its coffin. I smelled something wet, but not oceanic. I pushed myself up, the web ripping. I swung out at it and connected. I heard a gasp of expelled breath, but I was already on my feet and turning fast. My heel hit something with a sound like breaking glass.

A light flared, blinding me. I dropped low and went still. There were shapes in the light, beings moving slowly toward me. A storm raged under my skin, violence and the joy of violence on a hair trigger. I could feel myself grinning so hard it ached. My breath was pumping in and out, roaring in my ears as loud as music.

'Jayné?'

I turned my head toward the voice, ready to attack until something small in the back of my head said *That was Aubrey*. One of the hulking shapes moved toward me, and keeping myself from reaching out and snapping its neck was one of the hardest things I'd ever done. Aubrey swam into focus. His hair was wet, slicked against his scalp. His wide eyes shifted back and forth, and his hands were out before him in a placating gesture. I tried to understand what he was doing in my dream as my eyes adjusted to the light. Kim was behind him, one hand to her mouth like a caricature of surprise. Chogyi Jake stood behind Aubrey, his side toward me and carefully still. Oonishi was beside him, his mouth tight. I looked around me and found all the details of Oonishi's office in the sleep study unit. The filing cabinet I'd used for a barricade was on its side where the forced door had toppled it. The blanket I'd pulled over me hung in tatters across my shoulders. The huge flat-screen monitor on the wall was shattered, a single impact site radiating cracks to all edges. My backpack chirped, the cell phone letting me know I'd missed a call. Ex lay on the floor, his hands pressed to his solar plexus. He seemed to be having some trouble breathing.

'Um. Are you okay?' I asked Ex, still crouched and ready for a fight.

He rolled onto his side and wheezed softly.

'Jayné?' Aubrey said. 'Do you know where you are?'

I nodded. The traces of dream were still around my mind, but they were burning off quickly. I put down my hands.

'In the hospital,' I said. 'What . . . what are you doing here?'

'You started shouting,' Oonishi said, his voice tight with poorly concealed outrage. 'I couldn't get into the office, and I didn't want to explain you to security, so I called your boss.'

I squinted at him. I felt like I ought to know what he was talking about, but *my boss*? Chogyi Jake raised his hand

and I remembered. I squatted down beside Ex. His breath was regular, and I thought it was getting deeper. It was hard to be sure. The rage that had filled me in the dream was draining away fast, leaving a shaky near-nausea in its wake. I felt like I'd swum a mile and swallowed too much salt water in the process.

'I tried to call you. When I couldn't, I got the others,' Chogyi Jake said. 'We all came as quickly as we could.'

I looked at the file cabinet. One side was visibly bent in. My idea that it would wake me had been optimistic.

'Sorry,' I said, mostly to Ex and Oonishi, but also to everyone. 'I'm sorry. That wasn't supposed to happen.'

'I'm pleased to know it wasn't the plan,' Oonishi said.

I nodded toward the ruined monitor.

'I can replace that,' I said.

'What were you doing?' Chogyi Jake asked.

I sat back. The others came in closer, except for Oonishi. I swallowed to loosen my throat. I felt like an idiot.

'I needed to see it,' I said. 'The rider. The *haugsvarmr*. I thought maybe if I could talk to it, I'd be able to find out what Eric wanted from it. Even just a hint, you know? Maybe it wouldn't be so bad. Maybe it would be an angel, and so things with Eric wouldn't be what it looked like after all.'

'And?' Kim said.

I shook my head. 'It's not an angel,' I said.

With a grunt and a little help from Aubrey, Ex sat up. Even apart from the pain, he looked annoyed.

'Point—' he began, then gulped air and started again.

'Point of clarification? Eric used the Mark of Naxos to force Kim into a sexual relationship that wrecked her marriage. At minimum, that makes him a sociopath and a rapist.'

I blinked. Oonishi's eyebrows tried to join up with his hairline. Kim went a little paler as the word sank in. *Rapist.*

Of course, that was right.

'I mean I'm as disappointed as anyone,' Ex went on. 'But is there really room for debate over whether he was good or evil?'

'There's not,' I said. 'I wasn't thinking straight.'

'And coming here by yourself?' Ex said. 'I mean, yes, the thing's still bound by the interment, but that's like saying the tiger's in the cage. Still not what I'd call safe.'

'I get your point,' I said.

'If you want to work out your private life,' he said, 'maybe you could—'

'She got the point, Ex,' Kim said. 'Let it go.'

He leaned against the desk and muttered something about moral relativism I didn't quite catch. I stood up, plucking the ruined blanket off my shoulders and letting it drop to the ground. My backpack chirped again. The last threads of dream were gone, and my confusion vanished with them. A little wisp of my normal strength was coming back.

The hope I had been grasping at was an illusion, and knowing that—seeing the last vestiges of the life I'd known fall away past redemption—was actually a relief. I wasn't happy. I wasn't at peace. The bedrock I'd rebuilt my life on had turned to sand, but at least I knew that now. I didn't have to try to save it. There was nothing I could do to get it back.

'I think this is partly my fault,' Chogyi Jake said. 'When we spoke, back at the condo—'

'I know what you were saying,' I said. *We've all lost families and lovers and things that were precious to us, and we've all survived.* He hadn't meant us. He'd meant Eric.

He went quiet, his smile reading to me like a vote of confidence. Encouragement. Oonishi's gaze went from me to him and back again. I probably wasn't acting enough like an employee who'd just screwed up. That was fine. Oonishi's dreams had started us down the path, but his good opinion was so far down my list of things to clean up, I could barely make it out. This was my show now.

And I knew where I needed to start.

'Guys,' I said. 'Could you give us the room for a minute? Aubrey and I need to have a talk.'

19

They walked out quietly, Ex with a little help from Chogyi Jake. Kim hovered at the threshold for a moment, her gaze equal parts anxiety and exhaustion. When she closed the door, Aubrey and I were alone. He sat on the desk, his arms crossed. He looked older. I always knew there were threads of gray in his hair, but I saw them now. Sure, he looked tired, but more than that, he looked weary. I could still remember the first time I'd seen him, in the Denver airport holding up a sign with my name on it, spelled almost right. I remembered his empty eyes after our first, failed attempt on the Invisible College and the joy of seeing him come to after we'd taken them out. Holding him while he wept in the warm New Orleans night. Funny how many of our good times involved people dying.

'I should have called you,' he said. 'Or at least I should have told you why I wasn't calling you.'

'I get it,' I said.

'I didn't mean to be a shitheel. And I certainly didn't mean to drive you to this.'

'Don't worry about it.'

'I was confused,' he said. 'Honestly, I still am. What Eric did . . . it reframes a whole part of my life.'

'You know what?' I said. 'I actually totally know how that feels.'

He smiled and laughed.

'Yeah. You do, don't you,' he said. Then, 'Kim said you went to her place. Looking for me.'

'It seemed like a good bet,' I said.

'I wouldn't do that to you. I know I said some things in the heat of the moment, but I wouldn't run off to Kim and ignore you. I was very angry and confused and hurt, but I hope I wasn't a total jerk.'

'You weren't,' I said. 'Just a normal, garden-variety jerk. Still far from total. I've done worse myself.'

The air conditioner clacked and muttered. A computer hummed. My cell phone chirped again. The moment seemed slow and airless and over too quickly.

'You're not Eric,' he said. 'You're not like him. You didn't do the things he did. You shouldn't have to pay for his sins.'

'Yeah, but I do,' I said, trying to make it sound light. 'Ain't fair, but there you go. I know why you didn't go to Kim. And why you didn't stay at the condo with me. You're screwed, right? If you get involved with Kim again, try to make sense of what actually happened between you two and see who you are to each other, you're breaking up with me for something that's not my fault. And if you stay with me and go on like we've been doing? Well, that's not fair to Kim, right? Walking away from her knowing what happened means this time you're *choosing* to leave her. And it turns out for something that's not entirely her fault. You want to be fair, but you can't.'

'I don't think anyone's psychic well-being is really deter-mined by whether I'm sleeping—'

'Aubrey. I love you. And Kim loves you. And you're in a position where you have to pick between us, but you can't do it. So after long and sober reflection, you're going to leave both of us and strike out on your own. It's not great, but at least it's even-handed. Am I right?'

He took a deep breath and let it out slowly. Deep, unhappy lines etched themselves in his mouth and the corners of his eyes. The situation was unsalvageable. Even now, some part of me hoped that he'd say no, that he'd find some other alternative and make everything okay.

'It was that or a three-way,' he said.

Okay. That wasn't the kind of alternative I'd been think-ing of.

'You're joking,' I said.

'I am absolutely joking,' he said with a sad kind of smile that meant he had been, and also he hadn't. He wanted to be what I wanted and what Kim needed, and he'd resigned himself to failing us both. 'Two girls at once was never one of my big fantasies.'

'No?'

'Well, pleasant thought, I guess, but I always figured I'd wind up feeling like the host at a party, you know? "Doing all right? Can I get you anything? How about you? Everyone okay?"'

I laughed, and he blushed. There were only three steps between us. They seemed like an ocean until I took the first one. Then he was right there. I kissed him softly, opening his mouth with mine for what we both knew was the last time. We were both crying a little.

'Aubrey,' I whispered.

'Jayné.'

'You're fired,' I said. 'I'm breaking up with you. Me. With you.'

He leaned back, wiping his eyes with the back of his hand. He didn't understand.

'If you stayed with me,' I said, 'I'd always know you were thinking about Kim. And Eric. Wondering what it would have been like if you hadn't run into my uncle. You'd keep it hidden because you're a stand-up guy, but it would be there, and we'd both know it.'

'But—'

'I'm not going to live that way. Go where you want. Do what you need to do. But you're not welcome in my bed or with me. You understand? I'm telling you right now you've got no place here.'

His face was gray, but something deep in his eyes was glittering. It looked like hope. I was sad to see it there, and happy too.

'You're doing this so I'll stay with Kim,' he said.

'I don't care what you do,' I said. 'That's your business.'

'This is silly—'

'No sillier than ditching both of us out of a misplaced sense of chivalry,' I said. Then, more gently, 'You need someone to tell you it's over. That's me. It's over.'

He took a long, shaking breath. His fingers touched my cheek. I wanted to turn toward them, to press his palm against me. But then I would want something else, some other last thing for the last time. This was as good a boundary as any. I stepped away. His arm fell to his side.

'Fired, eh?' he said.

'Pink-slipped,' I said, fighting to keep the catch out of my voice. 'Let go. No longer with the company.'

'All right,' he said.

'The severance package is pretty good,' I said.

'No. Jayné, I can't—'

'It's Eric's money,' I said. 'After what he did to you—to both of you—you've got some coming. Besides, it would make me feel all magnanimous and stuff.'

'We'll talk about it,' he said.

'I'll tell the guys when we get back to the condo,' I said. 'Think they'll be okay with it?'

In point of fact, I thought Chogyi Jake already knew as much about it as Aubrey or me. And Ex would probably be quietly pleased, though he'd never show it. That was going to be a whole new box of problems, but later. That was for later.

'It's the right thing,' I said instead of answering.

The others were waiting in the hallway. Ex was standing up on his own now, even though he still had one hand protectively over his solar plexus. He looked annoyed. Chogyi Jake smiled at me and Aubrey both, and Oonishi glowered. Kim took a step forward, then paused. Her movements were sharp as a bird's. She probably wasn't quite sober yet.

'Right,' I said. 'Let's go home.'

The quiet hospital corridors felt colder than when I'd come in. Our footsteps echoed. We rounded a corner and almost walked into a security guard. He stared at us, clearly alarmed to find a bunch of people tramping through the dark hallways. I smiled and nodded. The elevator Oonishi led us to was different from the one we'd come down in. Deep enough for a gurney and equipment and medics to surround it, it looked more like a freight elevator. With all six of us inside, there was still enough room to break apart. Kim stood at the back, arms folded, and Oonishi beside her and Aubrey. Chogyi Jake and Ex and I were by the door. Like a single cell becoming two daughters, we were pulling apart.

It wasn't the first time I'd lost a lover. Depending on how I counted it, it was either the second or the third. But it was the first time that I didn't feel lost or confused. Sad, yes. Emptied. Dreading the moment when, still half asleep, I would reach for Aubrey and wonder where he'd gone. But I also felt calm and centered and certain, and that was new. I had to think that it came from having done what needed doing. When I looked at Aubrey, I thought I saw the same look in his eyes. Sad. Relieved. It was a peaceful kind of grief.

Kim looked from one of us to the other, confused. I figured he could tell her what had happened later. My cell phone chirped again, and I swung my pack around to get it out. Seven missed calls, six new voice-mail messages, and I'd slept through all of them.

'Third floor?' Ex said.

'There's a walkway to the parking structure,' Oonishi said. 'It's the only way to get there. They lock the ground-floor doors at midnight. You can get out, but you can't come back in.'

'What time is it?' Kim asked.

'Quarter to three,' Aubrey said.

'Jeez,' I said, checking the readout on the cell to confirm it, 'how long was I asleep?'

'Five hours, more or less,' Oonishi said.

'Weird,' I said. 'Didn't seem that long.'

The first message was Chogyi Jake wondering where I was and asking me to call him back. Then a number I didn't recognize. The elevator doors opened, and I stepped out into a dim hallway with arrowed signs pointing toward Pediatric ICU and Labor and Delivery Unit. A soft, artificial breeze stirred the flyer on the wall, 72-point Arial about Project Morning Air fluttering uneasily, and David Souder started talking in my ear.

'Something's wrong. Something's happening. I can feel it. It started an hour ago, and I thought . . . I thought maybe I was having an anxiety attack or a stroke or something, but I'm not. Something's coming after him. I . . . I can't explain this. Grandpa Del, I can feel it that something's coming *after* him. He's scared. He needs help.'

The memory came back, fleeting bits of the rider's consciousness I'd stolen in the fight: the dark room, the metal tank. *Hurry, she's killing me.* I didn't realize I'd stopped walking until Ex looked back at me. He started to talk, but I held up a hand, silencing him.

'I know you told me to stay away, but . . .' David said. His voice was shaking. 'Call me back. As soon as you get this, call me back. I'm getting in the car now. It's at least a couple hours down to Chicago. Just call me.'

The message had been left at ten thirty, almost as soon as I'd gotten to sleep. I said something obscene. The others clustered around me, questions in their eyes. I thumbed onto the next message. Chogyi Jake saying that Oonishi had called, and that he, Ex, and Aubrey were coming to Grace. An empty message from Ex's cell number. Kim saying that she'd gotten a call from Ex, and she was coming to the hospital. Then David again.

'Jayné, I don't know where you are, but I'm at Grace Memorial. It's a little after midnight. I know you said it was dangerous here, but I know that this is the right thing. Grandpa Del's in there. He's . . . talking to me.'

'That's not your grandfather,' I said to the recording. 'Come on, snap out of it. It's not *him*.'

'He's in trouble. Something's after him. A spirit or a ghost or something. Invisible, but it's burning. *Sonnenrad*, I don't know. It's really powerful, and I have to help him now. It's okay, though. It's going to be okay. I know where he is, and I know how to get him out. It's going to be all right.'

I fumbled with the buttons, calling him back. I was muttering obscenities under my breath. Down the line, David's phone rang. Once, twice . . .

'Hi, this is Dave Souder. If it's about a roofing problem, give me a call at the office. That number—'

I killed the connection.

'Problem?' Ex said.

'David Souder's here someplace,' I said. 'In the hospital. He got here two, maybe two and a half hours ago.'

'What is he doing?' Aubrey asked.

'Digging up his grandfather,' I said.

'What?' Oonishi said, raising his hands in bewilderment and annoyance.

'That's a real problem,' Kim said.

I pushed the cell phone into my pack and pressed my palms to my temples. I had to think. He was in the hospital already, within the rider's domain. Even if I could talk to him, I wasn't sure I'd be able to break the control it had over him now.

'Okay,' I said. 'We need to find him. The rider's able to guide him. Talk to him. It's probably worked out a plan to get David there as quickly as possible. Wherever the hell "there" is.'

'Civil defense ward under the north tower,' Ex said. 'Fifth level down, right underneath the fallout shelter.'

'Really?' I said.

'All this time you people were sleeping and figuring out your love lives, I was working. Remember?' Ex said. 'It's not spelled out on Eric's blueprints, but the implication's right there.'

'Okay,' I said. 'Once he gets there, how hard is it to undo the interment?'

'If he can get the coffin,' Chogyi Jake said, 'it's not hard at all. A little blood, the right words, and the intention.

It's like a balloon. All you have to do is make a pinhole and the pressure inside it does the rest. But reaching the coffin might not be easy.'

'But we don't *have* a north tower,' Oonishi said.

'You used to,' Ex said. 'It got incorporated in the new design in '48. You know how the floor numbers are different east and west of the operating theaters? That's because the new construction joined the north tower with the Campion office complex that was just east of it, and they used different—'

'Ex!' I snapped. 'Gold star for research later. Why won't the coffin be easy to get to?'

'Um,' Ex said. 'Because it's buried?'

'Probably under a concrete slab,' Chogyi Jake said. 'If he didn't bring a jackhammer or dynamite—'

'A tank of gas,' I said.

'There are plenty of ways to make something explode in a hospital,' Kim said. 'We've got a lot of tanks of pressurized gas, and most of them are oxygen.'

'What's cyclopropane?' I asked.

'It used to be an anesthetic,' Oonishi said. 'No one uses it anymore.'

'Because it kept blowing up?' I asked. Oonishi blinked. That was answer enough. 'Ex. Can you get us to the civil defense ward?'

'The plans were eight years old. If they haven't remodeled anything, then yes.'

'Let's go,' I said. Aubrey hit the elevator's call button, and the doors slid open immediately. Oonishi came in with us. As the doors slid closed, I wondered whether I should have told him to get out instead. The car dropped down, gravity shifting. I watched the numbers crawl: Two. One. G. L. B. B1. SB1. SB2. We were underground, and I imagined that I could feel the weight of earth pressing in against the air.

I'd underestimated the rider. I didn't get to do that twice. If we could reach David before it was too late, carry him out of the hospital, we'd be okay. We'd sedate him if we needed to . . .

The doors slid open on a hallway, fluorescent lights bright as noon, and green-white walls that kept every ray of it bouncing back. The ceiling was high, marks on the wall showing where a network of sound-killing acoustical tiles had once been. Pipes ran the length of the hall, turning at corners or vanishing into walls. I thought of blood vessels. Grace Memorial as a single, vast body more complex than any individual human within it.

'We're going to need to head north,' Ex said.

'Cool,' I said. 'Is that going to be right or left?'

'Left,' he said.

We walked fast. Signs in English, Spanish, and what I thought was Chinese pointed us toward the laundry, the film library, records storage. The mix of languages left me with the eerie feeling that I was in some universal ur-hospital, like I'd stumbled into a network of halls and tunnels that connected to infinity at the back. If I followed them long enough, I'd wind up in the basement of the Mayo Clinic or St Mary's in London or some tiny little hospital in the middle of Serbia. The pipes above us shuddered and clanked, locked in a conversation of their own. Ex led us left, and then right. We passed through a warehouse, chain-link fencing on both sides of a single hall making storage cells for ancient medical equipment. The skeletons of beds with cranks on the fronts, wheelchairs of rotting wicker with shredding rubber wheels. Cabinets of glass jars filled with foggy liquid and covered in dust.

'There should be a stairway over here,' Ex said. 'It can get us down to the fallout shelter. The civil defense ward is underneath *that*.'

'Have I mentioned that this is really creepy?' I said.

'We're going to be okay,' Aubrey said, and the lights went out.

The darkness was total. Suffocating. I felt a hand brush my arm, and I yelped a little. Then a deep throbbing came, resonating all around us. Once, then twice, and then a vicious wind whipped through the passageway, hot and damp and thick with the smells of old soil and corrupt flesh. To my right, a rat squealed in terror. The silence that followed was worse.

The lights flickered back on, dimmer and dirtier than before. They grew darker and brighter and darker again, like something breathing. A violent rattling passed through the pipes overhead, something huge sprinting one floor above us. We all looked at one another. No one needed to say it. We all knew what had happened; we were too late. David had reached the coffin. The *haugsvarmr*, the demon, the Beast Rahab was free. The hospital, taken over.

I thought for a moment I saw the cold, blue glow of a demonic fish swimming through the air at the end of the corridor. I heard the rider's voice in my memory. *I can't see you, but I know you're here. I can smell your skin.* The hair on my arms was standing up straight.

'Okay, new plan,' I whispered. 'Let's get the hell out of here.'

20

Retracing our steps, we were all quiet. The walls around us seeped with the threat of violence and a sense of something vast and implacable. Even our footsteps were quiet. Careful. Frightened as mice in a cat's bed. Chogyi Jake wasn't smiling. Oonishi kept speeding up or slowing down, unconsciously keeping himself at the center of the herd. Kim and Aubrey were walking side by side, neither looking at the other but their strides matching perfectly. Around us, the hospital changed.

At first, I thought it was only the low light, fluorescents buzzing and flickering as we passed them. It was more than that. The floors got damper, and the air thickened. The salt smell was somewhere between ocean water and blood. When we passed back through the storage cells, I had the feeling that the old equipment had moved, that it was still moving whenever I wasn't watching it. The pipes started dripping rust-brown water that burned a little when it hit the back of my hand. We got to the elevator faster than I'd expected, and paused there. There were five levels above us, just to reach the surface. I didn't care about getting to the parking garage. Anyplace with a window I could break and crawl out of would do just fine. But when I reached out for the call button, I couldn't quite do it. Somewhere in dim memory, there was a story about people getting into a haunted elevator and coming out as a thin, red soup.

Ex, at my side, saw me hesitate.

'Stairs?' he said.

'Stairs.'

We found the stairwell a few doors down, still marked by a glowing red exit sign. The door stuck when I tried to open it, but Ex and Aubrey pushed with me, and we got through. The railing was icy cold under my hand. I leaned in, looking up the central shaft. Two short flights to go up a story, twisting up for what looked like forever. Behind us, someone started shouting: a deep, angry sound. I started up.

I had felt the insectile press of riders pushing in against reality from the Pleroma or Next Door or whatever we called the abstract spiritual place they called home. At best, it had been like standing in a lake where fish sometimes blundered into me. At its worst, it was like being the egg in biology class videos about fertilization. This was different. Instead of the almost physical pressure, I felt like I was floating inside something, like if I pushed off from the concrete and steel landings, I could almost swim up into the air. Even the immediate solid touch of the railings and walls seemed unconvincing, and I heard voices talking just outside the range of hearing. Fighting. Weeping. Begging.

At the landing halfway to the ground floor, we paused. Oonishi looked winded, but he was the only one. He held up a hand, silently asking the rest of us to stop and let him catch his breath. I wondered for a moment what exactly we'd do if he had a heart attack or something right there. I didn't think I'd be taking him to the ER or dropping him with the night nurse at the Cardiac Care Unit. The thought skipped ahead of me into unsafe territory.

'Kim,' I said. 'How many people do you think are in the hospital right now?'

'We've got about five hundred beds,' Kim said. 'With night staff? I don't know. A little less than a thousand.'

A thousand men and women—kids, infants, newborns—who didn't know what was going on, only that all the familiar things around them were changed and changing. Would they think they were going crazy? That the sense of the hospital shifting, rusting, cooling around them was a kind of hallucination? Something rumbled deep in the earth, then a sound like metal shrieking.

'Okay,' I said. 'Anyone know what that was?'

'At a guess?' Ex said. 'Our hive-mind is figuring out that it's still trapped. May not be happy about it.'

'I can go on,' Oonishi said, still gasping. 'Really. I'm fine.'

The door marked G for ground level was green-painted steel with a bright crash bar. The exit sign above it looked like a promise. I pushed through. The hallway wasn't quite dark, but the lights were flickering and hissing. Something black was welling up through the paint and dripping down the walls, and the air smelled hot and close as breath. A heavy-set woman in pale green scrubs stood in the middle of the hall under a sign pointing us toward the Pediatric

ICU. Her hair and clothes seemed to float, as if she were underwater. Her eyes glowed a cold, deepwater blue.

I didn't think. My body leaped toward her almost without me, swinging through my shoulder, and sinking a stiff-fingered hand in her belly even before she screamed. Her breath went out of her in a gasp, and she folded over.

'Sorry,' I said, moving her to the side so the others could walk past her. 'Really, really sorry.'

'You think you can hold me, Santur?' she spat, her gaze skittering across me like she couldn't quite get me in focus. 'I owned you once, and I will own you again.'

I gathered the vital energy of my qi, drawing the heat from the base of my spine, up through my belly and my heart, and into my throat.

'Sleep now,' I said, pressing the words into her. Her eyes closed with an audible click. She started breathing deep and slow.

'Nice trick,' Oonishi said.

'You should see me get droids through Imperial checkpoints,' I said. 'Come on, let's . . . Hey.'

I pointed to the sign. Pediatric ICU.

'Isn't that on the third floor?' I said.

'It is,' Kim said.

'Aren't we on the *ground* floor?'

'I thought so,' Kim said, her voice uncertain.

Something screamed off to our left, huge, inhuman, and soaked in rage.

'If we're on the third, the walkway should be over here,'

Oonishi said, gesturing down the corridor at a set of closed staff-only doors.

I followed him, the others close on our heels, but as soon as we were through the doors and into the passage beyond, Oonishi stopped, his eyes wide and staring. A T-intersection offered us the choice of Nuclear Imaging to the left and Gastroenterology Clinic to the right.

'It's right here,' Oonishi said, putting his hand to the blank wall. 'The walkway's right *here*. GI and Imaging are on the second floor. They're nowhere near Pediatric.'

I pushed the fear and rising panic away. My hands were shaking, but I could ignore them. I'd break down later, if there was a later.

'Guys?' I said. 'Any thoughts? Is this the rider?'

'Could be,' Ex said, but he sounded unconvinced. 'The *haugsvarmr* might be changing the physical connections in the hospital or controlling our perceptions. Not my first suspect, though.'

'No?'

'More likely, the hospital is working in its aspect as a prison. The trap's sprung, so now it won't let the rider out. Or us. Or anyone. It's folded in on itself. There won't be a way out.'

There was a rushing sound, and a searing anger that wasn't mine washed over me. The others staggered under it too. And then just as suddenly, it was gone. Kim was weeping silently, but her expression was perfectly focused, and her voice didn't shake when she spoke. It reminded me why I liked her.

'Is there someplace we can hole up and make new plans? A secure area?'

'There's a locked ward in Children's Psych,' Oonishi said.

I felt a little sting of impatience.

'Because being locked in a haunted asylum for insane children is just what we need right now,' I said. 'Have you ever watched a horror movie? I mean, *ever*?'

'If we can get to the chapel, I think I can insulate us from the worst of this,' Ex said. 'For a little while, at least.'

'Beats standing here,' Aubrey said. 'Let's move.'

The nightmare maze of Grace Memorial opened up before us, shifting like something alive. I moved carefully, peeking through the wire-glass windows before I passed through the doors, glancing around corners before I turned them. The others followed behind, quiet and careful, going from closet to closet, hiding in the empty rooms, and scuttling for the stairwells. We were a handful of mice in a box with a thousand cats. We passed by wards of the sick and the dying, their eyes panicky, the alarms of their monitors sounding and being ignored. Twice, a nurse or doctor with glowing blue eyes appeared far down a corridor, head shifting and swiveling as they swam through the air, searching for us. For me.

The new, dreamlike architecture seemed not to have a pattern: a door that should have led to the staff cafeteria opened into a suite of empty examining rooms; the corridor leading to the ER dead-ended with a red exit sign glowing over the bare brick wall; a stairway leading down to the ground floor didn't have doors leading out. And with every turn we made, every new direction we set out in, the sense of the rider's seething rage and our own aching panic threatened to overpower us. If I'd had any other plan, I'd have called the whole thing to a halt. Instead, I pushed on. And then we turned a corner that promised to lead us to Women's Health and found ourselves facing the wood panels and metalwork holy symbols of the chapel. Ex actually whooped and jumped for the door.

He grunted.

'Locked,' he said. 'But under the circumstances, I think God would forgive us for kicking it in.'

'Relativist,' I said. Ex looked at me, his eyes wide with surprise, and then he laughed.

'Wait,' Chogyi Jake said, stepping forward.

He looked at the lock and the door frame, shaking his head like a car mechanic surveying an unfamiliar engine. He took out his wallet, plucked the American Express black card out, and bent it neatly back and forth on its longer axis. The plastic turned white and broke, leaving a thin, slightly hooked length that he slid between the frame and the door. He rattled the handle for about ten seconds while the rest of us watched. The door swung open.

'Misspent youth,' he said with a small smile, and I followed him in.

The interior of the chapel was simple, spare, and beautiful. Four rows of pews stood at respectful angles along a center aisle. A carefully nondenominational altar commanded the front, unadorned and a little blocky. A discreet door off to one side was marked as the chaplain's office. The ghost of incense touched the air, and the lights were warm and soft, without the sickly look the hallways had taken on. The whole place had a feeling of peace and calm and welcoming that didn't seem to belong to the hospital-prison I'd just walked out of. Ex closed the door behind us, locking it again, then began walking through the room, his fingertips on the walls, murmuring to himself or possibly God. I couldn't tell if his cantrips were making a difference or if it was just the sound of his voice and the calm of the architecture easing me back from the edge of panic. I walked down the center aisle, turned, and sat. The altar felt solid and sure against my back.

'Okay,' I said. 'What are we looking at?'

'The first two protections have failed,' Chogyi Jake said. He sounded tired. 'The *haugsvarmr* is still bound by the hospital, but it has much more freedom than it did before. More resources both in terms of people it can manipulate and objects it can control.'

'And when people try to come here?' I said. 'Come to work, come to visit family?'

'I don't think they'll be able to,' Chogyi Jake said. 'Grace is a different place now. It's not related to the world the way it was yesterday. If this goes on for very long at all, people will notice.'

'What's it going to look like from the outside?' I asked.

'The physical form of this hospital will still be there,' he said, 'but I don't think anyone will be able to get in, though it seems likely they'd try.'

'What about us? Can we get out?'

'Possibly,' he said. 'We can find a place that we know is near an exit in the hospital's usual configuration and then try to damp down the effects of the prison spells.'

'Calling Malkuth,' Kim said. 'Like in Denver.'

'Does that let the rider out too?' I asked.

'Possibly,' Chogyi Jake said. 'And if not immediately, it at least lessens the time during which the containment works. It's a rider. After being locked away for decades, it may still be weak but it will get stronger. The prison aspect is a network of spells worked into the hospital itself. Very complex, very powerful, but only spells. They will degrade with time.'

'And then it still gets out,' I said.

'It does.'

I leaned back, my head thudding against the altar. Ex finished his circuit of the room and came to perch on the back of a pew, his feet on the seat. In his black shirt and pants, pale hair pulled back, he looked like an eagle. Kim and Aubrey sat together in the pew across from him. They weren't quite touching, but they were closer than they would have been, I thought, if Aubrey and I hadn't talked. Kim still didn't know. It didn't seem like the moment to get into that. Oonishi paced at the back of the room, looking like a wax dummy of himself brought to life. Only Chogyi Jake sat on a front bench, his hands clasped before him.

'Worst case,' I said. 'What happens if it breaks free?'

Ex shrugged.

'It escapes, takes over a complex social structure. Political party, religious community, city. Maybe a country. Hard to say. Once it's in, it uses its power to gain more control. Maybe go back to the Ahnenerbe's plan. Yoke other riders either with mutual pacts or bindings fueled by death magic. So, five, ten years, you're looking at a wave of American genocide, massive spiritual possession, and probably a rider with nuclear launch codes,' he said.

I said something vulgar.

'Well,' he said. 'You said worst case. Being difficult to see magically gives you some protection, but you can't count on it. If the rider has access to a thousand pairs of human eyes, it will find us. And as soon as it's sure it can't find a way to squirm out past being confined, that's likely to be on its agenda.'

'Can it take control of *us*?' Aubrey asked.

'It already got me once,' Kim said. 'And that was before it got out if its grave.'

'If it can find us, it probably will,' Ex said.

'But we can break that,' I said. 'Just a little off-the-cuff cantrip did it before. Any of us should be able to do that, right? I mean, it's not like they're exactly being ridden. It doesn't take an exorcism to pop them free.'

'That was before,' Ex said. 'It'll be harder now. If it finds us and takes someone over, we have to be prepared to incapacitate whoever got the fuzzy end of the lollipop.'

The silence didn't last more than a few seconds, but it was soaked with dread. I hadn't even considered that Aubrey or Kim or Chogyi Jake might start glowing blue

254

about the eyes and come after me. I should have. If I'd been in the rider's place, it's what I'd have done.

'Let me see what I can do,' Ex said. 'The ward I've got up should slow it down a little, but maybe there's something I can use to give us some cover when we go back out.'

'I'm not going out there,' Oonishi said. 'Are you insane? If we're safer in here and we can't get out of the hospital, why the hell would we set foot out that door? The police are going to get here.'

'They will,' Chogyi Jake said.

'Then I say we stay right where we are and wait for the rescue workers,' Oonishi said. He had his arms folded across his chest like an angry five-year-old. I could almost smell the fear underneath his anger.

'They will try to free the people trapped inside,' Chogyi Jake said, and even the slight reservation in his voice told me the rest. *They may do more harm than good.*

'Ex?' I said. 'See what you can find. More protection's better than less. What about binding it? We're in here, we have some resources. Have we got enough to lock it back up?'

'It would be tricky, but maybe,' Ex said as he walked past me to the chaplain's office door. 'We'd need four people for the circle. And the coffin, assuming it's still intact. If we could get to the site where the coffin is, we might be able to consecrate it again. There was a fairly detailed description of the rite in Eric's papers.'

'I read that too,' Aubrey said. 'There are some sketchy parts, but we could probably fill them in. There was a passage about the Mark of Edjidan that would be a problem.'

'That was just the initial invocation,' Chogyi Jake said. 'With the rider trapped in the hospital, we might not need that layer at all. We could go directly to—'

'Who goes in the coffin?' Kim said. 'It's an interment. Someone would have to be buried with the rider.'

I'd forgotten that. We all had. Between the uncanny feeling of being trapped in Grace with the *haugsvarmr* and the natural urge to jump at any ray of hope, I'd been running five steps ahead and not paying attention to my assumptions. I lay my head back against the altar and let my eyes close for a moment. I had to stop this. If I hadn't bulled ahead without thinking things through, I wouldn't have been at Grace in the first place. Or at least I'd have had a babysitter on David Souder, and the rider would still be down in the dark where it belonged. Or if Aubrey, stuck in his confusion and hurt, hadn't bailed instead of talking things out with me and Kim. Or if Kim hadn't called us there in the first place. Or if Eric hadn't put the whole damn thing into motion years ago . . .

There was too much blame to go around, too long a chain of circumstance that brought us all here. I couldn't help blaming myself, if only because I wasn't responsible for anybody else's actions in quite the same way. But I had to stop now. I had to slow myself down, think things through, and not spend the thin sliver of time we had chasing after impossibilities.

I opened my eyes and sat forward.

'Okay,' I said. 'So if that's out, what else can we do?'

I looked from face to face, waiting for our eureka moment, the trick that would get us through in one piece. Something deep in the hospital bumped and shuddered like a submarine striking a reef. The light from the office behind me spilled out into the room. I heard Ex opening and closing drawers. Oonishi sat down at the pew farthest from me.

Chogyi Jake lifted his head. His eyes were calm and bright. His smile could have meant anything.

'I can go in,' he said. 'I will be the sacrifice.'

21

'No,' I said. 'Not going to happen. Find another way.'

My mouth had the penny-taste of fear. Aubrey's eyes went wide, and his lips thin and tight. The light behind me dimmed, Ex standing in the office doorway. Kim looked down. In context of the chapel, she might almost have been praying.

'There are no other bindings,' Chogyi Jake said. 'And even if there were, there isn't time.'

'It's not an option,' I said. 'Think of something else.'

'There must be . . .' Aubrey began.

Chogyi Jake turned up his hands, as if offering me something.

'We have very little time,' Chogyi Jake said. 'We have very little to work with, and no way to safely get other supplies. If we fail, many, many people will die. The longer we wait, the more likely that the rider will find us and kill us all. It's the right thing.'

'You're talking about dying. We're not doing that. We're just *not*.'

Chogyi Jake only lifted his eyebrows a little. *Then what?* We had to stop the rider before it broke out. We didn't have any other way to bind it. The stakes were as high as I could imagine. If the *haugsvarmr* got out and took over, one man's death was going to look like pretty small beer. But this was Chogyi Jake. This one was mine, and the world couldn't have him.

Only it wasn't really my call.

'If not me, who?' he said. He meant *We've all lost families and lovers and things that were precious to us, and we've all survived.* He meant *You can lose me.*

I felt like I was looking down from a sickening height. Vertigo, nausea, shock. Over my shoulder, Ex looked gray. His hand was on the door frame as if he needed it to stay standing. His gaze flickered down to mine, and I saw that all the same thoughts were running behind his eyes. And the same conclusions too.

'I can go,' Ex said. 'You stay out, and I'll go in.'

'And who performs the interment?' Chogyi Jake asked. 'You have the most experience with exorcism, and that's close to what we're doing here. You need to be on the outside, not trying to sacrifice yourself to save me. This is my own choice. Of all of us, you should respect that.'

The words seemed to have some reference I didn't understand, because Ex only hesitated, nodded, and stepped back into the office. I stood up, and the chapel seemed odd. I could see everything: the wood grain in the pews and walls, the subtle pattern in the carpet, the fold of cloth where Aubrey's collar wasn't quite down. It was the slow moment of perfect clarity in the middle of the car wreck; it was time going slow because my mind was running too fast.

I can't do this, I thought. And then, I have to do this.

'We'll go down,' I said. 'To where the coffin was. We might not even be able to. If it's broken or something.'

'That's fair,' Chogyi Jake said, standing up, and I realized I'd just tacitly agreed that if it could be done, we'd do it. I noticed he was only an inch or two taller than me. I'd always imagined him as bigger than that. A tiny dark mole perched at his collarbone. Surely I'd noticed that before. Sometime in the last year, I must have seen it the way I was seeing it now. I felt like someone was pressing a balled fist up under my rib cage. I couldn't afford to think about what that meant. This wasn't the time to pay attention to my feelings. Not if I was going to keep functioning.

Ex came out of the office with a pile of small objects in his hand, little origami pockets made from printer paper. Words in a script I couldn't read marked the center of each one, and something crackled against my palm as he pressed one into my hand. He closed his eyes, his fingers wrapping mine, and I felt a surge of warmth and energy from him. Magic. A little cantrip. When he opened his eyes, he looked tired and ill. And determined.

'Wear it against your skin,' he said. 'It'll make it harder for the rider to take you once we're outside the chapel.'

I nodded, and he moved on to the others. A little improvised talisman. The kind of thing we'd played at in school, writing the name of the boy we wanted to like us in the form of a cross so that God would notice it. We were storming Normandy Beach with BB guns and bottle rockets. We were doomed. I took the little cantrip and tucked it into the band of my jeans where my belt would keep it pressed against me. The others were doing things that were very much the same. Except for Oonishi.

'I'm not going out there,' he said. 'I don't know anything about this crap. I meant what I said. I'm staying here.'

Rage boiled up in me, raw and vicious and ready to kill out of hand. He had brought us here. All of it was his fault as much as anyone's. And now he wanted to step back from it and let everyone else suffer while he stayed safe. Well, screw that. We could tie him up, carry him down, and put him in the coffin. It would serve the bastard right and save Chogyi Jake besides. Aubrey pretended to cough. Oonishi looked at him, and then at me, and then flinched back.

Yes, I thought. I could do that. I could kill him. I could kill an innocent man because he was too much a coward to face down a rider. I wondered if that was what Eric would have done.

'Leave him,' I said. The contempt in my voice could have stripped paint. 'Let's go.'

Walking back into Grace felt like stepping into a septic tank. The air didn't have a smell to it besides the usual industrial freshener and the hint of rain still falling in some other world, but it felt filthy. The lights were dim and unsteady. Something huge rumbled far above us. Thunder or a collapsing girder. Or the rider's unreal fists beating at the physical walls of its prison. Its presence lay over us, pressing down. Smothering. I dreaded the moment it turned its attention toward me.

'Keep to the middle of the building,' Ex said. 'It's the part that should have changed the least. If we can get underground, it may not have changed much at all. No reason to switch the physical configuration if there's not a physical exit, right?'

'Fine,' I said. I wanted him to quit talking. I wanted it all over, quick before I could think about it too much.

We fell into a pattern; I scouted ahead, Ex following close, Aubrey and Kim behind him, then Chogyi Jake as rear guard. We turned a corner into a wide hallway. A gurney lay on top of an IV drip stand. A widening pool of blood and fluid meant that someone had been in it before it fell. A dark-skinned woman in a doctor's white lab coat and a thick-shouldered man with a gray-blond crew cut stepped out of a doorway, watching us all pass. Their eyes were wide and uncomprehending, but they didn't glow.

'It's all right,' I told them. 'We're taking care of it.'

'What is this?' the doctor asked, tears in her voice if not her eyes. She had a beautiful accent. Indian, maybe.

'It's the devil,' I said. 'But we're taking care of it.'

At the end of the hall, Ex stopped at a set of metal doors with a thin window in the side like something from a high school or low-security prison. A black plastic card reader was set into the wall level with the doorknob, glowering out with a single baleful red light. I could see a narrow stairway through the glass.

'Okay,' Ex said. 'If I'm right, this will get us down to the first subbasement. We'll need to go back toward the east to get down past that.'

His explanations were starting to annoy me, and I almost said so when my cell went off, Uncle Eric telling me from my pack that I had a call. Apparently the binding in the fifties hadn't taken blocking cell traffic into account. I scrabbled for it. I knew the incoming number.

'What?' I said.

'Jayné?' David Souder said. His voice was shaking. 'I'm in trouble. I think I'm in real trouble.'

'Where are you?'

'The hospital,' he said. 'Grace Memorial. I was an idiot. I didn't listen to you. I went back, and I thought I was saving Grandpa Del, but the thing that came out of that box . . . it was evil. I don't even know what it was. I ran. I just ran. I didn't even remember that I had a phone on me until just now. I usually leave it at work, and—'

'The hospital's all changed shape,' I said. I sounded bored and put-upon. I sounded bitchy. I didn't care. 'You're trapped. You can't get out.'

'And it's free,' David said. 'I can still feel it a little. It's so *angry*.'

'Just stay where you are,' I said. 'I'm in the hospital too. We're going down to put the rider back where it belongs.'

'You're here?'

'I'm here,' I said.

'Where?' he said. 'I think I'm on the fifth floor. Maybe the third. I don't know. But I can get to you. I can—'

'Stay where you are! Do you understand me? Don't move. Go find a chair and just *sit* in it!' I was shouting now. Screaming into the phone. I was losing it. I didn't care about that either.

The line was silent for three or four seconds. When

David spoke again, he sounded like he'd stepped back a few feet.

'Right,' he said. 'Got it.'

I dropped the connection and stuffed my phone back into the pack. The others were looking at me. Ex and Aubrey seemed shocked. Chogyi Jake, sympathetic. Kim turned away and wouldn't meet my eyes. An inhumanly high-pitched scream came from somewhere behind us, like a bat being pressed to death, then stopped with a loud, electrical pop.

'We waiting for something?' I asked.

Kim swiped her card through the reader. The red glow turned green. We headed underground. Our footsteps echoed in the stairwell, and no one spoke. Each small, cramped flight brought us closer to the fallout shelter and the civil defense ward, and I walked down the steps like I was in a bad dream. I didn't want to go, but I was going. I'd always thought of horror as the thing from the movies, the scary monster that jumps out from dark corners. I'd been wrong. Horror is doing something terrible because you have to. Killing your best friend, for instance. I kept walking, kept pressing myself forward. If I stopped, I didn't think I'd be able to start again. I couldn't stand to look back at Chogyi Jake—his graceful walk, the smile that always waited just at the edge of his mouth, the glitter of joy and amusement in his eyes. Even now, they were there. Muted, maybe. Dimmed. The idea that I would lose him here, tonight, was literally inconceivable; my mind kept skittering off it, defeated. He was so alive, so sure of himself.

We'd go home after this, back to the condo, and he'd make green tea, the way he always had. He'd gently call me on my bullshit. I couldn't imagine any other outcome.

Breaking up with Aubrey had been easy compared to this. It had been right. I'd been prepared, sure of myself, and in control. And anyway, he was just going back to his ex-wife. I was letting Aubrey go. He wasn't dying.

I was going to *kill* Chogyi Jake.

Or maybe it wouldn't work; maybe we'd get lucky and the coffin would have been blown to slivers. Maybe the ground itself would refuse to take the rider again. Chogyi Jake would be spared, and then . . .

And then.

When we reached the end of the last flight, I looked out the door. I'd expected it to be like places we'd been before, all storage and ducts and laundry services, but the subbasement looked a lot like the upper floors. Hallways twisted in nearly organic curves, the walls studded with signs directing us to Medical Records, Nuclear Medicine, Oncology, Pathology, or Facilities Management. The closed doors wore warnings against radiation and biohazards and intrusion by unauthorized personnel, along with the occasional taped-up Dilbert cartoon. Everything told us where we should go and where not to, the architecture itself pushing us like cattle in a slaughterhouse run. Just by looking, I couldn't tell if the magic affecting the rest of the building had warped the nature of the spaces here, or if they'd always been like this.

'We should be okay,' Kim said. 'There aren't any patient

care units down here. They try to keep the beds up where there's some sunlight.'

I nodded. Ex set off down one corridor as if he knew where he was going. I followed. I didn't notice particularly that Chogyi Jake had come to walk at my side. I didn't know how he could radiate calm, but he did. I looked over at him, then away. I heard him take in a long, slow breath and then let it out. In anyone else, it would have been a sigh. From him, it was just an invitation to breathe with him. I found myself walking in step, our feet swinging in the same arcs, our arms shifting like we were twins. And some part of the peace he carried with him began to seep through my anguish and despair. I wanted to reach out, put my arm around him, rest my head on his shoulder, and beg him not to do this thing. I didn't. I just tried to enjoy the walking.

I was so involved in myself, I didn't see the trap until we were in it.

The waiting area outside Nuclear Medicine looked like it had been lifted out of an airport. Rows of plastic-upholstered seats joined together at the hips stared at a dead television screen. An intake desk lurked behind a set of vertical security bars, rolled down for the night like it was a street-front shop in the bad part of town. Everything smelled like carpet shampoo. Just beyond, a set of double doors in fake blond wood paneling warned that people with pacemakers should remain outside. Ex was walking in the front of the group, and so he was the first to stop when the door swung open.

Five men came out toward us. Two wore the scrubs and lanyard ID cards of nurses, two had the cop-reminiscent uniforms of security guards, and one—a huge man with full-body tattoos, a shaved head, and easily a dozen stitches in his scalp—was in the breezy gown of a patient. Their eyes glowed cold blue-white, their clothing and hair floated. In the waiting room, the television stuttered and came on, the images a sickening montage that I'd seen before. Slaughter and brutality and the joy of the killing mob. The walls had changed. Instead of the carefully soothing paint and bright posters, they were bare concrete, stained by water and blood and time.

'Did you think I wouldn't find you?' all five men asked at once. 'Did you think you could hide? I've got you in my guts.'

I looked back over my shoulder. If we could run . . . Six other people—four men and two women—were behind us. Their eyes glowed too. One of the security guards drew his pistol.

'You are in one flesh, slave girl. I have come to take it from you and eat what comes out: you and her and all the others you travel with.' The voice was a chorus, but among the various voices, there was something else. Something more. The sweet, silky voice of the man from my dream with his hat and his old-fashioned suit. His voice grew out of all the others put together, and the effect made my skin crawl.

The little pocket of paper against my skin flared painfully, and I saw the others—Chogyi Jake, Ex, Aubrey,

Kim—flinch at the same moment I did. The glowing-eyed mob grunted in frustration, and the guard raised his gun. Years of action flicks had trained me to expect a deep, authoritative boom, but the report was small and dry as a firecracker. I heard the bullet hiss past me, but I was already in motion, my body sprinting forward with a scream that tore the air. The other guard drew his own gun, and the three unarmed men moved toward me like blockers on a football field. Someone behind me screamed, but I couldn't look back. Another pistol report came, and I rolled my weight, twisting my body and pushing my fist and qi together into one of the nurses' chests. I felt his ribs give way, but the other two were on me, their weight dragging me down.

The last time, when the rider had still been trapped, the mob had been made from men and women. Rage-crazed, yes, but only normal people. Now I felt the power of the rider surging through the hands of its tools, burning cold and implacable as hate. I was on my knees, arms twisted back and locked. If I tried to rise up, my elbows would break. Behind me, Kim screamed, and Chogyi Jake moaned. The two security guards stepped close, the paired pistols aiming at my head. I pressed out my qi in a scream. I might as well have kept silent.

Something loud happened, and for half a second I thought they'd shot me. The guard standing to my left crumpled, black blood spilling down his legs, and his eyes flickering white to blue to black. The guard standing to my right whirled just as the explosion came again. He went

down in a heap. A new voice rang out in the hallway, familiar and unexpected and obvious.

'I've got enough ammunition to take down every one
you put up, y'bastard!' David Souder yelled. 'I don't want
to, but push me and you know I will.' He racked another
round in his shotgun and stepped forward. Resting the
barrel on the shoulder of the shaved-headed patient who
had my right arm in a lock.

'You let them go or I will,' he said.

The room was silent. David's eyes were bright and glassy
and brimming with a fear that I recognized. He didn't
know whether he was bluffing either. I took two deep, fast
breaths, gathering my will into a ball of invisible power,
and pressed it out through my right hand. I could feel the
rider inside the patient's flesh, a cold pressure pushing back
at me.

'Kill them, then,' the mob said at once, and each of them
smiled. David's face went pale.

'Let go,' I said, and the man holding me shuddered. The
eerie glow went out of his eyes and he dropped my hand,
stumbling back.

'What the hell, man,' he said, his hands out toward
David's shotgun as if his fingers would stop the round.
'What the *hell*?'

I felt a short rush of pleasure. I could still break the rider's
hold on these people the way I had with Kim that first time. I
could take back what it had stolen. It wasn't strong enough to
keep them. Not yet.

The television screamed in frustration, then popped,

scattering sparks like a firework. The pressure on my other arm faltered, and I pulled myself free. Three men lay at my feet. The two security guards; one bleeding badly from the side, the other curled up in a fetal ball in a spreading pool of blood. The nurse I'd punched was fighting hard to draw breath, a white foam at the corner of his mouth. Their eyes were human. Their pain was human. When I looked back over my shoulder, the glow had gone from the back rank of the mob too. And the walls were painted again. The rider's influence had been withdrawn. Kim had blood on her mouth. Chogyi Jake was on his hands and knees, standing up slowly. The woman who'd been kicking him stepped forward to help him up.

'We need to get these three to the ER,' I said. 'Ex, can you—'

'Jayné,' Aubrey said. 'We have to go.'

I pointed to the fallen security guards.

'They've been shotgunned,' I yelled. 'They could die!'

'They could,' Ex said, coming toward me. 'But we have someplace we need to be, and the rider's getting reinforcements.'

I looked around, a sense of powerlessness washing through me. Chogyi Jake looked stunned, Ex grim. Aubrey and Kim stood with their backs together, unconsciously preparing for another wave of attacks. I turned to the shaved-headed man, pointing a finger at his chest.

'You,' I said. 'Get them help. You understand? You get them help, or I will track you down and finish the job!'

'Yeah, all right, lady,' the man said. He had a low growl

of a voice, a bear that had been punched in the throat too many times. 'Whatever you say.'

I turned to David.

'You just can't follow simple directions, can you?' I said.

'Apparently not,' he said. His voice was shaky, his face pale. Chances were good he'd just killed two men. The first time I'd seen anyone killed, I couldn't stop vomiting. He was holding together better than that, at least.

'Okay, then,' I said. 'Come with us.'

I couldn't fight the rider if every swing I took hurt someone innocent. I couldn't stand against the Beast Rahab without becoming a little bit like it. The good guys were the ones who protected the innocent, who stood on principle, who thought that failing in a just cause was better than championing a moral compromise. And it turned out that wasn't me.

I was the lesser evil.

22

One of the first cantrips I'd learned was how to bring my qi up to my eyes, brushing aside all illusion and sharpening my sight. My head ached from it now. The hospital around us seethed with malice. We had navigated the second subbasement without another encounter with the rider's victims, but at the cost of moving slowly through longer, harder routes. Ex had brought us to dead ends twice now, forcing us back along our path. The frustration of being lost in the maze made me want to scream. The fear that another ambush might be around the next corner. I'd given my paper talisman to David on the theory that the wards and protections Eric had put on me would give me some cover, and I didn't want the guy with the shotgun getting all glowy around the eyelids.

I wasn't the only nervous one.

'But how did you find us?' Ex said.

'I don't know,' David said. 'I mean, I knew you were going back to the place. With the coffin. I just started going there too, and then . . .'

'There are choke points,' Aubrey said. 'Any complex route is going to have places where the number of possible paths narrows down and places where it opens up again. The rider knew that too.'

'The rider headed us off at the pass?' Ex said.

'It could be at all the passes,' Kim said. 'All of them at once. And the chances are always pretty good of running into someone when you're going to the same place.'

Only Chogyi Jake didn't talk. Since the fight, his face had grayed, and he kept a hand pressed to his belly. I knew he was hurt and hurting. That I couldn't do anything about it only added to my frustration.

'But if there's a connection,' Ex said. 'If David and the rider are still in communication somehow—'

'Then every hallway between us and that coffin would be standing-room only with people trying to kill us,' I said. 'They aren't, so they aren't. Let it go.'

It took almost an hour, scuttling like rats, darting from shadow to shadow, to reach the thick steel doors with the faded trefoil on them. Fallout Shelter. The remnant of the good old days when the Russians were going to drop nukes on us at any moment and the worst thing you could be was a commie. It wasn't even my parents' generation. These were my grandparents' nightmares in fossil form, concrete and steel to keep what happened in Nagasaki and Hiroshima from happening here, built less than a decade after Truman had given the go-ahead to drop the bombs. The lock had been forced, and the air within smelled like burned cheese.

Inside, the shelter was like a dorm room writ large. Narrow bunk platforms on steel frames rose from the floor to the low ceiling. If there had ever been mattresses on them, they were gone now, leaving only a slightly rusted webwork behind. Eight sleepers to a bunk, eight sets of bunks in a row, fifteen rows to the end of the room. Dim lightbulbs glowed in cages hanging from the ceiling. It was submarine-tight, but almost a thousand people could have been packed in here, breathing one another's air as the nuclear slag that had been Chicago cooled four stories above them. Men and women and children, half of them sick or dying, buried alive.

Storage rooms lurked off to the sides. I wondered whether they still had palettes of food there, waiting since before my father was born. We walked through the tomb of the Pharaoh Doris Day, avatar of the 1950s. Dread curdled at the back of my tongue. A stairway at the end of the bunks led down. It was wide enough to carry a gurney down it. A faded sign had a blue circle inscribed with a white triangle and the letters CD—Civil Defense—and a bent arrow pointing down.

'That's where it is,' David said, pointing down the stairs. 'That's where I found it.'

'Okay,' I said, and gestured back at the open steel door. 'What can we do about getting that door closed and locked? I don't know how long this is going to take, but I don't want fifty pissed-off orderlies breaking in on us when the thing figures out what we're doing.'

'I'll see what I can do,' Aubrey said.

'Are there lights down there?' Ex said, squinting down into the gloom.

'There were,' David said. 'They didn't do too well when I broke the concrete, though. I had a lamp and a couple cans of fuel from one of these rooms, though.'

Ex motioned roughly that David should follow him and stalked away toward the storage rooms. Chogyi Jake sat at the top of the stairway, looking down. He was pale and wan. I had the urge to kiss his head, but instead I took out my cell phone and let it complain that it couldn't connect to the satellite. I went down the stairs by the electric candlelight of its display. Kim followed close behind, her footsteps soft and careful.

The ward was in ruins. Smoke clung to the walls like it was afraid to let go. Old boxes—wood, not cardboard—lay shattered on the ground, ancient rolls of yellowed gauze spilling out of the remains. A tangle of metal and wire bore a Profexray placard. Chunks of concrete were piled up among the boxes. A shovel leaned against the wall. The air smelled like overheated metal and fresh clay. I'd expected something richer. More like soil.

'Lot of work,' Kim said.

'He was motivated,' I said.

'And how are you doing?'

I turned and stared at her. In the dim light of my cell phone, she looked like her own ghost. There was no color to her face or hair or clothes. The cut on her lip where the rider's minions had beaten her looked black, the bruise around it gray. Her eyes glowed, but only with reflected light. I didn't know if the flood rising up in me was anger or laughter or raw disbelief.

'Sorry,' she said. 'Stupid question.'

'Yeah, well,' I said, turning away.

'I meant to say I'm sorry. All of this is my fault. I was

drunk and shooting my mouth off. I should have known better.'

'Don't sweat it,' I said stepping forward. The shadows twisted and danced every time I moved. A yawning mouth of earth, a thick pile of pale dirt. Crushed limestone at a guess. And only a couple of feet below the floor of the shattered concrete and twisted rebar, the box. The coffin. Its black lid was off, a collection of scattered bones catching the light; rib and skull, vertebrae and femur. The mortal remains of the architect. Part of me had hoped to see it in splinters, unusable. No such luck. Or maybe it wasn't luck. Maybe the Invisible College had built the coffin to withstand the worst they could imagine. A coffin to last until Judgment Day.

I squatted at the edge of the hole. It was too much work. Even if David had known exactly where to go, exactly how to generate an explosion that would shatter the floor, getting through the steel and concrete rubble would have been the work of days, not hours. The reinforcing steel bars alone would have . . .

I put my hand on one, and it snapped like a twig. The metal was brittle. Fragile. Rotten from being too close to the rider for too many years. I took a chunk of concrete and rubbed it between my fingers, feeling it come apart in my grip. The ward was more than destroyed, it was inflamed. The ground itself had been festering for half a century, rejecting the rider, pushing it out like flesh rejecting a splinter. The thought left me a little nauseated.

'We need to clear the air,' Kim said, and for a few seconds

I thought she meant that the smell of smoke was overpowering. Then I understood.

'We really don't,' I said.

'We're about to get into a very dangerous piece of magic,' Kim said. 'Group work. All of us together. If we're going in fractured and conflicted, it *will* break the circle. You wanted me to forgive you, and I . . . well, I didn't exactly get around to it. So here. You didn't do anything wrong. I don't hold anything that happened against you, and I really, sincerely want you to succeed and be happy. I don't think you need it, but if you still want my forgiveness, you've got it.'

She nodded once, more to herself than to me. She'd gotten through the words. I wondered when she'd started rehearsing them. I held up my hand to her. She hesitated for a moment, then took it. Her fingers were cold and thinner than I expected. I drew her down to sit next to me. Just beneath us, the coffin seemed to suck away the light. *Nomen mihi Legio est, quia multi sumus* shone on its side.

'I broke up with him,' I said.

'This isn't about Aubrey,' she said.

'No, really,' I said. 'I broke up with him. Upstairs. Before the rider even got out.'

'Jayné,' Kim said. Her voice was taking on a tone of real annoyance. 'This isn't. About. Aubrey. Okay?'

'Then what?'

She shook her head, a tiny movement that meant exhaustion and morbid amusement and sadness all at the same time.

'It's about me letting go of all the things that I could have done with my life and didn't,' she said. 'Aubrey's only one entry on that list.'

I nodded. Ex's voice came from above, a bark of pleasure and triumph. At a guess, he'd gotten a lantern working.

'It's very strange, thinking about what happened as rape,' Kim said. I was amazed that she could sound so calm. So clinical. 'I mean, I understand that it was. No consent means no consent, and it explains . . . how it felt. Not knowing that until years after the fact makes it strange. I wonder if it would have been easier if I'd been aware of it at the time.'

'You think?'

'I don't know,' she said. 'But it helps everything that came after it make sense. I had nightmares for years. I'd wake up convinced there was someone in the apartment. A man who was going to . . . Anyway, I didn't put that together with Eric until now. And now, it seems obvious.'

'I'm sorry for what he did to you,' I said. 'Not repentant. Just . . . sorry.'

'That's more than enough,' Kim said. 'That's fine.'

The rage in my heart was starting to flutter, the fire going out. I looked down at the coffin. The pale light glittered off the black surface. The bones seemed alien and unreal. They had more in common with rock than with human flesh and frailty. For a second, I felt the swelling, oceanic sorrow behind my own anger. A presentiment of what was going to come.

'I don't know if I can do this,' I said.

'Chogyi Jake, you mean?'

I've got the boy, boy, boy, boy down in the dark. Down in the dark he'll stay.

'How long do you think he was alive?' I asked, motioning toward the bones with my chin.

'Not long,' Kim said. 'Hours. Not more than a day, even with the rider. You can see where they carved sigils all along the inside. There?'

I did see them, now that she pointed them out. Hairline swirls and strokes that covered the inside of the coffin so thickly they became a texture. I imagined Declan Souder's hands clawing at those sigils in the darkness, screaming as the air grew thicker and closer and the rider raged, tearing through his mind. I wondered if he'd known, even as he designed the prison, that he'd end here, deep beneath it. I suspected that he had.

'I'm not going to be okay after this,' I said.

'I know.'

'Do we have to do it?'

'Yes, dear,' Kim said. 'We do.'

The lock on the main door to the shelter was bent past repair, but Aubrey had managed a decent barricade, two of the bunks turned on their sides and stacked one on top of the other, then the spaces where bodies would have slept filled with boxes and crates, the overall mass growing past the point where the door could be forced. Hopefully. Ex and David had encountered less luck.

'We have lights,' Ex said. 'The interment box is solid. It

barely needed anything. And I salvaged enough straight nails from those boxes, I'm fairly sure we can seal the coffin at all the critical points.'

'That sounds good,' I said.

'But we don't have a hammer.'

'What about a chunk of the concrete from down there?' David said. 'There were some pretty decent-sized bits.'

'Check,' I said, 'but be careful. A lot of it's crumbling. It might crack the cement instead of driving the nail.'

Ex shook his head, but he said, 'I'll look.'

'There's an old X-ray machine down there too,' I said. 'It might have something heavy enough to use. A bar or something.'

Below us, Aubrey and Kim were clearing debris away from the bared earth so that we could stand at the cardinal points: Kim to the east, Aubrey to the north, Ex to the west, and I'd take south. Chogyi Jake would be in the middle, with David standing guard to see that nothing interrupted. I could hear their voices coming up the stairway. Chogyi Jake was still sitting at the head of the stairs, his eyes closed, his head resting against the handrail's pole. He looked pale and sick and still, but his rib cage worked in hard, sudden bursts. Some meditation I'd never been taught. Something for warriors, maybe. For someone preparing to die.

I couldn't imagine what was going on in his head, so I tried not to think about it. It would only wind up with me going over, intruding, talking to him. If I thought I had anything that might comfort him, I'd have done it, but I only would have been trying to make him comfort me. David looked from him to me and then down.

'What else can I do?' he asked.

'Nothing,' I said. 'We'll start soon. It'll be over.'

'Yeah,' he said. 'It's almost six o'clock.'

'Long night.'

'They're coming in. Up there, the first bunch of people are probably coming in,' he said. 'Nurses and doctors. The guys who work the coffee bars.'

'Probably are.'

'This is going to . . . I mean, this is going to blow things open,' he said. 'Spirits. Possession. Magic. The whole thing.'

'No, it won't,' I said. 'They're going to show up. It'll be weird. Then we'll lock that bastard thing back down, and it'll go away. At most, it'll make the *Fortean Times*. The world isn't going to know what happened here, and it isn't going to care.'

David was quiet for a minute.

'What if it gets out?' he said.

I thought of Kim and Eric, the magic he'd used to wreck her life.

'They won't know it then either,' I said. 'It's just one of those secrets that keeps itself. Right up until you're in the middle of it.'

'He knew, though. Grandpa Del knew.'

'He did.'

'I screwed up his life's work.'

'Well, it's not like he told you to be careful. And really, even if he had, what would you have done?'

David squinted down toward the stairway. His wide face tensed and relaxed, and tensed again.

'Seriously,' I said. 'If he'd taken you aside when you were a kid or left you a letter or something. Told you that there were spirits from outside the world, and that he'd used his talents and abilities to lock one of the biggest and nastiest up by getting buried alive under a hospital, do you think you'd have been better prepared? Or would it just have been more evidence for a genetic component for your breakdown?'

'Yeah, probably that last one,' he said. 'A secret that keeps itself, eh?'

'I had to have proof too. When I found out? I got my clock cleaned by a *haugtrold* that had taken over this cop's body. Put the original guy into his girlfriend's dog.'

'Really?'

Despite everything, his voice had a sense of amazement. Wonder. Had I been like that? Awed by the truth behind the world. Overwhelmed by the sudden unveiling of a bright, dangerous version of everything that had been walking beside me the whole time. I probably had, but I couldn't quite imagine it now. I wondered what he'd make of it if I told him all my stories: the Invisible College in Denver. Carrefour in New Orleans. Midian Clark, vampire chef. The thing with that guy in London. I'd almost forgotten that one myself. I could imagine mistaking it for glamorous.

And, I realized, that was how I'd seen Eric. He'd known more. He'd done more. And so I'd made him into the hero of my own private comic book. Eric Heller, gentleman adventurer. Force for good. Decent human being. It hadn't had anything to do with the real man.

'Jayné.'

I looked up. Aubrey was on the stairs, hidden from the waist down by the drop. His hair was tousled from his work. He looked exhausted. We'd all been up for too long.

'We ready?' I asked.

'Ex says it's time,' he said.

'I'll hold the fort up here,' David said, hefting his shot-gun. In his wide hands, it looked almost small.

I walked to Chogyi Jake, kneeling by his side for what I knew might be the last time. His eyes were still closed, lost in meditation. His face was pale, and his breath quick and shallow.

'Hey, guy,' I said softly. 'You ready to do this thing?'

He didn't answer. I put a hand on his shoulder, surprised by how cool his skin felt.

'Hey. Chogyi. It's time. Are you—'

His body shifted, slouched, and spilled back onto the ground. His head made a hollow sound when it hit the floor. He didn't try to catch himself. I wasn't aware of screaming, but Aubrey, Kim, Ex, and David all appeared at my side. Aubrey gently moved me, kneeling by Chogyi Jake's body, pressing fingers to his neck.

'That's not good,' he said.

'What's the matter?' Ex asked. He sounded as much annoyed as concerned.

'Those guys back in the subbasement? They kicked him

harder than I thought,' Aubrey said. 'He's in shock. I think that means internal bleeding. I don't know how long he's been unconscious.'

'Well, get his legs up,' Kim said.

'But the ceremony,' I said. 'The spell. Can we still . . . ?'

'No,' Ex said. 'No, we have a problem.'

23

We stood over the body, looking at one another. Chogyi Jake lay on the floor, bleeding to death without spilling a drop, and I didn't know if I was relieved or frightened. Somewhere far above us, in a different world, the sky over Lake Michigan would be a robin's egg blue. The sun minutes from pouring down over the city. We were trapped in the dark. Weariness dragged at all their faces. It probably dragged at mine too. I wanted nothing more than to sleep for a day and a half and wake up to find out it had all been a bad dream. I couldn't go on. I went on.

'Can we revive him?' I asked. 'Just to get through the binding.'

'I don't know,' Aubrey said. 'If we had . . . smelling salts? Or something to up his blood pressure?'

'Kim?' I asked.

She shook her head.

'Not an MD,' she said. 'All I know is we put his legs up, get a blanket over him, and get him to the ER.'

He might almost have been sleeping, except that his breath was so fast and so shallow. Now that he was lying flat, I thought there was a little more color in his face. I had almost talked myself into believing I could stand to watch him die if there was a reason. If something came out of it. This? I couldn't do it.

'Okay,' I said. 'We have to get him back upstairs.'

'No,' Ex said. 'We have to go on without him. If we go back, it's going to find us, and then it's over. As long as we're in here, there's a chance.'

'What chance?' I said. 'What chance do we have? Because the way it looks from here, we're screwed.'

Kim murmured something too quietly for me to hear. Aubrey, standing at her side, turned to look at her.

'I say we go up and let the thing out,' I went on. 'Break the prison. I know it's a risk, but someone tracked it down and bound it before. We can do that again, but after we get Chogyi Jake to a doctor. After we find a different binding. After—'

'I said I'll do it,' Kim said. 'I'll go in. I'll . . . I'll take his place.'

'You can't,' Aubrey said.

Kim met his gaze. The darkness under her eyes was almost purple. The bruise on her face had darkened, and the cut lip was scabbed black. Her hair was a collection of greasy strings. She gave him a faint, weary smile, and for a moment, she was beautiful.

'It's okay,' she said. 'I can do this.'

If I hadn't known before, the anguish on Aubrey's face would have been enough to show me how much the thought of losing Kim broke him. Even with everything else, I found there was a small part of my heart that ached seeing him feel that strongly for a woman that wasn't me.

'Actually, you can't,' Ex said. 'You know how to channel your will. You've worked puts like this before. This isn't something I can do without experienced people at all four points on the circle.'

He was looking at me. His eyes were blue as gas flame. I could feel him wanting me to understand something, and if I hadn't been up all night, if I hadn't been wrung out four times in the course of a single day, if there had been *any* neurotransmitter left in my brain, I might have gotten it on my own. As it was, I needed a prompt.

'Ah. What exactly did you need this guy to do?' David asked.

I looked at him. Eager, worried, guilty over the part he'd played, and frightened of the beast he'd set loose. He was the only one here without any experience. He was the only one who could take Declan Souder's place. All I had to do was talk him into it. Now. Before Chogyi Jake died.

Lie to him, I thought. Tell him something that puts him in the box. Tell him we need a focus for our energy, that we need someone to hold the bones just right, something. Anything. Just put him in the place and get this done. An emotion I didn't recognize was rushing through me. I felt light. Unmoored. My chest was widening from inside, and it was wrapped around Chogyi Jake and the chance of getting him upstairs. I thought for a moment this was some new kind of panic, and then I recognized it. It was hope. It was relief. As sure as kittens in springtime, I was about to kill David Souder, and I was grateful.

I felt something spiritual give way with an almost

physical click. I knew something in me was broken, that it was going to be broken for a very long time. And I knew I wasn't going to lie to David.

'He was going to go into the coffin,' I said. 'We were going to drive the rider into him, then seal the coffin and bury it again. Put it back where it was before.'

David rocked back on his heels like I'd struck him. His gaze went to each of us in turn. He tightened his grip on the shotgun.

'It was what your grandfather did,' I said. 'It was his life's work. You saw the thing that came out of that hole. You've been living with it in your head for over a year now. You know what it's capable of.'

'You were going to kill him?'

'Bury him alive,' I said. 'It's called an interment binding. And it might be the only chance we have of stopping this thing.'

'But—'

'David,' I said. My voice was soft, but I could hear the steel in it. 'If there were another way, I swear I'd take it. But *you* let this thing out. You're the only one who can put it back. I need you to be as strong as Grandpa Del was. I need you to be as brave.'

He looked at me, his eyes filling with horror and panic.

'Please,' I said. 'We don't have much time.'

'What . . .' He swallowed and tried again. 'What would I need to do?'

'Lie back,' Ex said. 'Close your eyes. We do the rest. But you don't come out alive, and it won't be peaceful.'

David snorted, a deep sound, like a bull facing the toreador. His jaw slid forward a degree and his eyes narrowed.

'You can make this right,' I said. 'We'll *help* you make this right.'

He was quiet for a few seconds that lasted days. When he spoke, his voice belonged to a smaller man.

'Good thing I never had kids,' he said and tried a smile.

'Give me the gun,' I said.

He looked down at his hand like he was surprised to see it there. For a moment, I didn't know what he was going to do. Then he took it by the barrel and held the stock out to me. It was heavier than I'd expected.

'Grandpa Del could do it, right?' he said. 'I can't see myself doing less.'

'Thank you, David,' I said.

He nodded, but he wouldn't meet my gaze. I took his hand, and he let me lead him down into the darkness.

The open coffin lay in its shallow grave, the lid ready at its side. Ex set up the ancient-looking, hissing lanterns around the ruined ward, their filaments glowing a perfect white, too bright to look at. The shadows they cast on the walls didn't flicker. Grandpa Del's bones lay just to one side among the rotten concrete and fragile rebar. Ex murmured words that might have been Latin or something older over his handful of salvaged nails. His improvised hammer was a nine-inch length of galvanized pipe. Aubrey and Kim let bits of pale dirt fall from their hands, creating the circle like they were making a sand drawing. The broken boxes and twisted machinery stood in mute witness as David lowered himself carefully to stand in the coffin. It looked too narrow for him until he lay down to try it. Then it only looked almost too narrow.

He saw me watching him and grinned.

'I'm used to it,' he said. 'My first car was a VW Bug.'

I laughed. Chogyi Jake was at the top of the stairs, still unconscious. Still breathing. We were moving as quickly as we could.

'It's not so bad,' he said. 'Chances are pretty good I'd have killed myself anyway. If you hadn't come, I'd still be back at my place, thinking I was crazy, right?'

'Probably,' I said.

'So at least this way, it's not like nothing good comes out of it, right?'

Tell yourself that, I thought. For ten more minutes, tell yourself this is something besides hellishly unfair.

'You're a good man,' I said.

'Hey. Jayné. Could you do me a favor?'

'Anything.'

He sat up, his arms wrapping his knees. He looked like he was in a rowboat too small to reach the shore.

'Alexis. My ex. Tell her I did something real. Tell her I made a difference.'

There was a history in those words. A boy who'd met a girl, fallen in love or at least in bed. A wedding that was supposed to end with happily ever after and wound up in divorce court instead. Those were the bones of it, but they carried the flesh of a life on them. There had been a first time they'd met, a first kiss, a first fight. Maybe he was thinking right now of the moment when everything might have gone one way but instead fishtailed into another, or of the one thing he'd said that he regretted. The last kiss. The last thing he'd said to her.

All of those details that made it his life, his history, were about to be wiped away.

'I'll tell her,' I said. 'Promise.'

Ex surveyed the circle of dirt, his expression sour. He didn't find anything to object to. I watched David watching him, and I could see the fear in his eyes like fish swimming under ice.

'We should do this soon,' David said. 'Before I chicken out.'

'You won't,' Ex said. 'You're too strong for that. It's going to be okay.'

'I'm going to die,' David said.

'We all are,' Ex said. 'Sooner or later. This just means you'll see God's face before I get to.'

David blinked and managed an amused smile, then twisted in the narrow space, digging at his sock. A moment later, he handed my paper talisman up to Ex.

'Hey, if I'm supposed to get possessed, I probably shouldn't have this, eh?'

Ex's face went grayer. I wondered what would have happened if David hadn't remembered it.

'No, probably not,' Ex said.

'Okay,' Kim said. 'I think we're ready.'

'You should lie down, David,' Ex said.

Slowly, David lay back, folding his arms over his chest. I heard Ex whispering a benediction as he made the sign of the cross in the air. Then the four of us took our places at the cardinal points. Ex began chanting. Kim and Aubrey and I came in one at a time, like kids singing 'Row, Row, Row Your Boat.' The comparison struck me as hilarious, and I had to bring my focus back to the moment before I took out *nos dico vobis* and put in *life is but a dream*.

I couldn't tell if the shuddering was the power of the qi flowing among us, the rider becoming suddenly aware of us, or my own exhausted body. My eyes closed, and I tried to keep my intention tightened down to a single point. The flutter of up-all-night random thoughts was my enemy. I couldn't afford to worry about Chogyi Jake or the guards we'd hurt. I couldn't wonder what Oonishi was doing, or whether Eric had planned to do something like this, or what I was going to do about changing my ringtone. There could only be the words, cycling around all of us.

I became vaguely aware that I could feel the others: Kim and Ex and Aubrey. I knew that Kim's left knee was aching badly. I knew that Ex was suffering a headache that he hadn't mentioned. They were becoming part of my own body, unfamiliar and immediate and close. I'd never been part of a circle like this before, and the intimacy of it was startling. I felt Kim's desperate hope. Aubrey's guilt and confusion and discomfort at his psychic proximity to Kim and me at the same time, and I knew when he felt my amusement, remembering what he'd said about not liking the idea of a menáge à trois. And Ex. His mind was a furnace: powerful, unnerving sexual desire; guilt as black as ink; and a bone-deep resolve that felt like a mother bear ready to kill and die for her cubs. Our minds slid into one another, the barriers between us softening, weeping, being erased in the whirlpool of our combined intention. We reached out for it.

And then we had it.

The rider's howl was inaudible and deep as a well. Its rage raked cold teeth against us, tearing at our minds. It gathered itself and launched a furious assault on the combined mind we had created. I pushed back, or Ex did. Or Kim. It was a distinction without a difference. We shifted, pulling the rider down. I felt the words of the chant roughening in my throat. I wanted to cough, but I didn't dare to. My spine and knees ached, and I was sweating like I'd been put in a fire. It had to go down, into the coffin, into David's waiting flesh. I bared my teeth, forcing out the words. My jaw hurt. The rider didn't move. I felt it floating in the air that was either graveyard-still or hurricane-whipped or both. I knew that if I opened my eyes, it would be there, just like in the dream. Its inhuman fingers brushed against me, grabbing at me, trying to break my concentration. We could not make it move.

And then it slipped. It caught itself almost immediately, but it slipped. I felt the surge of joy from all of us, and our gestalt mind redoubled its effort. The rider threw images at us like stones. Worms crawling through living flesh. Fire-charred bodies. A naked woman stretched upon a cross while a pale man did something unspeakable. The smell of burning hair filled my nostrils. Of burning skin. The smell of the vast, cold ocean, lifeless as a desert, and more hostile. A woman's voice, soft and throaty, offered obscene things and a man's low growl threatened force. Every time it came too close to a weakness, every time one of us recoiled in fear or shame, the others flowed in. The rider could have broken any of us, but together we were more than four fragile, imperfect, wounded people.

Together, we were Legion.

The rider slipped again, and for a moment, David was in the unreal struggle too. I heard him crying out in the old civil defense ward, miles away from me and close enough to touch. He fought, pushing the rider away in mindless panic. I felt him drowning in the filth and ice water; I heard his heels kicking against the bottom of the open casket.

It's all right, we thought to him. This is the worst part. It's almost over.

David's scream was despair and fear. Something in our group mind reached out, and the rider recoiled. I felt David grow calm and his resistance fade. The rider slid into his flesh, unable to find a handhold. The silence was so sudden, it seemed loud. My eyes fluttered open.

The ward looked just the same. The lanterns were still glowing. The ruined boxes and machinery stood where they had been. Tremors shook my body, seeming to start in my belly and grow more violent as they radiated out my arms and legs. Aubrey, across the pit from me, was soaked with sweat. Kim's eyes were still closed, and I didn't need the magic of the ceremony to feel the raw exhaustion in her.

It was too much like my own. Ex only seemed a little more drawn than usual, a little harder. I could still feel my connection to them. I knew that if I pushed my awareness to the back of my mind, I could find my way into them all, and the knowledge was as eerie as it was comforting.

'Not done yet,' Ex said. 'Almost.'

I risked a glance down. David Souder was gone, and something demonic was staring out from him. His eyes glowed a cold blue. The light spilled out his nose. When he opened his mouth, his lips forming threats I could understand but not hear, his mouth was bright, his teeth sharp and glasslike, his tongue tar-black and unnaturally mobile. His fingers had sprouted extra joints. I knew that the man was in there, trapped behind those evil, luminous eyes, but I couldn't see him. All sense of David vanished, and the Beast Rahab, Angel of Shells, was in his place. Its presence still pressed against me like the chill of an opened door in the dead of winter. The sigils and marks that lined the coffin swirled with something that wasn't quite light. The prison was ready. All we had to do was close the door.

'Help me,' Ex said, but not to me.

Aubrey rose to his knees, and together he and Ex lifted the black plank of the coffin lid. Gingerly, they positioned it over the silent, screaming man.

It almost worked.

I couldn't tell which of them slipped, only that the lid twisted, and Ex bent hard, trying to catch it. Kim leaned forward, putting out her hand to steady him. Her leg went out behind, balancing her and scraping a break in the thin line of dirt. I felt the connection to the others vanish. With a shriek, David's spirit-ridden body boiled up out of the coffin, wide, meaty hands batting Ex away like they were slapping a fly. Kim screamed and Aubrey dropped the coffin lid.

The circle was broken, and the beast was loose.

24

I didn't think, didn't consider. I dropped back a few inches behind my eyes, and my body leaped forward, shoulder hitting the rider's side. It was like trying to tackle a wall, but the *haugsvarmr* stumbled. I swung around, driving my elbow in toward the small of its back, but the rider had already moved. It wore David's body like a shawl. I could see the force of its will making the air shimmer, heat waves off a highway, and I noticed again that David was really a very large man. Ex scrambled backward, cursing furiously. Kim and Aubrey stood caught between fleeing and fighting. The rider's hand shot out, grabbing me by the head, lifting me, and tossing me across the room like I weighed about a pound. I landed on my back, the wind knocked out of me.

While I tried to sit up, the rider turned its head, slowly taking each of us in. David's flesh was changing under its influence: the skin taking on a starlit glow, the mouth starting to protrude. I'd seen riders transform their mounts before, the spirit's nature curdling skin and blood and bone. This was no different. When it spoke, its voice was soft, friendly, and genteel. It made my skin crawl.

'So close, daughter-thing,' it said. 'You were so close. Do

you know what I thought? That you'd wrap yourself in the Mark of Forcas and hide until I slipped my leash.'

It laughed, a low and rueful sound. Its eyes shifted across the room where it had thrown me, its gaze skittering off me without quite managing to connect. I felt a stab of profound cold at the small of my back. It still couldn't see me. I tried not to move, afraid that any sound would give me away.

'I looked through every pair of eyes I could find in this piss-pot Carcer, and then I turned away. I thought you were my second problem. And you were doing *this*. It was good. Oh, it was very good. I am all admiration and fear. Trembling,' it said, laughter in its voice. It pulled one leg up from the grave hole and onto the shattered floor. David's jeans shredded when the rider bent its knee. It was getting bigger.

Ex crouched, and the rider turned to fix him with its gaze. It moved so quickly, it seemed like a jump cut made real.

'I know what you've got on those nails, boy,' it said. 'Come close to me with them, and I'll put them through your eyes.'

'Leave him alone,' I said. The rider's attention snapped back to me, homing in on the sound of my voice.

'You care about the meat? She did too.' It stepped up, the concrete crumbling under its weight. 'We don't have to do this, little one. You've fought bravely and well. I respect you. But it's over now. You can see it's over.'

It took a step toward me, and my body moved, curling over until I was on toes and fingertips, tight as a spring.

Aubrey and Kim were on the far side of the grave. He had a length of pipe in his hand: Ex's improvised hammer. Don't be stupid, I thought, trying to press the words through the air and into his brain.

'There are only two ways this ends,' it went on. 'You enter into a pact with me, or I bind you. Ally or slave, daughter-thing. It makes no difference to me.'

It was lying. The difference between pact and binding was the difference between contract law and slavery. If it was offering up a pact with me, it wasn't sure of the fight's outcome. I grabbed onto the thought that there might be some hope, something I could do that would defeat the beast. I didn't know what that was.

The rider took another step toward me. Aubrey handed the pipe to Kim and drew in a deep breath. The rider's head snapped up a degree, and then back toward Aubrey. The glowing eyes went round, and Aubrey's mouth opened wider than I thought possible.

The Oath of the Abyss rang out, Aubrey's soul forged into a weapon and shaking loose from his flesh. The only other time I'd heard it, he'd been saving my life. The rider stumbled, glowing fragments of its flesh skirling out from it like fireflies. It bared its teeth and screamed back, the roar of its voice drowning out even the most powerful magic any of us knew. The walls shook and dust swirled down from the ceiling. In the lamplight, it looked almost like snow.

Aubrey hadn't knocked the rider out, but he had knocked it back. This was my opportunity. Maybe my only one.

I felt myself jump, landing hard on the rider's back. It staggered forward as I wrapped my arm around its huge neck and squeezed. With my ears still ringing, I felt its chuckle more than I heard it. My legs locked onto the thing's back, holding it as close as a lover. Its skin shifted and bumped against me. I tightened my grip and hauled, fighting to cut off its air. If it needed air. My shoulders ached with the effort, and I felt something in me begin to weaken.

This, I thought, was the moment. Chogyi Jake had warned me, it seemed like a lifetime ago, that my protections would fail. And now I thought I felt them starting to go. It felt like despair. Desperately, the small part of me that watched the fighting tried to pull my qi up from my belly and press it out into my arms. It seemed weak and distant, a voice shouting in a windstorm. I closed my eyes, trying again. Not to control my body. The last thing I wanted now was Jayné-the-white-belt to start driving. I only pushed to feed the thing that was happening to me, support the spells and wards.

And the weakness and despair began to fade.

The rider lifted a huge hand. Its skin was black as the void and swimming with points of nauseating light. Its impossible fingers dug into my back.

'You're weak,' I said. 'Your days are gone.'

It tugged at me, trying to rip me free, but I was immovable. Something in its throat made a repulsive crunching sound under my arm, and it started to choke. The rider pulsed, its multiple soul gathering itself to break out of

David's body and flow back into the hospital and out of reach. I wrapped myself around it, making a net with my will. A prison. I was doing alone and on the fly what the four of us had struggled to do together.

I had the feeling it would work.

'I bind you, Daevanam Daeva. I bind you to the blood which you betrayed,' I shouted.

It swung me around, beating me against the walls. I felt the stab of a breaking rib like it was happening to someone else. Something like battle rage had flowed into me, lifting me up, widening me out past the confines of my body. The room around us seemed brighter now, even though there was no light. The rider spun, clawing at my arms and drawing blood. Ex and Kim were there too, beating at it with fists and pipe. Aubrey lay at the graveside, exhausted from his efforts. The rider swung hard, bending at the waist and knocking my head against the wall so hard my vision narrowed. For a moment, I was choking the man from my dream. I could smell the Brylcreem in his hair. He stumbled, falling to one knee. My feet hit the floor, and I took him by his collar and the waistband of his pants, lifting him over my head. Ex and Kim stepped back, their eyes wide and frightened. I took two steps to the edge of the grave and swung the body down hard enough that I was afraid I'd broken the casket. The dark wood held. I raised the lid up in one hand, keeping the other on the rider's chest.

And it was David Souder again. I could feel the rider within him; it hadn't gotten free. It had thrown its horse toward me like a shield. Human eyes looked up at me in horror.

'Wait!' he shouted.

I slammed the lid down.

'The nails,' I said. 'Give me the nails.'

Ex didn't hesitate. Seven long, silvery nails. The coffin lid thumped, David trying to push it open, but with his arms pinned to his sides, he had no leverage. I put the heads of the nails in my mouth like a carpenter.

'Kim!' Ex said. 'The pipe? Where's the pipe?'

I didn't have time. I knelt on the coffin, my weight keeping it in place, and put the first nail at the lid's dark corner. There was a rough hole where the previous one had been. I moved half an inch to the left, set the sharp point down. I gathered my will, drawing the power into my hand until I felt like I was about to catch fire. I screamed and drove my open palm onto the nail head. The metal slid home with a single blow. My palm was bleeding and bright with pain. I didn't care.

'Oh my God,' Kim said. I ignored her. I drove the second nail home. I could feel the coffin grabbing onto the metal and its cantrips, weaving a seal between box and lid that was more than the simple physical connection. After the third nail, David's struggles couldn't even make the coffin shudder.

'Stop,' Ex said. I looked at him, almost understanding the word. It was like something with a cognate in my language. 'Stop it, Jayné. We can drive the rest of them with a hammer. Just stop.'

Like a switch being turned off, the strength left me. Every muscle in my body trembled, and I looked around the room. It was like I was just waking from a nightmare, or just falling into one. I tried to say something, but there were still four nails in my mouth. I took them out, amazed by the blood soaking my hand and sleeve. My right palm looked like hamburger. I began to feel the pain, something huge and far away, but coming close quickly.

Had I done that? Driven nails with my bare hands?

'You beat it,' Kim said, awe in her voice. 'You really beat it. How the *hell* did you—'

'We'll finish it,' Ex said.

'Give me the pipe,' I said.

'We can—'

'Rider's trapped. In there. Get a gurney. Chogyi Jake. ER.'

Ex looked back at the stairs. He'd forgotten. I couldn't blame him, but I didn't have time to argue about it.

'Go,' I said. 'I can finish this.'

'Use a hammer,' Ex said. 'Kim. Clear the barricade. I'll find something to carry him on.'

'Aubrey—' Kim said.

'I'm fine,' Aubrey said. It wasn't true. I could hear the buzz in his voice, the fever, the price of magic. 'I'll be fine. I can help.'

Kim handed me the pipe, and they stumbled up the stairway, Aubrey leaning against her, Ex alone with his shoulders hunched against his own fatigue. The coffin beside me bumped and shuddered. I looked over at the black planes. The ceremony wasn't finished, but it was close. The danger had passed. Only a few ugly last details remained. I lifted the pipe in my bloody hand, picked up a nail. Four more. Just four more.

'Jayné! Stop!' David's screams seemed to come from much farther away than an inch of black-stained wood could account for. 'Please, wait. Something's wrong. It didn't work.'

I set the nail. My hands shook, and the pipe wasn't a great substitute for a real hammer. It took three tries before the metal started biting into the wood.

'It's not in here. Jayné, it's not in here. It got out before you closed the lid.'

I hesitated for a moment, wondering if it was true or a ploy to trick me into freeing it. The lanterns hissed out their steady light. The air didn't carry the oppressive, filthy feeling that it had before. I set the fifth nail and steadied myself. When I brought the pipe down, it only drove the nail about half an inch in, but the rider roared; David's pleading voice turned to a stream of impotent rage and despair. I sat on the coffin to keep it from shifting and spoiling my aim. When the nail was in, the shaking was less violent, the shrieking more muffled.

My hand was slick with blood and every swing of the fake, improvised hammer felt like the nail was going into me. Above me, Ex shouted something, and Kim's voice was a muttering reply. Something crashed, and Ex's voice sounded more pleased. The wheels of an ancient gurney squeaked in protest and then faded. They were getting

Chogyi Jake to help. My friends were leaving me and finding safety. I was alone in the deepest hole of Grace Memorial. Down in the dark, with only the lanterns, the sacrifice, and the beast.

I didn't know when I'd started weeping. Maybe I had been all along. Driving the last nails became a long, slow torture. The pain in my hand was constant now, the flares that came with the blows hardly noticeable through the constant roar of exposed nerves and torn flesh. I didn't have the strength, so I soldiered on with determination instead. I couldn't believe that a few minutes ago I'd done the same job with one bare-handed strike.

The screams and threats floating up from the coffin felt light and powerless as fluff. I went through the punishing steps of my chore almost without noticing them. When the blow sank the last nail, I stopped for a minute. I wanted to collapse, to fall asleep and never wake up. And never dream. I'd been sandblasted, left outside in a desert storm, shocked and abraded until I was clean and pure and skinless. I told myself it would pass. A few days to recover, and I wouldn't be empty. My brain would start working again. I would be able to feel something that didn't hurt. I watched myself crying from a distance, as if the sobs weren't related to me. The coffin still let out muted knocks and thuds, and far, far away, David Souder was screaming. He'd be screaming for the rest of his life. The best I could do now was make sure that wasn't a very long time.

I stumbled up out of the grave, banging my shin against the crumbling concrete edge. I found a roll of gauze and a bandage pack in a yellowed paper seal, sterilized and marked a year before my mother was born. I opened it, pressing the old cotton against the new wounds on my hand. It sucked up the blood hungrily. The gauze held it in place. It felt almost like I had a lace glove. I didn't have the strength to laugh at the incongruity. I hauled myself to the wall. The shovel David had used to dig the coffin out lay on the ground beside Declan Souder's scattered bones.

'Well,' I said to the empty skull, 'we did it. Just like the old days, eh? Evil defeated. Hell of a price, but we paid it. Go us.'

The skull didn't do anything. I hadn't expected it to. After all, it was just a lump of calcium phosphate. It didn't have dreams or hopes or regrets. It didn't have to live with what it had done. Still, I turned its eye sockets toward the wall. I didn't want it to see me.

I picked up the shovel.

'Hey.'

Ex stood on the stairway. The shadows clung to his eyes, and his cheeks looked sharper than I remembered them. Pale hair had escaped his ponytail, spilling down his face.

'What?' I said. It was the best I could manage.

'I got them on their way to the ER. Aubrey and Kim are with him. There's nothing I can do there.'

'Nothing here either,' I said. 'One shovel.'

I didn't want him here. I didn't want anyone here. I wanted my crimes committed in the dark, without witnesses.

'Never heard of taking turns?' Ex asked, coming down the stairs. 'What kind of day care did you go to as a kid?'

'Don't do this,' I said. 'Please. Go. I have to—'

I was crying again. I hated it, but I could no more stop than I could will myself not to breathe.

'You have to what?' Ex said.

'I have to kill him,' I said, then folded. My knees gave way gracefully, and I hunched on the floor, supported only by the shovel. The words kept spilling out of my mouth. 'I have to kill him. Oh God, I have to kill him.'

'Give me the shovel,' he said.

'No.'

'I can do this for you,' he said. His voice was so soft. So gentle. He wanted so badly to spare me this. To spare me something. Anything.

'No,' I said. The anger in my voice surprised me, but it also gave me a last sip of strength. 'Don't make this easy. Don't you *dare* make this easy.'

Ex smiled. He understood. So maybe his being here wasn't so bad after all.

'Come on, then,' he said. 'Let's get this done.'

He held out his right hand, and I took it with my left. My legs were rubber and string. We walked together, side by side, to the edge of the grave. The rider was screaming obscenities somewhere. And when it wasn't, David's weaker voice wailed piteously. I wasn't doing him any favors by waiting.

Ex stepped away from me, standing at the coffin's head. He took something out of his pocket—a bottle of something that looked like olive oil—opened it, and poured it onto the coffin lid. Then he put his hands out, palms down toward the grave. His voice was low and resonant and rich. Almost like he was singing a dirge.

'Per istam sanctam unctionem et suam piissimam miserecoridiam, indulgeat tibi Dominus quidquid per visum.' With this holy oil and His own mast gracious mercy, may God forgive you those sins which you have committed by sight.

Last rites. He was giving David last rites. There was no magic in the words, no sense of the human will bending the world to account. But maybe there was something, even if it was only hope and respect. I sank the shovel into the pile of dirt, lifted, and poured it onto the coffin. Then another. David screamed every time more dirt struck the lid. I closed my eyes and kept going.

'Per istam sanctam unctionem et suam piissimam miserecoridiam, indulgeat tibi Dominus quidquid per audiotum.'

It took me half an hour, but I filled the grave. I buried an innocent man alive. At some point, the screaming stopped being loud enough to hear and became something I only imagined.

It sounded just the same.

25

When I was still living at home, back even before I'd broken the news to my parents about going to a secular college, I found a picture in the back of an old book. I still remembered it now. Two boys in front of a wide, white fence. The color was off; all red and yellow and hardly any blue. They were both wearing pea coats and haircuts that made me think of the late 1960s. The taller boy grinned at the camera. He might have been seven or eight years old, and the rictus grin of his false smile looked charming. I could see where the cheeks would thicken, the flesh fill out, and a small, well-intentioned mustache grow in. I could see my father in the boy.

The smaller one wasn't aware of the camera. He was pointing at something off to his right, his eyes wide with wonder and joy. He would grow up to be, in Ex's words, at minimum a sociopath and a rapist.

There had to be a moment. Somewhere in the path between that little boy discovering the world with an innocent delight so powerful it could impress itself onto a fold of paper and a little light-sensitive chemistry and the man who wrote *Fucked her*. There had to be something that made it all go wrong. Not just a lost innocence. Something worse than that.

Becoming soulless, maybe.

'They tell me that spleens are, for the most part, optional,' Chogyi Jake said. A television across the hall burst into authoritative news-on-the-hour music.

'I'd heard that,' I said.

As soon after the operation as he'd been stable enough to move, I'd had him transferred out of Grace. Without my being his wife or his kid, it hadn't been as straightforward as I'd hoped. I wound up playing the employer card and throwing a lot of money at it, and the problem eventually went away.

The first time I'd walked into Northwestern Hospital, coming to see him even if it only meant watching him sleep, I'd had a flash of panic. The complexity of halls and elevators brought up a bone-deep terror that didn't have anything to do with the place. After a couple visits, I got a better handle on the new space. Coming to see him today, I hadn't had anything more than a little mild anxiety.

'I hear they had to put six units of blood into me,' he said.

'That's what they tell me.'

'I don't actually know how much that is.'

'The word *massive* came up,' I said. 'They were apparently fairly angry at Kim and Aubrey for not getting you in sooner.'

Chogyi Jake smiled. He'd been in the hospital for three days, and he looked a million times better. The gray tone of his skin was gone. His hair was growing out. His smile seemed to carry a meaning behind it instead of just being a habit of the flesh. Even the gown he wore looked less sickly. I didn't know whether it was because he wore it like a meditation robe or he'd been sucking up to the nursing staff for a better class of patient-wear.

'You explained that you were saving the world?'

'Not really,' I said.

'Well, there's the mistake,' he said. 'If they'd just told the surgeon more about the circumstances . . .'

'They'd all be in for psych evaluations, even as we speak,' I said. Chogyi Jake nodded and laughed, then twitched and lay back, a hand pressed to the incision site on his belly.

'Only hurts when I laugh,' he said.

'Really?'

'Well, that and when I take a dump, but I was being polite,' he said. 'How are things at Grace?'

'Weird,' I said. 'Go figure. Kim said there's going to be a bunch of new policy announcements in the next couple weeks, but I don't have any idea what they are. I would have thought invoking evil spirits was already considered inappropriate workplace behavior.'

'There's nothing else they can do,' Chogyi Jake said.

'Yeah. One weird night, no explanations. I'm not sure what I expected of them.'

'And the rider?'

'It's in there. There's still weird stuff going on. Oonishi's screwed. He's shutting down his study until Kim can re-create the Invisible College's spell that I broke. Quiet it down a little.'

'I'm sorry to hear that,' Chogyi Jake said. 'He's doing interesting work.'

'Yeah, well. He can try again next year.'

Chogyi Jake nodded and lay back on his pillow. Outside his window, the high air was a hazy white.

'Seems like a long time,' I said.

'It can be,' he said, and from his tone of voice, I knew we'd changed subjects. I heard Kim again, from when we'd first arrived. *What a difference a year makes.* Or a day. Or a moment, if you pick the right one.

'How are you?' he asked.

'We're leaving the country. Me and Ex. Aubrey's staying here. You heard about that, right?' I was talking too fast.

'I did,' he said. And then, gently, 'It might be awkward, you and Ex being alone together for an extended period.'

I chuckled. It was cute, Chogyi Jake treating me gently, not pushing me, with him being the one in the hospital bed. He knew we were both hurt.

'Yeah, I can handle it. Anyway, Ex thought it would be a good idea to be a little hard to reach for a while. Burying someone alive as a ritual sacrifice is still a felony last I checked. There are going to be a lot of phone records between him and my cell, and I don't really want to explain to the judge why this time it was different. My

312

lawyer said that forcing any inquiries to be international would give her enough time to make it all disappear. If we need it to. You can catch up with us when you're okay to fly. I mean, if that's all right?'

'Absolutely. But, Jayné. How are *you*?'

I was having nightmares every night, and sometimes during the day. I could still hear David shrieking. Anything that hissed like the lantern in the civil defense ward or had the weird burned-cheese smell of cyclopropane residue sent me into a tailspin. I was having trouble keeping food down. Sometimes I woke up thinking I was still going to have to kill a friend of mine, and when the dream faded, I still felt *grateful* it was David trapped down in the dark.

David, who had been a lot like me.

'I'm fine,' I said.

When I was born, Eric would have been in his early twenties. Was he already corrupted by then? Had his soulless moment passed? When I turned sixteen and suffered my lost weekend, had he helped me hide it from my father out of affection, or was there another file out there like Kim's, only with my name on it, that told a different story?

But my mind kept going back to the picture. The little boy.

I suspected that Eric had started as someone not so different from me. Well intentioned, so far as he really knew his own intentions. A little lonely, maybe. On his own. He'd discovered the occult world of riders and magic. He'd been caught up, and it had broken him.

I imagined there was a moment when the boy had stopped and the man begun, but that was probably wrong. More likely, it was a series of things. Small steps that added up to something terrible. Maybe he'd been tempted by something. Wealth, since he'd clearly managed that part pretty well. Or love. Or power.

Or maybe he'd had to do terrible things that he'd believed were right until they didn't seem terrible anymore. Maybe he'd compromised himself until being the lesser evil seemed like being second place. I could imagine that happening.

'Hm,' Kim said. Even her little, nonverbal interjections were clipped and controlled. She looked at the papers with all the passion of someone reading a phone bill. If I hadn't known better, I wouldn't have guessed that she was holding the key to a new life.

'You don't have to do this,' Aubrey said for what must have been the hundredth time. He still didn't look good. The Oath of the Abyss showed in his face and the way he moved. He was less connected to his body than he'd once been. It would be easier for him to get sick, even harder to recover. He'd die younger, from something he'd have been able to fight off, except for me and Eric. I wondered, if it had gone another way, if I'd have kept him with me, even knowing that he'd hurt himself if it meant protecting me. If I would have let him.

The condo was, if anything, more stripped down than when we'd arrived. Lake Michigan floated outside, the water stretching to an obscure horizon until it turned into sky. I liked it better during the daytime. At night, the lake was too dark.

'It's nothing,' I said. 'And by nothing, I mean it's not one percent of what I'm working with. Or a millionth of what Eric owes you guys.'

'And yet enough to live on for the rest of our lives,' Kim said. She put the papers back down on the table and stroked her chin like she might have started growing a beard.

'Or to fund your own study,' I said. 'Something real. You know. Basic.'

Kim's smile was so small and so brief, it was easy to think it hadn't been there.

'Alepski and Namkung are going to wet themselves,' she said.

'But you're rebuilding the Invisible College's make-it-shut-up spell first, right?' I said. 'So that anyone else who goes looking for the rider won't find it.'

'That's first priority,' Kim said. 'But if I've got my own funding, there's no reason I can't do a little work of my own on the side.'

I smiled. We were almost done. Aubrey looked at me, and I raised an eyebrow. It was almost fun to watch him not know what to do. He'd been so sure of himself for so long. A week ago, I'd thought that losing him would be the worst thing ever. Now that the time had finally come, it wasn't. I was sad. I was going to miss his constant company. I wished things had gone differently.

I had bigger problems.

'I told Harlan that you two would both be taking care of the condo,' I said. 'He's still pretty much sloppy happy to do anything we want. He knows you're legit. If you want it repainted or anything, he's probably good for it.'

'I'm not sure I can live in your house,' Kim said. 'Taking money from Eric's estate is one thing. I deserve that. Being kept by my ex-husband's ex-girlfriend is too strange.'

'Until you find someplace better, then,' I said with a shrug. 'Or you stay at your place, and Aubrey can stay here. Or whatever. Up to you. I'm not using the place. You can stay here or not. Whatever you want.'

'But if you come back here—' Kim said.

'I won't.'

The tricky thing about innocence is you don't know you've got it until you've lost it. You think that you're worldly and experienced and maybe a little jaded, but you're not. You find out something about the world or about yourself, and it changes everything. Puts everything up for grabs again.

I had a year as the luckiest girl in the world. From my twenty-third birthday to just after my twenty-fourth, I was the heir to the magic kingdom. Sure, there were monsters in it. Sure, it was dangerous. But it came with a ready-built set of friends and allies, and my wise old uncle before me had left bread crumbs for me to follow, right? I just had to figure out what he'd have wanted me to do, follow directions, and everything would work out right. Looking back on it, the idea seemed frail and naive and I wanted it back. I really wanted it back.

Eric fell from grace with the world, and along with everything else, he'd left me the chance to do the same thing. I could follow his path and become the person he'd been. I'd wanted to, until I saw where the path ended. I felt older. I felt hurt and lessened and more frightened. And more alone. I'd lost my faith in my uncle, and losing faith in God had been easier. If God wasn't what I'd thought, then He was just a story people told themselves to get through the night. If Eric wasn't what I thought, then anything was possible.

Eric wasn't what I thought. Anything was possible.

I'd spent what seemed like a lifetime living the question *What would Eric do?* That was gone, and all that was left were *What am I going to do?* and *What will it cost me?* I left something in the darkness under Grace. Part of my innocence. Part of my soul. Which word I chose didn't really matter. It was gone, and I would never get it back.

And even that wasn't my biggest problem.

Going back to London felt strange. It didn't seem like going home so much as going back to a friend's place. There wasn't the sense of exploration, of discovering something new. I'd been in these rooms before, slept in this bed, woken up to the same neighbor with a kink for bhangra music. The weather was gray and cool. The leaves had already changed color. Living with just Ex was strange too. I kept expecting him to be Aubrey or Chogyi Jake. But he drank coffee instead of green tea, and none of his stories were about exotic wasp larvae. It wasn't unfamiliar, just strangely small.

We were sitting on the couch watching TV. The rain pattered against the back windows. A British police car with its two-tones siren passed by like something out of a BBC murder mystery. I wondered what Helen Mirren was doing these days. And between one breath and the next, I knew I was going to tell him.

'I shouldn't have won,' I said.

Ex looked over at me. He frowned. He always frowned.

'The fight with the *haugsvarmr*. I shouldn't have won.'

'The guilt's hard. I know that, but—'

'Ex. The circle broke. I didn't have you three to help me. Even with Aubrey pulling the Oath of the Abyss. I shouldn't have been *able* to win.'

'The wards that Eric put on you—'

'You mean the ones we can't find? The ones we haven't reinforced in the last year and who knows how long before that? Those wards?'

Ex crossed his arms.

'Those wards,' he said.

'Spells are magic,' I said. 'And magic fades. You told me that. Magic fades, and I'm getting *stronger*.'

'All right,' Ex said.

There should have been a flash of lightning, a crack of

thunder. The rain just kept dripping. The TV show went to commercial. I felt Ex's gaze on me like I was a puzzle he couldn't quite fathom. I took a deep breath, sighing it out slowly. When I spoke, my voice sounded weirdly calm and matter-of-fact. You know. All things considered.

'I think I have a rider.'

Acknowledgments

I would once again like to thank Jayné Franck for the use of her name; my editor, Jennifer Heddle, for her attention and support; and my agents, Shawna McCarthy and Danny Baror, for making this project possible. And also Carrie Vaughn, whose friendship and intellectual company have made this a more interesting book.

extras

www.orbitbooks.net

about the author

M. L. N. Hanover is an open pseudonym for Daniel Abraham, author of the critically acclaimed Long Price quartet. He has been nominated for the Hugo, Nebula and World Fantasy awards. He also writes science fiction (with Ty Franck) as James S. A. Corey. He lives in New Mexico.

Find out more about M. L. N. Hanover and other Orbit authors by registering for the free monthly newsletter at www.orbitbooks.net

if you enjoyed
VICIOUS GRACE

look out for

KILLING RITES

also by

M. L. N. Hanover

1

'So, Miss Jayné,' Father Chapin said, pronouncing my name correctly: Zha-*nay*. Either he knew a little French or he'd been coached. 'You believe you are . . . *possessed?*'

'Yes,' I said.

He wasn't what I'd expected. I only knew a few things about him—that he'd been my buddy Ex's mentor back when Ex had still been studying for the priesthood, that he ran some kind of Jesuit exorcism squad, that he was presently working just south of the Colorado border in the Sangre de Cristo Mountains of northern New Mexico. It had left room for me to imagine some kind of Old West demon hunter. If he'd walked into the ranch house wearing a black duster with a Sergio Leone movie soundtrack playing in the background, it would have been closer. Instead, he looked like someone's pharmacist or grocery manager. Close-cropped, wiry white hair, a beard that was more a collection of individual whiskers each doing its own thing, and watery blue eyes that were a little red about the rims. He was a small man too, hardly bigger than me. His shirt was dark to match his slacks, and he didn't even have the Roman collar.

I felt cheated.

He took a sip of the coffee I'd made while we waited for him. It was a little after six at night, and already an hour past sundown. If he was anything like me, the caffeine would keep him awake until bedtime. The pine log burning in the fireplace popped, scattering embers like fireflies inside the black metal grate. Above us, shadows danced between the vigas.

'What leads you to suspect this?' he asked.

'All right,' I said, took a breath, blew it out. 'This goes back a little way. About a year and a half ago, my uncle died. Got killed. Murdered. It turned out he'd left me everything he had, and he had a lot. Like more than some small nations a lot.'

'I understand,' Father Chapin said.

'It also turns out that he was involved with riders. Demons, or whatever. We call them riders. Spirits that cross over from Next Door and take people over. Like that. I didn't know anything about it, so I was flying blind for a while.'

'How did you discover your uncle's involvement with the occult?'

'There was a guy staying in one of his apartments. He turned out to be a vampire.'

'The *varkolâk*,' Ex said. 'Midian Clark. I mentioned him before.'

'So there was that,' I said. 'But then I started getting these weird powers, you know? Wait. That sounds wrong. I don't mean like I can fly or turn invisible or anything. It was just that when someone attacked me, I'd win. Even if I really shouldn't have. That, and everyone tells me I'm sort of invisible to magic. Hard to locate. We figured that Eric—that's my uncle— had put some kind of protection on me.'

'What did it feel like?'

'What did what feel like?'

'When you felt you should have lost in some conflict, but didn't.'

'Oh. It's like my body just takes over. Like I'm watching myself do things, but I'm not really driving that car.'

'I see. Thank you. Go on.'

I looked over at Ex. He was sitting at the breakfast bar, looking down at the couch and overstuffed chairs like a bird on a perch. His white-blond hair was tied back in a ponytail and he wore his usual basic black pseudo-priestwear. Looking at Father Chapin, I could see where his fashion sense came from.

I wished the others were there too—Chogyi Jake and my now ex-boyfriend Aubrey. Kim. The ones who'd been there from the beginning. I wasn't sure what to say that I hadn't already told Father Chapin. I felt like I was at the doctor's office trying to explain symptoms of something without knowing quite what information mattered.

'It isn't fading,' Ex prompted.

'Yeah. That's right. It's not,' I said. 'The guys always told me that magic fades, you know? That when someone does some sort of mojo, it takes upkeep, or it starts to lose power. We were looking through my uncle's things for months, and we never found anything about putting protections on me. We never used any kind of magic to keep them up. But instead of getting weaker, it seems like I'm getting stronger.'

'Have you found yourself taking actions without intending to?'

'Like what?'

He took another sip of coffee, his thick white eyebrows knotting like pale caterpillars.

'Walking places without knowing that you meant to go there,' he said. 'Picking up things or putting them down. Saying words you didn't expect to say.'

'No,' I said. And then, 'I don't know. Maybe. I mean, everyone does things like that sometimes, right?'

'Have you been sexually active?'

'Excuse me?'

'Have you been sexually active?' he asked again with exactly the same inflection.

I shifted on the couch. The blush felt like someone had turned a sunlamp on me. When I glanced over at Ex, he wasn't looking at me. I didn't want to go into any of this, but I especially didn't want to talk about my love life with Ex in the room. We'd both been pretty good about ignoring that he wanted to be part of it. Hauling out the fact that he wasn't seemed rude.

Still, in for a penny, in for a pound.

'A couple of times in college. And since last year, I had a boyfriend for a while, yes,' I said. 'Aubrey. But we're not seeing each other anymore.'

'Why not?'

'It turned out that my uncle—the one I inherited everything from?—wasn't exactly a good person. He used magic to break up Aubrey and his wife. To make her have an affair with my uncle. The phrase *rape spell* came up. When we figured that out, Aubrey kind of needed to go resolve that with her.' I paused. 'It's not really as *Days of Our Lives* as it sounds.'

'No other sexual activity?'

'None,' I said.

'Are you Catholic?'

'No.'

'What is your relationship with God?'

I shrugged. 'Well, we used to be really close, but then I went away to college. The whole long-distance thing was really a drag, so we're kind of seeing other deities.'

No one laughed. I felt my own smile go brittle. I shook my head and tried again.

'So, look, my parents are evangelical. We went to church all through my childhood, but the older I got . . . it just didn't work for me. I decided to go to a secular college. Took a while to save up the money, but . . . Anyway, I haven't been to church since then. Haven't talked to my parents either.'

Father Chapin's smile was a relief, if only because it meant he was skating over the 'seeing other deities' comment. I was a little bit annoyed with myself for wanting him to like me as much as I did.

'What did you study?'

'I majored in prerequisites,' I said. When he looked

quizzical, I said, 'I dropped out after a couple semesters. Then Uncle Eric died. Since then, I've been kind of busy.'

The old priest sighed, wove his fingers together on one knee, and leaned forward. I had the feeling we'd just been making small talk and he was ready to get into the real business. I didn't know what he was going to talk about if my messed-up family, my faith breakdown, Eric's death, and my sexual history were just the warm-up.

'Xavier tells me that you have recently killed a man.'

'Who's Xavier?' I asked. 'You mean *Ex?*'

'He tells me the man was an innocent and willing sacrifice, and that you—'

'All this stuff started a long time before that,' I said. 'It's not related.'

'Still, to take such an action could have—'

'It's not related,' I said again, and my voice shook a little. My heart was racing. I felt a pang of anger at my body for reacting so obviously. Wasn't I supposed to be the cool-as-a-cucumber demon hunter?

'I'm not here to judge you, young miss,' he said. 'I know something of the circumstances.'

'Then you know I've been seeing this freaky shit a long time before Chicago,' I said. 'If I've got a rider, I've had it since at least last year. Maybe longer.'

'Yes,' Father Chapin said. 'Yes, I understand. Thank you for your candor.'

The pine log popped again. The quiet got awkward.

'So, what do we do?' I said. 'Is there someplace we should

go and get our exorcism on? Some kind of rite to keep things together until we're full power? What?'

Father Chapin looked pained. He scratched at an eyebrow with the nail of his right pinky, smiling down toward the coffee table as he spoke.

'There are many things we will need to do. Little steps. Little steps to be sure that our action is right, yes? Move forward with our eyes open.'

'Great,' I said, clapping my hands on my knees. 'Where do we start?'

'I would consult with Xavier, please. For a moment.'

When I didn't hop up immediately, Father Chapin looked embarrassed, and I had the sense it was more for me than himself. *This is* my *problem* hunched at the back of my throat. *Anything you can say to Ex, you can say to me.*

'Just for a minute, Jayné,' Ex said.

'Sure,' I said. 'No problem.'

I walked out of the den, heading for the kitchen. But at the last minute, I turned right instead. Down the hall, and out into the December night. After the warmth of the ranch house, the air was like a sharp slap. To the southwest, the lights of Santa Fe were glowing against a sparse covering of cloud. The stars overhead were brilliant and crowded in the sky. A meteor passed over, a thin silver-white light, gone as soon as I saw it. I stepped out to a stretch of rough wooden fence that divided the scrub and stones near the house from the scrub and stones slightly farther away from it, sat on the top plank, crossed my arms, and waited.

It had been a little over two months since I'd killed an

innocent man. I'd had a good reason—saving-the-world-from-madness-and-war-level good—and he'd known what we were going to do. He'd gone into darkness of his own free will. But I was the one who'd put him in the box, driven in the nails, and buried him and the thing living in his body while they screamed and begged. Me. Little old Jayné Heller. My palms were almost healed. There wouldn't even be much of a scar. According to my lawyer, the police weren't investigating. It was a missing persons case, and it probably would be forever. Once upon a time, there was a man named David, and then one day, for no particular reason, there wasn't.

I hugged myself closer, the cold pressing into my skin. I'd bought an overcoat when we were in London—soft black wool that went down to my ankles—and I thought about going in to get it.

The days since then hadn't been the best of my life. I wasn't sleeping enough. I had weird spikes of anxiety and fear that felt like I'd accidentally gunned the gas with the car in neutral. I didn't know if it was the aftermath of my very bad day in Chicago or more evidence for my new theory of why I kept winning fights I should have lost.

From the moment I'd told Ex my suspicion that I had a rider in me, I felt like I'd fallen into a wheelchair that he was pushing. He'd arranged for the ritual tests in Hamburg that we'd tried with spectacularly inconclusive results. He'd orchestrated the trip back to the States—plane tickets, car, hotels. He even drove on the way up from Albuquerque International Sunport to Santa Fe.

He'd brokered the meeting with Father Chapin and his cabal of Vatican-approved exorcists. He'd made them sound like the ninja SWAT team of God. And maybe they were, but right now, sitting on my fence, I felt more alone than I had since I'd left college. I heard the front door open and close on the other side of the ranch house, then a car door. An engine came to life. Tires punished the gravel. I watched the headlights curve over the landscape of piñons and cactus without ever seeing the car itself. I figured it was safe to go in, but I didn't. A few minutes later, the door behind me opened. I heard Ex's footsteps coming out toward me, and I smelled the hot chocolate before I saw it. He had a cup for each of us, complete with half-melted marshmallows.

The news was going to be bad, then.

He leaned against the fence, looking out toward the smudge of light that was Santa Fe.

'He's in the middle of something right now,' Ex said. 'There's an Akkadian wind demon that's been possessing people all through the northern part of the state and up into Colorado. They've tracked it through almost three dozen cases. Father Chapin says they've got a rite coming up that's going to stop it for good.'

'Okay,' I said.

'They've been chasing this thing for months.'

He sounded defensive. I waited. I'd known Ex long enough to tell when he was working himself up to something. I let the silence push for me while I sipped the hot chocolate. It was good, but he always put a little too much cinnamon in it.

'There's some work we can do, though,' Ex said. 'So that we're ready when he's done with that. Hit the ground running.'

'This is the part I'm not going to like, right?'

'Yeah,' Ex said. 'It is.'

I popped what was left of the marshmallow into my mouth and talked around it.

'Lay it on me, Preacher Man.'

'There's someone in Taos he'd like you to talk with.'

'Another priest?'

'A psychiatrist.'

I laughed. The amusement didn't reach down as far as my gut.

'It's not about you,' Ex said. 'It's standard. It didn't used to be, but . . . well, it is now. People come to him and say that they're hearing voices or that demons are trying to control them or . . . anything really. What he does won't help people who are mentally ill, so it makes sense to have someone do that kind of triage. And he doesn't know you. All he sees is your history.'

'And what does my history look like?'

Ex's sigh plumed out white in the freezing air.

'It looks like someone with a very controlled, fairly sheltered childhood who's been through a lot of changes in a very short time. Just falling into that kind of money can put lottery winners into therapy. Then there's everything else. It wouldn't be strange for someone who has been through all the things you have to be . . .'

'Mentally ill?'

'Shell-shocked.'

'Great.'

We were quiet for what felt like a long time. The moon was new, a starless spot in the star-strewn sky. The breeze was no more than a breath, cold and dry. For as long as I could remember, I'd had dreams of being in a desert not entirely unlike this one. I wondered now if they'd really been my dreams. Maybe they belonged to something else that was living in my skin. Or maybe that was really mine, and everything else in my life was the falsehood. I thought I was a woman, but maybe that was a mistake.

I bit my lip, pulling myself back from that train of thought.

'You know I'm not going to do it, right?' I said.

'Yeah, I figured.'

'So do we have a Plan B?'

'Sort of,' Ex said.

'What's it look like?'

'Step one: Make a Plan B.'

'Let's get inside,' I said. 'I'm freezing.'

He took my hand, steadying me as I got down. He kept hold of my fingers for a few seconds longer than he needed to, and I let him. My plan to tour all the properties Uncle Eric had left in my name and catalog everything I could find had gone off the rails when I'd been called to Chicago. In the aftermath, we hadn't gotten back to it. But of places I'd actually seen, the New Mexico ranch house was one of my favorites. It sat alone on fifty acres of undeveloped wilderness, a single gravel road the only way in or out. It had power from the grid and utilities from the city, but there was also a generator and a well. The walls were white stucco that caught the desert sunlight, glowing yellow at dawn, pink and red and gold in the five o'clock winter dusk. And there was a patio that looked out to the west, catching the gaudy, improbable sunsets that had been different every day I'd remembered to look. I couldn't imagine myself living there. It was too isolated. But I could see curling up there to lick my wounds for a few weeks. A few months. Years, maybe.

I went to the kitchen and poured out the hot chocolate now well on its way to tepid. Ex went to the front room and stirred the fire with a black iron poker. The floors were red brick with thick Navajo rugs over them. My cell phone rested on the couch next to the leather backpack I used as a purse. It said I had one new message. The number was Chogyi Jake's, and I told myself I'd call him back later. After dinner, maybe. A demon-ridden mob had beaten him a good three-quarters of the way to death in Chicago. All his news would be about recuperating, which I didn't want to know. All mine would be about my quest for a first-class exorcist, which I didn't want to tell him. It didn't leave a lot in the middle.

'I could be wrong, you know,' I said, sitting on the couch. 'Maybe there's another explanation. The whole thing about having a rider on board could be crap I made up, and I'm scaring myself for no reason.'

'I'm not willing to take that chance,' Ex said. 'It fits the data too well. If we can't figure out what's going on and

Father Chapin won't help us, then I'll find someone else. I'm not giving up on him yet, though. He'll be in a better position after he's done with this thing with the wind demon. If I can just get him to look at you himself, try a few cantrips and pulls to see what's there to see, he'll change his mind.'

'You're sure of that?'

'I'm not.'

'I thought this guy was your Yoda.'

Ex smiled toward the fire. In the flickering shadows, he might have looked sad. It was hard to tell.

'He taught me most of what I know about riders. The occult. I trained with most of the men he's working with now. I was going to be one of them.'

'So what happened?'

Ex shrugged. The fire muttered to itself. When it was clear he wasn't going to say anything more, I stopped waiting.